A Reckless Seduction

"You should not look at me like that," she said, clucking her tongue.

"Like what?"

"Like you wish to devour me."

He did wish to devour her. "You do look a little like a cream puff, sittin' there."

Now she was staring at *him*.

"You shouldn't look at me like that," he told her, still holding her hand.

"Like what?" she breathed.

"Like you're about to do somethin' you ought not to."

It was probably just the liquor, but he could see smoky seduction in her gaze, like she wanted to do something completely reckless. Maybe kiss him.

This work is a work of fiction. Names, places, characters and incidents are the product of the author's imagination or are used fictitiously. Any resemblance to actual events, locales or persons, living or dead, is coincidental.

NATIVE HAWK

Copyright © 2016 by Glynnis Campbell

Cover design by Tanya Straley & Richard Campbell
Formatting by Author E.M.S.

Glynnis Campbell – Publisher
P.O. Box 341144
Arleta, California 91331

ISBN-13: 978-1-938114-35-9
Contact: glynnis@glynnis.net

Published in the United States of America

NATIVE HAWK

CALIFORNIA LEGENDS BOOK 3

DEDICATION

For my Grandma Alma
who loved a good Western
and gave me her Singer treadle sewing machine

Other Books by Glynnis Campbell

THE WARRIOR MAIDS OF RIVENLOCH
The Shipwreck (novella)
Lady Danger
Captive Heart
Knight's Prize

THE KNIGHTS OF DE WARE
The Handfasting (novella)
My Champion
My Warrior
My Hero

MEDIEVAL OUTLAWS
Danger's Kiss
Passion's Exile

THE SCOTTISH LASSES
The Outcast (novella)
MacFarland's Lass
MacAdam's Lass

THE CALIFORNIA LEGENDS
Native Gold
Native Wolf
Native Hawk

ACKNOWLEDGMENTS

Thanks to
Mia Sara and David Boreanaz,
My dad, for all the stories about stagecoach robbers,
My mom, for teaching me how to sew on a treadle machine,
My BFF Lauren Royal and father-in-law Dick Campbell,
for attempting to teach me five-card draw,
My stepmom Betty, for educational field trips in Shasta,
Ernesto Pavan for his brilliant Italian brainstorming,
My friends at the Gold Nugget Museum—
Joan Dresser, Becky Dresser, and Al Abrams,
The Hoopa Valley Tribal Council for their
amazing Hupa Online Dictionary,
and all those who refuse to judge by the color of one's skin
but rather by the content of one's character

CHAPTER 1

PARADISE, CALIFORNIA
SPRING 1875

Catalina Palatino Prosperi Valentini di Ferrara clutched her *caffelatte*-colored silk parasol in one tight kid-gloved fist. This was it—the end of her journey.

The buggy driver stepped down to fetch her trunk from the back. She took a single calming breath of fresh, pine-scented air. Then she peered down the main street of her new home.

Despite her uncle's descriptions, Paradise wasn't quite what she'd imagined when she'd dreamt of coming to America from her villa in northern Italy.

For one thing, she'd never seen so many buildings made of wood. They butted up against each other like wardrobes squeezed into a too-small room. Their names—The Adams Hotel, Clark's Dry Goods, The Red Dog, Assay Office, Pair-o-Dice Saloon, The Parlor—were painted above the doors in large, gaudy letters.

In Italy, her centuries-old stone-walled family estate

dominated a grassy slope overlooking rolling vineyards. But this town, surrounded by thick evergreens, looked like it had sprung up in the middle of the forest. The street was bare earth, full of ruts, so wooden walkways connected the shops for foot traffic.

There was a lot of foot traffic. Or maybe it only felt that way because she was receiving so many stares. It seemed every man who passed Catalina ogled her as if they'd never seen a woman before.

Self-conscious, she straightened her jacket and smoothed the wrinkles from her traveling dress. Was there a tear in her skirts? Was her sleeve smudged with dirt? She'd been wise to choose the cocoa-and-cream ensemble, considering the amount of dust the buggy had kicked up on the journey.

At least the voyage had been shorter than the one her uncle had taken during the Gold Rush twenty-five years ago. There hadn't been a railway or a stagecoach then. He'd traveled by ocean liner, steamboat, and mule.

She wished he were still alive. At least then she'd have one friend in this new land. She didn't truly remember her uncle, since he'd left when she was an infant. But he'd corresponded to her father every week by letter. She'd read those letters so many times, she felt as if she knew him...and California. It had been his love of this little mountain town that had inspired Catalina to follow in his footsteps. One could make a new beginning in this new place, he had written. And that was exactly what Catalina intended to do.

Her heavy trunk suddenly landed with a thud on the ground beside her, startling her and sending up a puff of fine dust. She clapped her hand to her bosom.

The driver took off his grimy hat and wiped his brow with his forearm. "Whatcha got in there, ma'am—a boat anchor?"

She frowned. A boat anchor? Was he serious? Why would he imagine she was transporting an anchor? How odd.

Catalina could speak English passably well. She'd made a point of learning it over the last few years—ever since, for Londoners, a season in Italy had become all the rage. But the English that Americans spoke sometimes seemed to be a completely different language from that of London.

The driver apparently didn't expect an answer. He left to fetch the porter from The Adams Hotel.

She glanced down at her trunk. No anchor. But everything else she owned was inside.

It was remarkable how little she possessed, considering her noble lineage and her family's wealth. But most of that wealth was tied up in property and agriculture. The Ferrara vineyards produced some of the best Albana wine in Italy, and the woodlands on the estate were thick with valuable truffles. She could purchase anything on her father's account.

Actual coin, however, was not so easy to come by. She'd barely been able to scrape together enough to pay for the journey. Besides, if her father had suspected her intentions— to leave her home and her family to pursue her dream of designing clothing in America—he wouldn't have given her a single *lira*. As the daughter of nobility, he expected her to simply marry the titled man of his choice and give him heirs.

She restlessly tapped her fingers on her parasol handle, gazing down the street again as she waited for the porter. A few women ambled along the wooden walkway. She studied them with narrowed eyes.

Their dresses were out of date and ill-fitting. One woman wore a drab, plaid, slope-shouldered dress that looked like it had been made during the presidency of Abraham Lincoln. Another sported a high-necked day dress made out of faded red linsey-woolsy, with a frayed bonnet tied under her chin. A young lady in an oversized blue crinoline swayed from side to side like a big bell.

Catalina clucked her tongue. Her talents were definitely

3

needed here. Once she located the dressmaker's shop, she'd start work immediately. Within a few months, the ladies of Paradise would be wearing her latest designs and setting fashion trends all over California.

Her spirits lifted, she ignored the gray-suited man who stopped to stare at her in open-mouthed shock. With a half-smile and a dip of her beribboned brown hat, she followed the driver and porter as they hefted her trunk and entered The Adams Hotel.

When she was finally settled into her room upstairs, Catalina propped her parasol against the wall, tossed her hat onto the feather bed, and peeled off her gloves.

The first thing she had to do was assess her finances. She emptied the coins out of her reticule and then dug to the bottom of her trunk for the satchel of money she'd brought, spreading it out atop the coverlet.

The currency still confused her. It seemed like she'd brought a great deal of *lire*. But since she'd arrived in America, and particularly in California, everything had cost much more than she expected.

Figuring the cost of the coach and the hotel, she only had enough funds left for two weeks of lodging, and that was if she ate like a bird.

Obviously, she needed to find employment as soon as possible.

She put the money back in the satchel, hiding it in the trunk, and then turned to look at her reflection in the mirror of the dresser.

Considering her long journey, she didn't look too dreadful. A splash of cool water on her face, a few loose strands of her hair tucked in, a dab of perfume behind her ear, and she'd be ready to interview for a position.

She examined her jacket, from the dark cording along the edges to the tiny tucks beneath the bust and the perfectly turned cuffs. She perused the sleek, cocoa-colored skirt, gathered up into trim, flat panels on the sides and finished with cream cording. She whirled to make sure her bustle was straight and that the pleated train was centered.

It was suitable. The dress displayed her talents without *braggadocio*. Anyone with an eye for clothing would note her attention to detail, her sense of color, her clever stitchery. Yet it wasn't so ostentatious as to be inappropriate to the position of a dressmaker.

Her position. It was curious, this fall from grace she'd taken. In Italy, she belonged to a noble family. She dressed in the finest silks and velvet. Her complete collection of apparel filled several wardrobes.

But in America, she was only a woman like any other woman. She'd brought just what she could squeeze into one trunk. She would have to earn her way into this new life on her own merits.

Nothing had ever sounded more exciting.

With renewed enthusiasm, she poured water from the pitcher into the bowl on the dresser, washed her face, smoothed her black chignon, and carefully pinned her hat on again. Then, pulling on her gloves and grabbing her parasol, she left to explore Paradise.

Half an hour later, her élan became somewhat diminished. First, she'd received numerous impolite stares. And second, in her quick tour of the town, she'd passed two dry goods stores, a school, a jewelry shop, a number of saloons, a bakery, an assay office, a barbershop, a boardinghouse, two churches, a blacksmith's forge, and three hotels. It seemed Paradise had no dressmaker's shop.

Considering the outdated and poorly tailored dresses she'd seen, she should have realized the clothes were homespun.

Returning to the covered porch of The Adams Hotel after her rounds, she closed her parasol, looping it over her arm, and flicked open her silk and sandalwood fan. Perhaps the lack of a proper dressmaker here was a *good* thing, she thought, fanning herself. Perhaps that was just what the town needed. If she somehow managed to start up her own shop, she would have no competition.

But it took a lot of capital to start a shop. Even if she lived and ate in a boardinghouse and took in hand sewing, she couldn't make enough money to earn her keep. In a town where the women did their own sewing, only bachelors would pay to have their sleeves altered, their trousers patched, or their shirts hemmed by hand.

If only she had her sewing machine, things might be different.

It had been heartbreaking to bid farewell to the thing in Italy. But it was too heavy to bring. Besides, as far as anyone knew, it didn't actually belong to her. Since her father would never have allowed his daughter to toil like a common servant, Catalina had pretended to order the machine for their housekeeper, Paola. Many a late night, she'd crept down to Paola's quarters to sew by candlelight, rocking the treadle with such practiced skill that it sounded like the clickety-clack of a speeding train.

Her father assumed Paola sewed all of Catalina's beautiful gowns. But the truth was Catalina had been designing and making her own clothing for years, right under his nose.

She sighed, rapping her fan closed against her palm. A good dressmaker's shop would have had at least one sewing machine. With a good treadle, a dress that might take all day to sew could be finished in an hour. An industrious seamstress could make a decent living as a dressmaker with that kind of speed.

Of course, the women of Paradise probably didn't spend as much money on their clothing as titled ladies did in Italy. In Ferrara, sumptuous attire was expected as a display of prosperity. Indeed, with the money that her cousin had spent on a wedding gown last year, Catalina could have purchased *five* sewing machines.

She opened her fan again and waved it slowly in front of her face, deep in thought as she gazed down the street. Most of the women on the boardwalks were dressed in simple fabrics—calico, muslin, linsey-woolsey, gingham.

After a moment, it came to her. She could design *affordable* dresses. After all, much of the cost of a dress depended on the fabric. And Catalina knew how to cut a pattern to get the most out of a piece of cloth. She could think of clever ways to use inexpensive cloth where it would never show while saving richer velvet, silk, and fine lace for beautiful trim and accents. She could even take old dresses—like that awful maroon monstrosity the woman walking toward her was wearing or the yellow calico sack on the young lady with her—and re-style them into something more fashionable.

She didn't realize she was staring until the two began whispering furiously behind their hands and looking in Catalina's direction.

She politely lowered her eyes and rapidly fanned her warm cheeks.

Suddenly, to the disapproval of the woman in maroon, the young girl in yellow broke away and scurried directly up to her.

Catalina froze. What did she want? Had she guessed that Catalina was secretly ridiculing her clothing?

"Pardon me, ma'am," the girl blurted before the frowning older woman could stop her, "but is that a..." She looked about for witnesses, then lowered her voice to a murmur. "A bustle?"

"Agatha!" the older woman barked, picking up her ugly skirts and making her indignant way forward.

7

Catalina exchanged a conspiratorial, amused glance with young Agatha.

"Is it?" Agatha's brows shot up in delight.

Catalina nodded.

Then the old woman grabbed Agatha by the elbow. "Come along, Agatha." She dismissed Catalina with a rude perusal from her hat to her shoes and back up again. "I won't have my daughter palaverin' with one o' your kind."

Catalina was stunned. She had no idea what palavering was. But she recognized an insult in any language. Her uncle had warned that, in some circles, foreigners were not welcome. She just hadn't expected rejection to come so soon. After all, she'd been in Paradise less than an hour.

Still, Catalina had never been able to keep silent in the face of an insult. Her father said her temper was a curse. Already the blood simmered in her veins.

She narrowed her eyes. "What does this mean—my kind?"

"Women who wear..." The woman thinned her lips, then spat out the word. "Bustles."

Catalina blinked in surprise. "What?"

"Disgustin'," the woman grumbled, yanking on Agatha's arm.

"But Ma!"

"Come along, young lady."

"Aww, Ma!"

Catalina didn't mean to laugh as the woman dragged her daughter off, but the situation was ridiculous. The woman didn't care that she was a foreigner. She just didn't like the way she was dressed.

Her laughter caught the attention of several pedestrians. They turned to look at her with a mix of expressions ranging from curiosity to confusion, from appreciation to disgust.

Now that she thought about it, she hadn't seen a single woman in this town wearing a bustle. No wonder they were all staring at her. They'd probably never seen such a contrivance.

How strange she must look to them. And yet they thought nothing of strutting about in enormous, stiff crinolines and poke bonnets that were decades out of fashion.

Deciding that now was as good a time as any to allay their fears that she might be "that kind" of woman, she planted the point of her closed parasol on the boards in front of her, cleared her throat, and addressed the town as a whole.

"Hello! Yes! My name is Catalina, and I am wearing a bustle!" she announced, bringing all of the main street to a halt. She pivoted to the side to give them a good look at her profile. "It is the fashion in Italy, worn by all the finest ladies!" She turned this way and that, allowing them to see the back of her dress as well. Then she called out, "I am a designer of clothings! If you wish me to design a bustle dress for you..."

Almost in unison, the mortified citizens averted their gazes and lowered their heads, shuffling on about their business.

Catalina frowned. How unfriendly these people were. She didn't expect to be welcomed like a long-lost cousin. But she deserved at least a bit of courtesy.

She sighed. It would have been easy to be discouraged. Here, with no friends or family, things looked bleak. But she hadn't come this far to slink back to Italy like a dog with its tail between its legs.

Certainly, fitting in to a town like Paradise was going to be a challenge. But it wasn't impossible. It was simply a matter of having a positive attitude, making a few minor adjustments, and then employing sheer force of will.

Just like fitting into a corset.

Chapter 2

If no one wanted a bustle dress, and if there were no dress shops, Catalina would just have to seek a position elsewhere until she could afford to buy a sewing machine.

She'd never tried to get a job before. But she'd seen her father interview staff. She knew what sort of things impressed an employer.

She straightened her jacket and prepared to enter Clark's Dry Goods.

Just before she reached the door, she felt someone's eyes on her. She peered discreetly from under the tipped brim of her hat. At the farthest end of the boardwalk, a woman all in burgundy watched her with keen interest. Her bright red hair was piled high beneath a feathered hat, and her neckline was cut low enough to be more suited to the ballroom than the street. Catalina wondered why the woman was staring. Was she fascinated by Catalina's bustle as well?

But by the time Catalina opened the door to the dry goods store and looked back, the woman had disappeared.

Catalina went into the store. At the back, behind the counter, a man in an apron was polishing his spectacles. *"Signore* Clark?" she asked.

There were two customers in the store, a pair of men in jeans and flannel shirts who were looking over the jars of liniment. As she breezed past, the blond man backed out of her way. The bearded one let out a low whistle.

"Well, good mornin'," the blond crooned, letting his gaze drip down over her.

She gave him a curt nod and proceeded to the counter.

The skinny and balding Mr. Clark fumbled his glasses onto his face and looked up with a start. "Can I help you?" he squeaked.

She flashed him a friendly smile. "Yes. I am seeking a position."

"A position? You mean a job?" he said, rapidly blinking his eyes. "Here?"

The blond chuckled as he came up behind her. "Well, well, Henry, it must be your lucky day."

She ignored him and spoke to Mr. Clark. "Yes. I can read and write. I can settle accounts. And I am good with peoples."

"I bet you *are* good with peoples, darlin'," the blond continued.

Catalina furrowed her brow. The blond man reminded her of her spoiled cousin Alessandro, who believed he was as irresistible as Adonis.

She went on. "I can order supplies, stock the shelfs..."

"Can you lift a twenty-four pound sack o' flour too?" the blond jeered. His companion giggled.

Her eyelids flattened, but she only tightened her fist around her closed parasol.

"I am not lazy," she told Mr. Clark. "I am always on time. I—"

Mr. Clark held up his hand to stop her. "Much obliged,

11

ma'am, but I don't need help. My son does my stockin', and my wife keeps the accounts."

Catalina tried not to show her disappointment. "I see. Well, thank you for your time. I will go now."

"Hey, you want a job with Calvin and me, workin' at the Curtis Ranch?" the blond offered with a leer. "I bet you could tame those randy stallions faster than—"

She raised her hand and slapped the words right out of his mouth.

His eyes widened in shock as he cradled his injured cheek.

She swept past him on her way out, closing the door behind her.

Perhaps she should have used more discretion. But, as she'd learned from watching her father, it was best to let bad-mannered people know who was in charge from the very beginning.

So, straightening her shoulders, she proceeded to the Assay Office next door.

There was no work available at the Assay Office. Nor were there any positions open at the bakery. She sidled discreetly past the Red Dog and Pair-o-Dice saloons. The boardinghouse could offer no pay, only free room and board in exchange for labor. The hall already had a caretaker. The barbershop would hire no women. And the Hill Hotel had enough Hills to fill all the available positions.

There was just one more business on this side of the street. It was at the spot where the woman in burgundy had disappeared. The beautifully scrolled red letters rimmed in gold above the door said simply The Parlor.

As soon as she turned the brass handle on the heavy oak door and stepped inside, she gasped in wonder and delight. This was the kind of elegance to which she was accustomed.

Here she fit in perfectly. Here she felt right at home.

The ceiling was high, like that of her family's villa. A

staircase led up to a balcony with a carved wood balustrade that looked down on the first floor. The large salon had a bar on one side and was filled with plush sofas and chairs which were upholstered in scarlet velvet to match the walls. An enormous mirror took up most of the wall behind the bar, reflecting the brilliant chandelier that hung from the ceiling. Flowers were placed in the middle of a few card tables and elsewhere around the room in vases of crystal. The scent of roses and lilacs mingled with traces of whiskey and tobacco, filling the salon with a pleasant aroma.

No one seemed to be here. She wondered where the woman in burgundy was.

As she gazed around the salon, it suddenly occurred to her that this might be a private residence. *Santo cielo!* Had she trespassed into someone's home, without even ringing the bell?

Before Catalina could slip away, she heard a woman's voice calling from the next room.

"You're startin' a little early, hon," she said as she swept into the salon. "The girls don't get up and around till—" She stopped when she laid eyes on Catalina.

The woman was older than Catalina had first assumed. The way her face was painted had made her look younger, at least at a distance. This close, the lines around her eyes were visible, and her cheeks were obviously rouged. Her burgundy dress was a bit worn in places, but it was well-fitted to her body. The velvet dipped with risqué daring at her neckline, clung to her waist, and flared smoothly over her hips. Her feathered hat perched at a playful angle atop her graying red hair. And a large ruby pendant sat upon her bosom. In this exquisite room, her formal clothing didn't look out of place at all.

"I'm sorry," Catalina said. "I did not realize this was—"

"Well, well." The woman placed her hands on her hips and

smiled. "If it ain't the lady with the bustle. How do you do?"

"Good morning," she said, still perusing the luxurious room.

"Come on in. You like the place?"

"Very much. It is beautiful. It reminds me of my home."

The woman coughed. "Your home? Well." She squinted. "Where do you call home?"

"Ferrar-..." Catalina caught herself before she slipped and revealed her true title. "Ferrazzano, in Italy."

She didn't want anyone to know exactly who she was or where she came from. If her father heard a young lady by the name of Ferrara had been found in America, he would track her down and bring her back. But she was also keenly aware of bringing further shame to her family name. According to her father, she was already a disgrace. She'd spurned suitors and engaged in artistic pursuits instead of marrying the man of his choice like an obedient daughter.

"Italy," the woman repeated.

She was studying Catalina, discreetly sizing her up from head to toe. Not that it made Catalina terribly uncomfortable. After all, she did the same thing all the time. One could learn a lot about a person from the way they dressed.

If the woman was as discerning as Catalina, she'd realize Catalina was a woman of quality who took care with her appearance.

"Would you care for a cup o' coffee? I just put a pot on."

Catalina smiled and nodded. Finally, someone in this town was offering her hospitality.

From the next room, which Catalina assumed was the kitchen, the woman called out, "What brings a lady like yourself from Italy to this neck o' the woods?"

Catalina frowned, puzzled. She wasn't sure what a neck of the woods was. "I am a designer of clothings."

"So I heard." The woman entered with a tray. On it were a

14

pot of coffee, two flowered bone china cups and saucers, spoons, a small pitcher of cream, and a bowl of sugar. "But why California? Why Paradise?"

She set the tray on a low table and gestured for Catalina to have a seat.

"My uncle came here twenty-five years ago for gold," she said. "He said it was a beautiful place, a place to make a fresh start."

The woman gave her a calculating glance as she poured the coffee. "So is that your plan—makin' a fresh start?"

"*Si*, yes." She didn't know why, but she felt like she could confide in this woman. "My father did not wish for me to design clothings."

"Is that a fact?" The woman added sugar and cream to her coffee and stirred it.

Catalina had quickly learned that American coffee was very different from what she drank in Italy, but she decided she could make a fresh start with coffee too. She mimicked the woman's formula.

"But you had to pursue your dreams, right?" the woman guessed.

Catalina brightened. Here was a woman who understood her. "Exactly! It is my passion. How can I let it waste away?"

She took a sip of coffee. It wasn't too terrible.

"Mm." The woman eyed her for a moment over the top of her cup. Then she lowered the cup into the saucer. "Folks call me Miss Hattie, by the way."

"Miss Hattie, I am very happy to meet you. My name is Catalina."

"Catalina. I like that."

Catalina beamed. At least *that* part of her name was real.

Miss Hattie picked up her cup again and wrinkled her brow in concern. "You know, just between you and me, I don't think there's a big market for bustles in this town."

Catalina lifted a brow. "Not yet."

"So how are you plannin' on drummin' up business?"

"Drumming," Catalina echoed. "I do not know this word."

"How are you goin' to get customers?"

"Oh. I need first to buy a sewing machine. Then I can make dresses much faster, and hopefully, I will get customers. But…"

Did she dare prevail upon Miss Hattie for a job? Could the woman possibly have need of help? She didn't seem to have household staff. She'd made the coffee herself.

"But?"

"I do not have the money to buy a sewing machine yet. So I must find other work."

Miss Hattie stopped with her coffee halfway to her lips. "Other work?"

"Yes. Do you…know of anything?"

Miss Hattie looked at her long and hard then, gazing into Catalina's eyes as if she were peering into her soul. "You're a very pretty girl."

"Thank you."

"Pretty girls like you don't grow on trees."

Catalina blinked. That was true. It was an odd thing to say. Pretty girls also did not hatch from eggs.

Finally, Miss Hattie sat back with a sigh and said, "And you seem like a very *nice* girl."

"Thank you."

"From a nice family?"

"Yes." Despite her father's tyrannical nature, he was a decent man.

"Yep, that's what I thought," Miss Hattie said, shaking her head. Then she let out another sigh and said, "Tell you what. I can't offer you much, but I've been shorthanded since one o' my girls got herself in the family way. I may be mad as a March hare, but I'm goin' to offer you a job."

Catalina almost spilled her coffee. She didn't understand half of the words, but she definitely understood the offer. "You are?"

"It won't be much," Miss Hattie warned. "I can give you a dollar a day to start, plus room and board."

Catalina thanked her enthusiastically, hiding her disappointment. At a dollar a day, it would take almost three months to make enough for a sewing machine.

Still, she was grateful. It wasn't such a long time to wait when it came to realizing her dream.

She was proud of the fact she'd landed her first job and in such a beautiful house. She'd do whatever it took to buy that sewing machine, even if it meant doing clerical work, such as keeping Miss Hattie's household accounts, writing correspondence, managing her servants.

"You'll start with the housekeepin'," Miss Hattie told her, "washin' laundry, polishin' furniture, waxin' floors."

The smile froze on Catalina's face. Those were not just menial tasks. They were servant's work. And yet, what had she said? Whatever it took.

Miss Hattie added, "So I hope you have some plainer clothes to wear. It'd be a shame to ruin—"

From upstairs, a door swung open with a loud creak. Catalina looked up. Emerging to lean on the balustrade was a curvy woman with bright gold hair, clad in nothing but her camisole and drawers.

"Betsy!" Miss Hattie called up. "You're up early."

Betsy yawned and scratched between her ample breasts. "Casey took off around midnight last night." Her eyes roved over Catalina. "Who's this?"

"New girl," Miss Hattie said.

Just then, a second door opened. Another woman came out. This one, a brunette, was dressed in just a corset. When she turned with a laugh to drag her male companion out of the room, he slapped her bare bottom with his palm, and the woman shrieked.

Catalina's fingers tightened on her coffee cup.

"Jesse!" the brunette scolded with a giggle. "You stop that!" He pinched her buttock, making her squeak. Then he put on his hat. "Next Friday?"

Miss Hattie called up to him, "As long as you got the gold, sweetheart!"

One by one, the doors along the balcony opened. Men of various social standing, judging by their attire, emerged from the rooms. Some of them grinned and tipped their hats to all the ladies before tromping down the stairs. Some of them shuffled away like shadows, their hats pulled prudently over their brows.

The ladies mingled on the balcony, as if chatting in their corsets in public was perfectly acceptable. A few of them lit cigarettes and began puffing away. Most distressing to Catalina, between them, they probably wore less than seven yards of fabric.

Catalina couldn't budge. She felt like a fool. How could she not have realized this was a *bordello?* If she'd thought the town was scandalized by her bustle, what would they think of her working in such a place?

But it was too late to refuse Miss Hattie's offer. Catalina needed the money. Besides, she thought, staring at all the half-naked ladies on the balcony, they looked like they could use a good seamstress.

She'd just have to be cautious. She didn't dare let the upstanding women of Paradise know she was employed at a *bordello.* Her reputation as a dressmaker might suffer.

She took a fortifying gulp of coffee. Whatever it took, she thought again. She supposed she should be thankful Miss Hattie hadn't hired her to do...what the ladies did.

CHAPTER 3

Drew Hawk lowered his gaze discreetly to the pretty lady in red. Beside her were her three sisters. Though he was much obliged to see them, he kept his feelings to himself. He wouldn't let his face betray a thing.

He glanced up at the three men sitting around the poker table in the Winsome Saloon.

He was pretty sure Harvey, the one twirling his mustache, would fold.

The eyes of the bearded fellow next to him, Jim, widened the slightest bit. He might have a decent hand.

Billy, the bare-faced third gent, was working his lips, like he was getting ready to spit. He probably didn't have shit.

It had been a good night for Drew. After two hours, most of the money had moseyed its way over to his side of the table.

He'd have to leave Shasta in the morning. Being a gambler was a bit like selling snake oil. Once you drained a town dry of its wealth, you were smart to skedaddle to the next.

Harvey stopped twirling his mustache long enough to recklessly plunk his last two silver dollars in front of him.

Jim wiped at his beard in indecision. Finally he let out a sigh. "Aw, hell." He tossed out two dollars of his own, which left him two.

Billy picked up his shot glass and slugged it back with a vengeance. "I'm in," he snarled in reckless defiance, shoving two dollars forward. "Call."

Drew calmly spread the four lovely queens on the table, kicking the unnecessary jack aside with his little finger.

"Criminy," Harvey muttered, tossing his useless cards in front of him.

Jim showed his hand—three tens, a seven, and a five. "Damn it."

The young firebrand Billy slapped his cards face-down onto the table. "You're a cheat!" He looked for confirmation from the other players. "That damn half-breed cheated! That's the only way he could have won so much!"

It wasn't the first time Drew had been accused of cheating by a sore loser. Nor was it the first time his mixed blood had been used as a slur. Under the table, his hand moved to hover over his holster as the firebrand staggered to his feet.

"Now, simmer down, little brother," Jim said.

Little brother? Hell, were the two of them related? Just as a precaution, Drew soundlessly slipped his Colt out of its holster.

"I reckon he's right, Jim," Harvey snarled. "I ain't never seen a man win so much in one night."

"Yeah!" Billy said, weaving on his feet. "He was cheatin'. And you know what we do to cheaters." He sloppily pulled out a Remington derringer.

Drew ran his thumb over the hammer of the Colt, cocking it silently. In the condition young Billy was in, he probably couldn't hit the broad side of a barn. But Drew didn't like to take chances.

"Whoa, little brother!" Harvey warned, scraping his chair back as he stood. "You don't want to be doin' that."

Shit, were they *all* related? If Drew had known that, he wouldn't have let the game go on so long. It was one thing to take a man's money. It was another to impoverish a whole family.

"Easy, Billy," Jim told his little brother. "Put the gun away. Let's settle this fair and square."

With a touch as light as a feather, Drew caressed the trigger with his fingertip. He wanted to be ready, but he didn't want to jump the gun. Usually these things worked themselves out with no shots being fired.

"Look, boys," Drew said calmly, "I don't want to make trouble. I swear I wasn't cheatin'. Sometimes it's just the luck o' the draw. How about I buy us a round o' drinks and we call it a night?"

Drew saw Jim's gaze narrow in suspicion. No doubt he'd noticed that only one of Drew's hands was on top of the table. And he could probably guess where the other hand was.

"Billy," Jim said, rubbing at his beard, "put the gun down. He's right. We can settle this peaceful-like."

Billy chewed on that for a little while. Finally, with a curse of disappointment, he reluctantly shoved his Remington back into his holster. It took him three tries.

Drew eased the hammer on the Colt quietly back into place, holstered his weapon, and waved the saloon girl over. Walking out of town without a bullet hole in his gut was well worth the price of four whiskeys.

Jim leaned over to whisper something to Harvey. Harvey nodded, plucked his hat off the rail of his chair, and smashed it down over his thinning hair.

Drew eyed him with suspicion. "You goin' somewhere? The whiskey's comin'." He nodded at the saloon girl and held up four fingers.

Harvey got up. "I'll be right back." He pushed his chair in and headed out the door.

Drew smelled trouble. Maybe it was time to bid them goodnight.

"Aw, hell," he said after Harvey was gone. "I clean forgot. I got a pretty little lady waitin' for me. What time is—"

He reached for his pocket watch. Before he could draw it halfway out, Jim scraped his chair back in a panic and shot to his feet. The movement startled Billy, who tipped over backwards in his chair. Drew had his Colt whipped out and cocked before Billy's head hit the floorboards with a sickening thud. Meanwhile, Jim was struggling to untangle his own six-shooter from its holster.

Drew still hoped he wouldn't have to shoot somebody. Billy was out cold. And it looked like Jim had the shooting skills of a four-year-old.

Unfortunately, the bartender spotted the flash of Drew's Colt and decided to intervene. From the corner of his eye, Drew saw the barrel of a rifle swing up over the bar.

Drew ducked, which turned out to be unnecessary. The bartender's shot was a warning blast only, fired at the plaster ceiling.

The crack of the rifle got everyone's attention. Jim responded reflexively, unfortunately before his gun was clear of the holster. He shot a chunk out of his big toe.

Still, Drew didn't fire. He might be a fast gun. But he never wasted ammunition.

For everyone else in the bar, however, two shots were a call to battle. Those who had guns pulled them out. Those who didn't armed themselves with broken bottles.

Before all-out war could break out, the front door of the saloon crashed open. A sour-faced giant of a man barged his way in.

At his heels was Harvey. "See, Pa? I knew he was trouble."

Pa? Drew scowled. Was all of Shasta just one big, happy family?

"What the hell is goin' on?" Pa boomed.

Then Drew noticed the star on the big brute's vest.

"You old fools!" the big man barked. "Put away your guns." He shook his head. "Pete?"

The bartender answered. "Just another poker game gone bad, sheriff."

"Is that so?" He scoured the room. When he saw Billy passed out on the floor and Jim limping around with a bloody foot and wrenching at his stuck pistol, a curious look came into his eyes.

Disappointment.

Drew realized a powerful man like that was probably ashamed to have such inept, sniveling cowards for sons.

Jim's face was white, and he grimaced in pain. But his beard quivered with rage over his misfire. "He was cheatin', Pa, just as bold as brass."

Harvey chimed in. "It's like I said, Pa. That no-good half-breed has been takin' our money all night."

The sheriff snorted, then peered down at Billy. "He all right?"

Jim was more concerned with his own bloody foot. "Aw, hell, he just passed out. He'll be fine."

Then he gave Drew the once-over. "What's a half-breed doin' in my town?"

"Just passin' through," Drew said.

"Like a bank robber's just passin' through?"

"Naw, not me," Drew said in his best aw-shucks voice. "I'm just visitin' from Hupa, over yonder."

"I don't care if you're Shasta born and bred," the sheriff said, pointing a sausage-sized finger at him. "We don't allow cheaters in this town."

"That's right," Harvey echoed.

"Oh, I wasn't cheatin', sir."

The sheriff closed his eyes to slits. "I got three men that..." He glanced down again at his son, unconscious on the floor. "Two men that say you were."

Emboldened by his father's bravado, Harvey chimed in, "I'll swear to it before the judge."

The sheriff looked again at his offspring. His mouth curled down. He'd probably just as soon sweep this whole incident under the rug. His sons weren't half the man that he was, and he probably didn't want anyone else knowing it.

With a sigh, he said, "Oh, I don't think we need to go to court."

Drew was happy to hear that. He wouldn't stand a chance in court. It would be his word against the sheriff's. No half-breed in his right mind would take those odds.

Then the man added, "We can just take care of this little problem ourselves."

Even that was fine with Drew. To be honest, in a situation like this, he didn't mind folding. He'd consider himself lucky to give back his winnings to the sheriff's boys and call things fair and square. He wasn't above cutting his losses and moving on. And he sure as hell wasn't looking for a fight.

"You gonna hang him, Pa?" Harvey asked with far too much enthusiasm.

Jim's eyes lit up at getting payback for the humiliation of having almost shot himself in the foot. "That'll teach the thievin' son of a bitch."

To Drew's alarm, the sheriff didn't rush in with dissent. And Drew quickly read in the man's eyes that he wasn't interested in a diplomatic solution. His sons' honor had been compromised. He'd like to pretend it hadn't happened. But barring that, he wanted to make sure it wouldn't happen again.

Hanging him is exactly what he planned.

Drew was tempted to draw his gun and shoot his way out of this predicament. But he never wasted bullets when he could use his fists. And he never used his fists when he could use his wits.

Before the sheriff could say the words to condemn him, Drew grabbed the edge of the table. He wrenched it up and tipped it over forward, forcing the lawman to dodge back. Cards and money scattered. Silver coins rolled across the floor. Some of the opportunistic denizens of the saloon dove forward, eager to claim their share of the loot. Others battled them for it.

In the chaos, Drew dropped to the ground, snatched his hat from its perch on his chair, and jammed it down over his head. Then, using the rolling round table as a shield, he scrambled toward the door.

"He's gettin' away, Pa!" Harvey cried.

Drew plowed forward with the table, bowling over the sheriff before he could reach for his gun.

"Shoot him! Shoot him!" screamed Harvey, blocking his way.

Having had about enough of Harvey, Drew grabbed his duster from the coat rack by the door and then used the rack to sweep the man's feet out from under him. Harvey went down with a satisfying squeak and a crash. And Drew made his escape.

Once outside, he donned his duster and headed directly for the closest competing saloon. Nobody would think to look for him there. They would guess he'd hightail it out of town. But like *Xontehl-taw*, Trickster Coyote, Drew had always found stealth and brains more useful than speed and brawn.

Sure enough, as Drew slipped into the Shasta Saloon, an angry mob burst out of the Winsome, with the sheriff at the fore. Drew quickly headed for the back of the establishment, where a piano player was making a big ruckus. Taking up residence in the corner beside the piano, he pulled his hat down over his eyes and slouched against the wall, as if he'd been standing there for hours.

In twenty minutes or so, he'd slip out of Shasta in the dark, going by way of the deer trails that wove through the mountains. If his luck held, he wouldn't get killed by a mountain lion on the way.

Sheriff Jasper Brown wheezed as he stared off into the dark of the woods with his revolver drawn.

"Shit."

The half-breed was long gone.

Scrambling up behind the sheriff were his two good-for-nothing sons.

"Did you get him, Pa?" Harvey hissed.

Jasper grimaced, thinking for the hundredth time that if only he hadn't joined up to fight in that damned War Between the States, maybe he'd have some real sons instead of the lily-livered brats his shrinking violet of a wife had raised.

"Did you, Pa?" Jim asked.

"Too dark," Jasper gasped out. "Liable to get killed, shootin' in the dark."

"Aww, dang it," Harvey whined like a petulant child.

Jasper would have liked to wallop him with the butt of his pistol right about then. But he'd promised Priscilla that he'd take care of the boys after she passed. He'd kept that promise for the last six years, even though they weren't boys anymore and ought to know how to fend for themselves. At least they ought to know not to fraternize with Injuns.

Jim slapped his hand on his holster, as if he actually knew how to use the pistol in it. "We can start out bright and early tomorrow."

Jasper bit back his real opinion about that—that he'd

rather take his chances in a pit full of rattlesnakes than hunt outlaws with his trigger-happy, foot-shooting son.

"Sure," he grunted.

Harvey hitched up his trousers with a sniff. "Leastwise we got our money back."

"It ain't about the damn money," Jasper snarled. "It's about honor."

"Yeah, Harvey," Jim chimed in, giving his brother a shove. "Don't you know nothin'?"

Harvey shoved Jim back.

Jasper jammed his gun into its holster and grabbed them both by the scruff of their necks. He resisted the urge to knock their heads together.

He supposed he'd have to spell it out for them. "I won't have it bandied about that the Brown boys were beat at poker by a damn Injun. Do you know what that would do to my reputation?"

The boys gave him a blank look.

Harvey licked his lips. "Actually, Pa, he was a half-breed."

Jasper growled, gave them a good shake, and let them go, walking off in disgust. "It don't matter. I'll hunt him down tomorrow and put an end to it."

What the boys were too stupid to understand was that the natives around here tended to get uppity. And if they started getting it into their heads that they might get the upper hand against lawmen, who knew what would happen? Just a few years back, not that far from here, the Modocs had made a stand against the U.S. Army and nearly won.

There would be no Injun war in Shasta, not on his watch. And the only way to prevent that was to subdue insurrection—before it happened.

If there was one thing he'd learned fighting in the War Between the States, it was that white men didn't dare give an inch or they'd lose a mile.

Hell, they'd lost a mile already, surrendering to the Negro-loving North. Freed slaves were running loose all over his good country.

If Jasper had anything to say about it, they'd go back to the way things were when he was his boys' age. Back then, there was a bounty of five dollars on every Injun scalp a white man collected.

His sons were savvy enough not to chatter at him on the return walk to the Winsome Saloon. Now all he had to do was collect his youngest boy, take him home, and sober him up.

When he swung open the saloon door, it was still a busted-up mess. But all the drunks were gathered around his boy. And the town doctor was crouched beside him.

Jasper's jaw tensed, and the coppery taste of fear hit his tongue. He barged forward, hauling men out of his way.

"What's goin' on?" he growled at the doctor. "What's happened to my boy?"

The doctor looked up at him with fearful eyes and slowly shook his head.

For the space of a heartbeat, Jasper was stunned. Then he decided the doctor didn't know shit. He shoved the man aside and crouched by Billy himself.

"Come on, Billy," he demanded, grabbing him by his suspenders and giving him a good shake. "Wake up!"

Billy's head lolled backward. He felt as limp as a stillborn calf.

"Wake up, damn you!"

He gave Billy another shake. But already he was starting to realize this was no drunken stupor. His son was gone.

There was deadly silence in the saloon.

Jasper's heart began burning like a smoldering coal. He'd broken his promise to Priscilla. He'd lost one of her boys. He'd lost her little Billy.

He clenched his teeth together hard enough to crack them.

He didn't dare surrender to the strangling ache in his throat. If people glimpsed a weak spot in him, he'd never hold sway over the town again.

So instead of a sob of grief, he snarled, "Who did it? Who did this to my boy?"

The bartender, frowning in concern from behind the bar, said, "Word is he just fell backwards and cracked his skull."

Jasper gave him a cold stare. That wasn't how it had happened. No boy of his was going to die from some drunken accident. Someone had to pay.

Beside him, Jim was rubbing his beard in agitation.

Harvey offered, "I saw what happened. It was Jim's fault. He stood up all sudden-like and Billy just—"

"You're full o' shit! It was that half-breed!" Jim yelled. "He's the one that did it! They was arguin' over that poker hand, and...and...he drew his gun!" He shoved at Harvey. "Remember? Remember he drew his gun?"

"Maybe," Harvey agreed.

Jasper nodded. That was good enough for him. Before anyone in the saloon could naysay him, he stood up with his hands raised.

"If the half-breed did this, then it's my duty to bring him in for justice. Me and my boys are gonna go after him in the mornin'." He didn't relish taking his sons along, but if they were underfoot, at least he'd be able to keep them from getting killed like Billy.

"I'm deputizin' you, Nate," he said to the bartender.

"Sure thing, Sheriff," Nate replied, untying his apron.

Then Jasper nodded to the doctor. "You put my Billy in a good pine box, Doc. I ain't comin' back till I get the son of a bitch who did this."

Then he left the saloon and headed home in the dark, where no one could see the wet in his eyes or the vengeance in his heart.

CHAPTER 4

Twenty-seven dollars.

That was how much Catalina had made since she'd begun working at The Parlor.

On her hands and knees in the secondhand blue calico frock and apron she'd altered to fit, she scrubbed at a stain on the polished wood floor. In one corner, a fiddler sawed out merry songs. At the nearby tables, men played poker, cursing when they lost a bet, crowing when they won.

She'd learned to ignore the sight of half-naked women on the balcony and the catcalls and bad language from the men downstairs. She'd even learned to sleep with a pillow over her ears so she wouldn't hear the sounds of fornication coming from the rooms next to hers.

And she'd prayed every night to receive absolution for frequenting a *bordello*, reminding god that if he saw fit to gift her with a windfall of money, she would immediately give Miss Hattie her notice.

So far, he had not.

Catalina had fully intended to hold herself aloof from the

fallen women who worked at The Parlor. To be a well-respected dressmaker, she couldn't afford to be associated with what some referred to as soiled doves.

But she'd been unable to resist the friendly overtures from two of the nicer ladies, who considered themselves Catalina's guardians.

Emily, whose grin could light up a room, had given her the dress. Anne, who always had a mischievous twinkle in her eye, made sure Catalina knew all the latest gossip.

In the end, she was grateful for their friendship. Some of the other ladies were not so welcoming. They saw Catalina as a threat and were openly hostile.

Sitting back on her heels, Catalina mopped her brow with the back of her forearm.

How the ladies could be worried about her stealing their "regulars," she couldn't imagine. Catalina had no interest in pursuing their line of work.

She tucked a loose curl behind her ear and resumed scrubbing the floor.

She still had moments when she doubted her decision to leave Italy and struggled with homesickness.

She missed her friends.

She missed her family.

She missed the way the sunlight fell across the Ferrara vineyards.

She missed the music of her language, the cold, velvety sweetness of gelato, the sight of starlings forming beautiful shapes against the azure sky.

She missed the taste of freshly dug truffles.

That was what she missed most—the truffles that grew in the woods around her home. She closed her eyes, imagining the musky, earthy flavor.

"Well, my word," she suddenly heard from behind her. "I see you found yourself a position."

She craned her head around. It was the obnoxious blond man from the dry goods store, the one she had slapped across the face.

"Looks like a real nice position." His eyes slithered over every curve of her body. "Not so high-and-mighty now, are you, Missy?" he said with a sneer, reaching down to give her bottom a familiar pat.

Her blood boiled. But before she could heave the entire bucket full of soapy water over his thick head, Miss Hattie intervened.

"Why, Delbert Akins," she said, sweeping up to take him by the arm, "we haven't seen you in weeks."

"Howdy-do, Miss Hattie."

"You know, Mary's been pinin' for you."

"Is that a fact?" His eyes slid to Catalina. "Well, I might have somethin' else in mind today."

Miss Hattie blinked, feigning ignorance. "And what would that be?"

"I kind o' like the looks o' your new girl."

"Catalina?" Miss Hattie forced a laugh. "She ain't for sale."

"Name your price," he said. "Three dollars? Four? Every woman's for sale. It's just a matter of for how much."

Catalina stiffened. She was definitely *not* for sale...at any price.

"You'd be wastin' your money," Miss Hattie said.

He shrugged. "It's my three dollars."

Three dollars—just for spending a few hours with a man. It took Catalina *three days*, working from dawn to dark, to earn such an amount.

She forced her attention back to her work. Dipping the rag into the bucket, she wrung it out with a twist and a squeeze, imagining it was Delbert's neck.

"Trust me, Del, you don't want her," Miss Hattie said.

"Says who?"

"Honey, she wouldn't know a tallywag from a polliwog."

"I could teach her...real fast."

"Yeah, I'll bet you could," Miss Hattie agreed, "but then who would scrub my floors?" Before he could come up with another argument, she called upstairs, "Mary, honey! Look who's here!"

Mary thankfully obliged by opening her door with a gasp of delight. "Delby, sweetie!" She gave him a childish pout. "I thought maybe you'd forgotten all about little old me."

"How could I forget you, darlin'?"

She came out to the balustrade and gave him a coy smile. All the men downstairs voiced their appreciation. Apparently, one glimpse of Mary in her ruffled pantaloons was enough to persuade Delbert to forget all about Catalina. He shoved two silver dollars into Miss Hattie's hands and took the stairs two at a time.

When he was gone, Miss Hattie sidled up next to Catalina and murmured, "Sorry about that, honey. Delbert's a bit...persistent. But Mary knows how to handle him. I'm sure he'll leave you alone now."

Catalina nodded. It wasn't that she couldn't defend herself. She was perfectly capable of cutting a man down to size with a few sharp words or a kick between the legs.

But she was afraid such behavior would not be agreeable to Miss Hattie. Miss Hattie treated her clients as if they were kings, even the ones who acted like peasants.

It wasn't the first time a man had mistaken Catalina for one of the prostitutes. Most of the men were mortified and apologetic when they realized their error. But to be honest, a few times she'd wondered how sinful it would be to pretend she *was* one of them. In one discreet evening with a few gentlemen, she could make half a month's wages.

Emily even suggested that Catalina might get herself a

regular. Some of the ladies considered themselves kept women. They had men who visited so often, they were almost like husbands. A girl could make a nice living that way and even make believe she was in love.

But of course Catalina would never do such a thing. She couldn't live with herself if she did. If she ever gave herself away like that—and at the moment she had no interest in such a distraction—it would be to one man only, in marriage, a devoted man with whom she would spend the rest of her life.

The women who worked here didn't seem to consider the lasting consequences of what they did. They were young and beautiful now. They had companionship and amusement. They could have any man they wanted.

But what would happen when they grew old, when the men chose younger, prettier companions? Who would come to their side then? Who would share their laughter and tears when they were gray and wrinkled?

The stain on the floor was faded now, so she dropped the rag in the bucket and hauled herself to her feet. There was just enough time before supper to pick fresh wildflowers for the salon.

Just as she lifted the bail of the bucket, she heard a gasp and a loud crash. Jenny, the young saloon girl, who couldn't get used to the men pinching her backside, had dropped a tray...again. Shards of crystal burst on the wooden floor. Wine made red rivers across the planks, dissolving into the shoreline of carpet. Jenny's cheeks were flaming as she mumbled out an apology and fled the salon in tears.

Catalina sighed, looking at the mess. Now she'd have to forego the flowers. It would take her an hour to clean up every splinter of glass, and she'd never get that dark stain out of the rug.

She glanced up at the closed doors on the second floor and tucked her lip under her teeth.

In a single month, plying the trade of the ladies upstairs, she could make enough money to buy a sewing machine. Then Miss Hattie could hire someone else to scrub floors and polish furniture, and she'd never have to do it again.

She tried not to think about it as she slogged the bucket across the floor to the crimson lake that was soaking into the carpet.

Drew Hawk wasn't listening. He was too busy looking over his shoulder as he and his twin brother, Chase Wolf, headed on foot to the Redding stage stop.

Chase was jawing on again about the vision he'd had and the message from their dead grandmother. Apparently, the vision had told Chase to go to the ranch where their grandmother had been kept as a servant. That was why, for the first time since they were infants, they were venturing south to the little mining town of Paradise, the place that had once been the land of their father's people, the Konkow.

At least that was why his brother *Chase* was on the journey.

Drew had his own reasons.

They might be twins, but he reckoned their looks were the only thing they had in common. The blood of their native father seemed to flow in his brother's veins while Drew had the spirit of their white mother.

His brother was a decent, honorable man. He was an upstanding member of the tribe. He lived on the Hupa reservation, where they'd both been raised, and he earned a respectable income from his work as a blacksmith.

Drew, on the other hand, couldn't wait to leave home and go to the big city. He'd never cottoned to the peaceful ways of the Hupa. He preferred to have a poker deck in his hand, a

Colt in his holster, and the open road under his feet. He was as restless as a rolling stone.

Although lately, he felt more like a loose cannon.

His last escapade proved that. He'd been lucky to get out of Shasta with his neck intact. But it looked like his luck might not hold out.

He'd learned that the Shasta sheriff's son, Billy, had done more than knocked himself out in that fall. Word was he'd hit his head so hard on the saloon floor that he'd never woken up. They'd put him in a pine box the next day. The crazy thing was the sheriff was blaming Drew for his death.

He blew out a long breath.

Chase misread Drew's sigh. "You know, it's not too late for you to turn back."

"Turn back? Why would I do that?" Hell, if he turned back now, he'd run straight into the sheriff's posse on his trail. He'd made the mistake of telling the boys in Shasta he was from Hupa. They'd know right where to find him.

Chase glared at him pointedly. "You keep looking back like you've got a hankering to go home."

"I'm just...watchin' for *minim'millediliw.*"

Chase snorted in disbelief. They both knew there weren't any mountain lions around at this time of day. They walked another five steps before he quietly added, "All I'm saying is you don't have to come."

"O' course I do." Drew bumped him with his shoulder. "Who else is gonna keep you out o' trouble?"

He was teasing, of course. Chase never got into trouble. If he ever did, Drew was the last one he should depend on to get him out of it. But it was the same lie he'd told their folks— that someone had to watch over Chase.

The truth was Drew needed to get out of Hupa fast, and he had to get his identical twin out of there too. A case of mistaken identity could mean they'd string up his innocent brother for a crime neither of them had committed.

Going along on Chase's vision quest was as good an excuse as any to leave the reservation. It sure beat either of them twisting at the end of a rope.

The thought made Drew wince. It was too easy to imagine a noose around his neck. He adjusted the strap on his knapsack and cast another anxious look over his shoulder.

"What the hell are you looking for, brother?" Chase demanded. "And don't tell me wildcats. What is it? Someone following you?"

Drew scoffed. It was unnerving the way Chase could sometimes tell what he was thinking—unnerving and inconvenient. "Prob'ly the little filly I left back in Shasta." He winked. "I think she might have been startin' to hear weddin' bells."

Chase growled out a sigh. Drew knew Chase had no patience for his romantic escapades and didn't understand Drew's special affection for the ladies.

Drew was a heartbreaker. There was no denying that. He adored women, and they were drawn to him like ants to honey. But most times he didn't take things any further than a kiss on the cheek.

He might be a silver-tongued flirt in the saloon. He might buy a lady a drink or offer to cover her bet when she lost.

But though he was a risk-taker when it came to poker, he played his cards close to his chest when it came to matters of the heart.

It was probably because his parents had such romantic beginnings. They'd built a bridge between two very different cultures—whites and Konkows. Against all odds and a heap of disapproval on both sides, they'd managed to make it work.

His mother had left civilization.

His father had left his tribe.

But they'd taken refuge in Hupa so they could raise their

half-breed twins in peace. Sakote, their father, doted on his white wife, and Mattie's eyes still lit up when she gazed on her native husband.

Drew wanted that kind of love—eventually.

In the meantime, he'd put up with having a reputation as a ne'er-do-well and a womanizer, flitting like a greedy *xontah-yayliwh*, bumblebee, from flower to flower. People never understood that it was just the kind of life a poker player led, especially when you were a *good* poker player. You had to keep moving.

One day he'd settle down, build a big ranch house with a white picket fence, fill it with a brood of little Hawks, and wake up every morning to a warm and welcoming wife who was as pretty as a bisque doll.

But for the moment, why would he chain himself to one town and one woman when females and fortune were always calling from around the bend?

"There it is," Chase said, nodding to the stage stop ahead.

He and Chase had come from Hupa yesterday by wagon. Today they'd take the stage from Redding to Chico, and then hire a buggy to take them up the hill to Paradise. The trip would take all day. But that was fine with Drew. He'd just as soon sneak into town after dark. Nothing attracted quite as much attention as a pair of six-foot-tall half-breed twins. And the last thing he wanted to do was attract attention.

Drew resisted the urge to glance behind him one last time. With any luck, the sheriff would guess Drew was in the next state. He'd never dream that the man he was looking for was currently less than a dozen miles from the Winsome Saloon.

He flipped his pocket watch out. It was 6:30. The stage left at 7:00.

It would be after midnight when they arrived at their final destination. He wondered if there'd be any good late night card games in Paradise.

CHAPTER 5

It was past midnight, and Catalina was still working—mending a tear in Anne's petticoat.

Jenny's accident with the wine tray had robbed two hours out of Catalina's day. Slivers of crystal had found their way under the furniture and, a few times, into her fingers. The stained carpet had to be rinsed and blotted dry several times. It turned out that Jenny had dribbled ruby wine on her yellow silk dress as well. Only by drenching and blotting it repeatedly with vinegar was Catalina able to lift out the spot.

But there would be no extra time to catch up tomorrow. Her responsibilities filled every waking hour.

She sat sewing by candlelight in her room. Through her door, which was slightly ajar, she could hear men's voices coming from the salon downstairs. She furrowed her brow. They were very late. The ladies were already tucked into bed with their partners for the evening. There were no prostitutes left.

But that never stopped Miss Hattie from being hospitable. She made a bottle of whiskey and her company available at all hours. As the madam liked to say, you never knew when a lonesome millionaire might come waltzing into The Parlor with more dollars than sense.

Catalina yawned. She couldn't hear what the two men were talking about. Their conversation was muffled. At one point they raised their voices and seemed to be having a disagreement. She hoped they weren't expecting to find a companion at this time of night.

She knotted the last stitch three times and snipped off the ends of the thread. Holding the petticoat close to the candle, she examined her handiwork. It should last...at least until one of Anne's less careful lovers tugged at her drawers a little too eagerly.

Catalina gave her head and the petticoat a brisk shake. She didn't like to think about such activities, not when they involved her friends. She flipped the thimble off of her finger, draped the petticoat over her shoulder, and wearily rubbed her eyes.

She didn't wish to disturb Anne and her gentleman caller, so she planned to leave the garment on Anne's doorknob.

The men were still arguing downstairs. The last thing she wanted was to attract their attention as she crossed the balcony.

She glanced at her bare feet. It was too much trouble to put her boots back on. Besides, she could steal down the hallway more quietly without her shoes. So she rose and slipped carefully out the door.

She glanced down briefly at the salon, just long enough to glimpse Miss Hattie hovering over two black-haired men seated there. Then, tiptoeing along the hallway, she hooked the mended undergarment over Anne's doorknob.

As she turned to go back, she could hear the men's conversation. One of them was trying to talk the other out of going somewhere in the middle of the night. While they were distracted, she crossed the balcony and stole back into her room, closing the door softly behind her.

She untied her apron and tossed it over the chair. Her dress followed after. Because of the kind of labor she'd been doing of late, she'd stopped bothering with her usual layers of undergarments, corset, and bustle. She simply stepped out of her single white petticoat, shook it and draped it atop her dress.

She caught her reflection in the mirrored dresser. How much she'd changed since she'd arrived in Paradise in her impeccably tailored cocoa-and-cream ensemble. Clad in only a camisole and drawers, she didn't look very different from the ladies of the evening.

She rose and took the pins out of her hair, one by one, placing them in the crystal dish on top of the dresser, letting the black curls fall over her shoulders.

Then there was a knock at the door.

It was probably one of the clients who'd gone to the outhouse and returned to the wrong door. It wouldn't be the first time it had happened. She'd peer out through a crack in the door. He'd instantly realize his mistake. Then she'd ask him whose room he was looking for and steer him in the right direction.

But when she cracked opened the door, it was Miss Hattie.

Her heart sank. What had she forgotten to do? She'd already undressed. She was exhausted. Couldn't it wait until the morning?

But Miss Hattie had a curious expression on her face, the same expression she'd had that first day they'd met, as if she were judging Catalina's character.

"*Si?*" Catalina asked.

"You've been here almost a month, ain't that right?" she murmured.

"Yes."

"And you seem to be...fittin' in real well."

Catalina tapped impatient fingers on the door. Couldn't this wait until tomorrow? She answered with forced courtesy. "Thank you."

Miss Hattie chewed at her lip.

Catalina frowned. Miss Hattie was usually quick and clever, but at the moment she was struggling for words. What was bothering her?

Miss Hattie leaned closer to the crack of the door and whispered, "How would you like to make a little extra money?"

Catalina's shoulders drooped. There were already too few hours in the day. How could she possibly add another job to her schedule?

Miss Hattie hastened to add, "I don't want you doin' somethin' you ain't ready for. Lord knows it's not everyone's cup o' tea."

"Cup of tea?" Did Miss Hattie want her to start serving tea in the salon instead of scrubbing floors? That might be a pleasant change.

Miss Hattie beckoned her closer with her finger. Catalina leaned in until their faces were inches apart and she could see every wrinkle in the madam's powdered face.

"How would you feel about...havin' a gentleman caller?"

Catalina's brow furrowed. "What do you mean?" She was afraid she knew exactly what Miss Hattie meant.

"Like some o' the other girls."

Before Catalina could respond with an outraged outburst, Miss Hattie held up her palm.

"Now hear me out," she whispered. "You don't have to do nothin' you don't want to do. I won't think any less of you. You won't lose your job. And you won't lose your room and board. But I know you need cash. And *you* know how much money the other girls are makin'."

Catalina's jaw was clenched so tight, she feared it would crack like a china cup. Still, she couldn't deny that the lure of all that coin was strong.

She paused for one, two, three seconds, pretending to think it over out of courtesy to Miss Hattie. But in the end, she couldn't do it. She straightened and announced, "No. I'm sorry. It is not possible."

From the hall, she heard a man's deep voice. "I'll pay you double."

Her eyes went wide. She hadn't realized the prospective "gentleman caller" was right outside her door.

Miss Hattie's eyes widened as well, and she hissed at Catalina. "Lordy, I told him you cost five dollars. That's already more than double what Sophie gets. He's offerin' you *ten*. Look, I know you're a smart young lady—"

"No!" Catalina said firmly, loud enough for the man to hear. "I am not for sale."

"Fifteen," the man called out.

Miss Hattie was almost apoplectic now. Her face was red, and she pressed her face through the crack in the door with new desperation. "Catalina, no one's ever offered fifteen before."

She hissed, "I do not care if he offers me the moon and the stars. I am not that kind of a woman."

Even as she said the words, she imagined all those lovely silver coins drifting through her fingers onto the floor. She almost wished she *were* that kind of a woman. To think a man was willing to pay fifteen dollars for her...

Miss Hattie could have burned holes into Catalina with her fierce glare. She probably thought Catalina was the most stupid woman she had ever met to turn down such a fortune. And the truth was, Catalina almost wondered if she didn't agree.

"Look," the man outside said, sounding a bit exasperated, "I won't even knock boots with you if you don't want to."

Miss Hattie almost fainted at that.

He continued. "All I want is a soft bed and someone warm to share it with."

Catalina arched a brow. He'd pay her fifteen dollars just to sleep next to her? She'd slept beside strangers on the journey to California...and had to pay for it herself...a whole dollar.

But he'd said "warm." That meant he would want to lie close to her.

She angled herself so she could take a quick peek over Miss Hattie's head at the man in the hallway. All she could see was his black hair and the square edge of his jaw.

Miss Hattie tried one more time, muttering, "He seems like a real gentleman, Catalina, like a man of his word. He's a handsome young fella. I think you'd like—"

"Eighteen dollars," the man offered.

Miss Hattie blinked in disbelief, and Catalina's brows shot up. Eighteen dollars? The man must either be crazy or very, very tired.

Miss Hattie whispered furiously at her. "If you don't take this offer, Catalina, you'll regret it. Never in my born days has anyone offered eighteen dollars just to spend the night with—"

"Twenty!" Catalina blurted out, immediately covering her mouth with her hand. She couldn't believe she'd said that. What was she thinking?

"What?" Miss Hattie burst out, unable to disguise her amazement.

The man in the hall exclaimed in disbelief. "Twenty?"

A long silence hung in the air like a storm cloud.

Miss Hattie's eyes gleamed at the prospect. But Catalina was still reeling from her outburst. What had possessed her to make a counter offer? She could only hope it was such a ridiculous price that no man in his right mind would accept it.

"Fine," he said, "twenty."

Catalina gulped. Surely the man hadn't agreed to her offer. Surely for twenty dollars, he was going to expect...something more than sleep.

"You will not make the sex with me?" Catalina reminded him, calling to him over Miss Hattie's head.

"Yes. No. Fine."

"Also, I do not want to take off all my clothings."

Miss Hattie frowned. She clearly disapproved of Catalina's conditions.

He grumbled something. "Fine."

"And I would like a bottle of whiskey," Catalina added. She'd doubtless need fortification for the night ahead.

"A bottle o'...?" He sighed. "All right."

"Okay. Fine," Catalina said, though it came out on a squeak. *Ahime!* What had she done?

She closed her eyes, blew out a breath, and straightened her shoulders.

It would be fine. Everything would be fine. He had promised her no sex. It was only one night. And tomorrow she would have twenty whole dollars.

Surely she could survive one night with a stranger.

Then again, she hadn't counted on the stranger being so bold and handsome and irresistible.

CHAPTER 6

Drew knew he wasn't playing with a full deck when he agreed to that offer. Nobody north of San Francisco paid a whore twenty dollars. And nobody but a shriveled old man paid a whore just to look at her.

Hell, he couldn't even believe he was frequenting a brothel when all he really needed was a place to stay for the night. But what had made him raise the stakes so high? He was behaving like a greenhorn gambler, wagering big money on a blind hand.

No, not quite blind. Even the quick glimpse he'd caught of the lady from downstairs told him she was something special. Her black hair shone like satin. Her close-fitting dress revealed sleek curves that would fit as perfectly in his hand as those of his Colt forty-five. And her bare feet were more seductive than the collective cleavage of all the saloon girls at the Winsome Saloon.

Once he heard the exotic sound of her voice from behind the door—deliciously throaty and foreign—he was sold.

Besides, he knew women. She was toying with him. He'd

agreed to her terms—no "making the sex," no removing all her "clothings." But he was sure that was all part of some cat-and-mouse game of seduction. Everyone knew a man wanted most what he couldn't have. Playing hard to get was a surefire way to goose up the price. Hell, the madam was probably in on it.

Besides, it was a safe bet that Drew Hawk could get any woman out of her knickers with a single come-hither look. One provocative whisper, and he'd have her eating out of the palm of his hand.

"It's all settled then," the madam agreed. She turned to him with a pretty convincing poker face, considering he'd just offered her ten times the going rate for a shady lady in Paradise. "Give me the twenty dollars, and she's all yours till mornin'. I'll throw in the whiskey for free."

"Much obliged." He had a stash of money in his knapsack, so he rummaged in it and dug out the right silver. For a split-second, he wondered if he'd been too hasty. After all, he'd only caught a fleeting glimpse of the shady lady. What if she had the face of a mule?

But then he supposed he was a gambling man. He dropped the coins into the madam's palm.

The instant the madam opened the door wide, he felt like he'd been dealt a royal flush. The breath deserted his lungs. All he could do was gape. The lady could have demanded *fifty* dollars. It would still be a bargain.

She was as pretty as a bisque doll. Enticing ebony ringlets caressed her cheeks and cascaded over her shoulders. Her skin had a lovely glow, warm and vibrant. Her lips were rosy, her chin had an adorable cleft, and a tiny, kissable mole resided beside her mouth. Her eyes were wide and wild, like dark honey.

She gave a tiny gasp. She was fully clad in her underclothes. But she still clutched one defensive arm across her bosom and splayed her other hand in front of her nether parts as if shielding them from his view. For a sporting lady, she was pretty good at playing innocent.

When he finally found his voice, he gave her a slight nod. "Howdy, ma'am."

She gulped in response.

"May I come in?" he asked.

Why he was being so hesitant, he didn't know. Maybe he was just dumbstruck by her beauty. But he'd paid his twenty dollars. The room and the lady in it were his for the night.

"Catalina!" the madam scolded. "Let the gentleman in."

She blinked, as if suddenly waking up, and backed away from the door. She fidgeted with her garments as he entered the room. He dropped his knapsack against the wall.

"I'll be right back with the whiskey," the madam said.

Then there was a drawn-out, awkward silence while they waited for the madam to return.

After a moment, the lady attempted to strike a casual pose, resting one hip against the dresser. But she knocked over a few small bottles on the marble top. She turned away to right them, glancing up at him in the mirror.

It wasn't his fault that his gaze dropped to her lovely backside. But in her reflection, her brows drew together in disapproval.

He looked away with a sniff, whacking his hat against his thigh a few times. Then he tossed it toward the coat rack beside the door...and missed.

Shit. He never missed. What was wrong with him? He retrieved his hat and hung it on the peg.

Finally, he broke the silence. "My name is Drew, Drew Hawk."

"Mr. Hawk." She gave her head a quick nod.

A smile tugged at his mouth. Mr. Hawk? That was awfully

formal for someone who planned to share a bed with him. "Call me Drew."

"Drew."

He liked the way she said it, with a little flick of her tongue over the "r."

She turned to face him then, but another long quiet ensued. Her eyes flitted over the furniture in the room, anywhere but on him.

Damn, she was beautiful. She had a figure like an hourglass, curved in all the right places. It made his loins ache just to look at her.

He cleared his throat. "Your name is...Catalina?"

She nodded, then volunteered, "Catalina Alfredo Romanesca di Lasso Ferragamo—"

The madam swept in with a bottle of whiskey and two glasses, interrupting her mid-name. "Here you go."

To his surprise, Catalina...Etcetera...rushed forward to seize the whiskey. Apparently, she was eager to start her night of drunken revelry...minus the revelry.

She poured herself a finger of whiskey and slugged back half of it at once. Then she gasped and began coughing.

"Whoa, little lady," he said.

The madam slipped out then, closing the door behind her, probably so the coughing wouldn't wake up the whole place.

He wasn't sure if Catalina's wheezing gasp that followed was from the burn of the whiskey or the fact that there was now a closed door between her and the madam. But she looked genuinely worried.

He started toward her, intending to clap her on the back a few times to make sure she wasn't choking. Her eyes wide, she backed up against the dresser.

He furrowed his brow. He'd thought the woman was playing coy. But now he wasn't so sure. Was she actually scared of him?

He'd seen his brother Chase get this reaction out of women before. His growling bear of a twin could frighten women just by walking into the room.

But Drew was nothing like Chase. Drew was a friendly fellow. With a wink and a smile, he could charm the stockings off a schoolmarm.

Of course, he wasn't exactly smiling at the moment. And she wasn't exactly a schoolmarm. Maybe he wasn't smiling because he was still in shock that he'd paid twenty dollars to spend the night with a lady who said she didn't want to have relations with him, even more shocked that he still felt like he'd gotten a pretty good deal.

But he'd paid for a body to warm his bed. He couldn't get a good night's rest while the woman lying next to him was shivering with fear...or choking on whiskey. He'd have to convince her he didn't mean her any harm. He might be ruthless when it came to gambling, but when it came to matters of the heart, he was as gentle as a kitten.

"There's no cause to be scared o' me."

"Scared?" She straightened. "I am not scared." Then she angled her head to look at him uncertainly, arching a fine brow. "Should I be?"

Drew could think of several reasons a woman should be afraid to be in a room alone with a stranger. But he didn't need to tell her the risks of her own profession.

"Not o' me," he told her. "I've never raised a hand to a woman in my life." Then an ugly thought crossed his mind. "You ain't nervous 'cause I'm a half-breed, are you?"

"A what?"

"A half-breed."

"What is this—half-breed?"

If she didn't already know, he wasn't much inclined to tell her. But something about that tiny furrow between her brows told him he should tell her the truth.

50

"I'm half white and half Indian," he admitted. "My father's a Konkow."

"Konkow," she echoed.

He liked the way she said it. He liked the way she said everything, even "half-breed." Her voice had an intoxicating rough edge to it, as well as a fascinating accent.

"You don't mind, do you?" he asked.

She shrugged, puzzled. "You did not decide how you were born."

"Right." He liked that answer. "So where are you from, Miss Catalina?"

"*Italia.* Italy."

He reached behind her for the whiskey and his glass, and she stiffened. He decided she was the most skittish hooker he'd ever seen.

The soiled doves he'd met were experts at seduction and usually in a hurry to ply their wares. In fact, he suspected most times they didn't get as much pleasure out of it as the men did and just wanted to get it over with.

But this one didn't seem in a hurry to do anything.

Not that he'd let that put him off. It just made seducing her more of a challenge.

He poured himself a shot, swirled it around the glass, and then tossed it back.

She followed suit, but wound up gasping and choking again.

"You all right, ma'am?"

She nodded, but her face was red and her eyes were watering.

"You ever drink whiskey before?"

She closed her eyes and shook her head.

He grinned. What on earth had made her order a whole bottle, he didn't know...unless...

His grin faded. "Wait a minute. You ever done...*this* before?"

"This?"

"Slept with a man?"

"Of course," she choked out, almost too insistently. "Yes, yes. Many times. Many, many times."

The lady couldn't bluff worth a damn.

It was obvious now she wasn't playing an innocent. She *was* an innocent. In fact, if he had to bet, judging by how jumpy she was, he'd say she had no experience whatsoever.

"Many, *many* times?" He narrowed one eye at her. "So you know what to expect?"

"What to expect?" She poured herself another shot of whiskey. Her hands were shaky, but she managed a smile. "Not too much—what you call it—snoring, I hope."

"Snorin'?"

"Back home, my brothers snored," she said with forced humor, holding the whiskey glass in both hands and staring down into the golden liquid. "Sometimes they kept me awake all night."

Drew frowned. Her brothers? He reached out to take the glass from her. "Have you ever slept with a man *here*, in The Parlor?"

She bit her lip and looked up at him with soulful brown eyes. "To be honest, Mr. Hawk, you are my first."

Damn. He was afraid of that.

"Before now, I am the housekeeper," she told him, pouring whiskey into the second glass. Then she raised it in a toast. "But do not worry. Tonight, I am The Lady of the Evening."

She said it as if it were a noble title.

He gave her a rueful smile. Something had definitely gotten lost in translation. Clinking his glass to hers, he shook his head and tossed back the whiskey.

She contemplated her glass, considering whether she should try another gulp.

If the lady weren't so adorable and it weren't so late, Drew would have marched straight down to the madam, given her a sound scolding for trying to pass off a virgin as a whore, and gotten his money back.

Catalina was obviously new to this country. He wondered if she even knew she was working in a house of ill repute.

She was lucky it was Drew and not some two-bit drunk who'd paid for her tonight. At least Drew had some respect. Though the raging bear in his trousers would be very disappointed, he'd do the gallant thing and leave her alone.

But it was late. He didn't have anywhere else to stay. His brother was off on some wild goose chase, and god only knew where he intended to sleep. Drew had already paid handsomely for the room. It would have been a waste of a good feather bed if he left now.

Maybe if he drank half the bottle of whiskey, he could forget about the pretty little untouchable lady who'd be sharing that feather bed with him tonight.

CHAPTER 7

Catalina's gentleman caller topped off her whiskey and poured another for himself.

"What did you say your full name was?" he asked.

She didn't want more whiskey. She could still feel the burn of the last shot in her throat.

Her name? She didn't remember what she'd told him before. But she never used the same name twice anyway. "Catalina Margarita Riccio di Santanella Abrizzio."

He cocked a suspicious eye at her, but didn't say anything. And Catalina thought if he kept looking at her like that, she'd *need* another drink of whiskey.

Drew Hawk was not all what she'd expected. She figured he'd look like the rest of the regulars—plain, ordinary, middle-aged—manageable and non-threatening.

And even though she'd gotten herself into this unnerving predicament, she expected she could get herself out of it. She'd observed how the ladies of the evening dealt with their clients. Besides, he'd promised not to have intercourse with her. How difficult could it be?

Then tall, dark, handsome Drew Hawk had come striding into her room as if he belonged there. Oozing masculine confidence, he'd taken her breath away and left her speechless. He appeared to be a bit travel-worn, but he was well-dressed, in snug brown wool trousers, a white cotton shirt, a brown brocade vest, a long oilcloth duster, and quality leather boots.

Yet despite his civilized attire, he looked nothing like a manageable regular. In fact, he looked about as manageable as a wild stallion.

His hair was black like hers, and the thick curls teased at his neck. He was clean-shaven, though it looked like it had been a few days since he'd shaved. His skin was a rich golden color, and his teeth shone white against his face when he smiled. But it was his dark, sparkling eyes that captivated her. They were so compelling that she couldn't look into them for too long, fearing she'd lose herself in their shimmering depths.

"Cheers," he said, handing her a glass and clinking it with his. "This time, just sip. Watch me." He winked, making her heart skip.

Maybe she needed that whiskey after all.

He took a small sip to show her.

She raised the glass to her lips in imitation, taking a tiny sip. Then she caught her reflection in the mirror and choked again. *Santo cielo!* She was standing beside the tall, handsome, fully dressed man in nothing but her camisole and drawers, with her hair loose over her shoulders, sipping whiskey. She looked just like all the other soiled doves of The Parlor. How quickly she'd become a fallen woman.

"You okay?" he asked with a chuckle. It was a delightful sound.

She nodded.

But she was still startled by the difference in their size. How she ever dreamed she could manage such a man, she didn't know. He was so big, he could carry her off in one arm.

"Just how do you plan to finish off that bottle if you keep chokin' on it?" he teased. He tossed back the rest of his glass and set it, empty, on the dresser.

While she cautiously sipped at the contents of her own glass, he boldly seated himself on the edge of her bed.

She stiffened, suddenly feeling violated. This was *her* room. A stranger shouldn't be sitting on her bed.

Then she remembered the twenty dollars he'd paid for the privilege.

Was it really so terrible to have him here? He wasn't doing her any harm. He'd promised not to bed her. He wasn't even insisting that she get undressed.

Still, his presence was affecting her. She wasn't sure whether the warm glow in her cheeks was from the whiskey or the thought of the man making himself at home in her room.

He waggled one of the bedposts, as if testing its strength.

She gulped down the whiskey all at once and instantly poured herself another. This time, she managed not to choke, but she winced as it seared a path down her throat.

"So what brought you to California, Miss..." He screwed up his brow. "Tell me your name again?"

What had she told him before? It didn't matter. He wouldn't notice it was different. Besides, after tomorrow, she'd never see him again.

"Catalina Isabella Fortuna di Rosetti Cesare Bertolini."

He smirked. There was a knowing twinkle in his eye. "If I had a name that long, I might not remember it either."

She couldn't stop the color flooding her cheeks. She hoped he'd think it was from the whiskey. To be honest, she wasn't sure it *wasn't* the whiskey. It was starting to warm her in the most curious way.

She took another sip. This time she let the liquor swirl over her tongue. Beneath the fire of the whiskey was a sweet taste, almost like caramel.

"If it's all right with you, I think I'll just call you Cat."

"Cat?"

He shrugged. "Sure."

"Like the little animal?"

"Yeah."

A giggle escaped her. She clapped her hand over her mouth, trying to catch it, but it slipped through her fingers.

"Is that funny?" he asked.

She nodded. It was—a little. She peered at him over the top of her glass. "You are Drew Hawk, yes?"

"That's right."

"And the cat, she hunts the hawk."

He chuckled. "I suppose so." Then his eyes twinkled, like a spark at the heart of a coal, contained yet dangerous. "Unless it's a little cat like you. Then the hawk swoops down and carries her off."

She gasped. But to her surprise, the gasp turned into laughter. This whiskey was having a strange effect on her. She took another drink and arched a challenging brow at him, declaring, "I may be small, but I am fierce."

He sank back onto his elbows and gave her a lazy grin.

Something melted inside her. Maybe it was the magic of the whiskey. Maybe it was a trick of the lantern light. But Drew Hawk suddenly looked very attractive. She didn't think it would be so bad to sleep next to him.

"Maybe you'd better take it easy with that whiskey," he suggested.

She didn't think so. It made her feel more brave and sure of herself.

"Maybe you should drink *more,*" she decided, filling his glass and handing it to him.

He didn't drink it. Instead, he set it down on the bedside nightstand. Then he rose, towering over her, and took off his duster.

Her fingers tightened on her glass. He'd told her she could keep her clothes on. He hadn't said anything about *his.* She'd seen men in all stages of undress since she started working at The Parlor. But she hadn't been this close to one. And she'd never been alone in her room with a man—dressed or undressed.

"Think I can make it this time?" he asked her, bunching his duster in one hand and nodding toward the coat rack.

She frowned and shook her head. The oilcloth was too heavy.

But he gave her another wink and tossed his duster, collar first. It caught perfectly on the hook of the coat rack, which tipped for a precarious instant and then righted itself.

"*Bravo,*" she said, drinking to his success.

But when she turned back to him, she saw what he wore under his duster. A heavy leather gun belt hung low on his hips. The holster was knotted with rawhide around his thigh. In the holster was a large pistol.

The whiskey glass clacked against her teeth as she stumbled back a step. He didn't seem like a cold-blooded killer. But she didn't know him. And the fact that he had a gun within reach...

Miss Hattie usually didn't allow strangers to take their guns into the rooms with the girls. She must have overlooked his weapon in her excitement over the twenty dollars.

"Don't you worry, Cat. It's just for protection," he volunteered. "Here, I'll take it off, all right?"

He untied the rawhide thong and unbuckled his gun belt. Then he wrapped the belt around the holster and set it on the nightstand next to his whiskey.

But taking off his gun didn't trouble her nearly as much as him taking off the rest.

Drew knew by the tension in Cat's jaw that she'd prefer he keep his clothes on. But he damn well didn't intend to sleep in his boots. She'd just have to put up with his bare feet. Hell, he'd grown up in Hupa, where everyone ran around barefoot.

He sat down on the mattress and crossed his right ankle over his knee. Then, with a scheming glance, he began tugging at the heel of his boot, grunting and grimacing as if it were stuck fast.

After watching him for a moment, she asked, "You need help?"

"I'd be much obliged, ma'am."

She knelt before him, took his big boot in her small hands, and pulled, inching it off slowly.

"So..." she asked, nodding to his Colt. "Are you a gunfighter?"

He chuckled. "Naw."

"That is too bad."

"It is?"

"I would sleep much better with a man who is a good shot beside me."

"Well, I *am* a good shot. At least I can keep the varmints at bay."

She screwed up her forehead. "Varmints? What is this..." She was interrupted when the boot slid off. She set it aside.

"Varmints," he said. "Pesky critters?" She still looked puzzled. "Never mind. Don't you worry. I'll keep you safe." He gave her his left foot. "This one's usually a mite tighter."

She rubbed her palms together, then braced them on his boot. She pulled and pulled. But he was enjoying the sight of her, so he flexed his foot to make sure the boot wouldn't come off.

Her brow was furrowed in concentration, and the tip of her tongue was wedged in the corner of her lip. The strap of her camisole had slipped down her shoulder, and at this angle, he could glimpse the subtle shadow of cleavage between her breasts.

After a few minutes, she began muttering something in her language, something he was pretty sure were curses. So he finally took pity on her and let his foot go limp.

At the same moment, she wrenched at his boot with a vengeance. It popped suddenly off of his foot, and the momentum knocked her backward.

He inhaled sharply as she rolled onto the Persian rug. He hadn't meant to do that.

But then she began to laugh, lying there on the rug, clutching his boot to her like a hard-won prize.

And then *he* began to laugh.

Their laughter tumbled together like dice in a cup, spilling out to fill the room.

After a while, it subsided, and she sat up, wiping at her watering eyes. Drew was left breathless at the sight of her in a puddle of white lace, still cradling his boot.

He wondered if she knew how beautiful she was. Maybe where she came from, *all* the ladies were that beautiful.

"You should not look at me like that," she said, clucking her tongue.

"Like what?"

"Like you wish to devour me."

He did wish to devour her. "You do look a little like a cream puff, sittin' there."

"A cream puff," she repeated, lighting up. "I know this. They have the cream puff at the bakery."

She gave him his boot, and he offered his hand to help her up. Her hand felt warm and small in his, but she had a strong, steady grip.

Now she was staring at *him*.

"You shouldn't look at me like that," he told her, still holding her hand.

"Like what?" she breathed.

"Like you're about to do somethin' you ought not to."

It was probably just the liquor, but he could see smoky seduction in her gaze, like she wanted to do something completely reckless. Maybe kiss him.

CHAPTER 8

It was probably just the whiskey, but Catalina felt giddy. It was the first time she'd felt so deliriously happy since she'd left Italy. She liked this American, Drew. He was funny and handsome, with his swarthy skin and big white teeth and hearty laugh.

"You are very pretty, Mr. Drew Hawk," she blurted out.

"Pretty?" he said with a grin. "Why, ma'am, in some circles, those are fightin' words."

She didn't know what that meant. But the fact she'd made him smile again made her heart beat faster.

He laughed, and she laughed at his laughter.

Then he took off his jacket and began unbuttoning his vest.

Her breath caught.

He didn't seem to notice.

"So what brought you to California, Cat?"

"I..." She hesitated, wondering how much of his clothing he planned to remove. "I came to make a new start."

Her nostrils flared as she watched him unbutton the vest, exposing the crisp white shirt beneath. She didn't think she'd ever seen such broad shoulders. She forced her gaze away.

"A new start. In a brothel?" he asked.

"No!" she hastened to say. "No, no."

"Then what?"

He unfastened the last button and slipped the vest off carefully so as not to spill the contents of the pockets, hanging it on the bedpost.

"I am a designer of clothings."

He tugged his white shirt out of his trousers. She swallowed.

"Ah, well, that explains it," he said.

"Explains what?"

"Why you can't seem to take your eyes off my clothings." He gave her a crooked smile.

She felt the color rise in her cheeks. She'd been staring. She knew she had. And he probably knew it had nothing to do with the cut of his shirt.

"So if you're a designer," he said, "why are you workin' at The Parlor?"

He started unbuttoning his shirt. She tried very hard not to look. But she didn't do a very good job of it.

She was definitely feeling the effects of the whiskey now. Her eyelids were growing heavy. But it was a rather pleasant feeling. And when she spoke, her voice came out low and husky. "To be a dressmaker, I must have a sew-" Her breath caught as she saw how deftly he managed the buttons. "Sewing machine," she finished.

He paused. "You can't just..." He made a stitching motion with his hands.

A giggle bubbled up inside of her and nearly escaped. If that was how Drew sewed, he was lucky his clothes did not fall apart.

"It is too slow," she explained. "But to get a sewing machine, I must have money."

"Money? How much money?"

"With the delivery?" The vee of his shirt was widening with each button he unbuttoned. It was quite distracting. "Almost one hundred dollars."

"A hundred dollars?" he said, incredulous. "That's as much as a pair of pearl-handled revolvers."

"Miss Hattie gave me a position as a housekeeper." She absently coiled a lock of her hair around her finger. "But it is only one dollar a day. It will take me many days to make enough money."

"Which is why you decided to fleece me for twenty days worth o' wages in one night?" he teased.

"Fleece? I do not know this word."

"The hell you don't," he said, laughing.

He finished unbuttoning his shirt, took it off, and hung it on top of his vest. Now there was only a single thin layer of white cotton undershirt to keep him from being indecent.

Looking at him with languid eyes and a limp jaw, she reached for the whiskey bottle again. How many glasses would it take to make her stop thinking about what was underneath that undershirt?

When he unbuttoned the top button of his trousers, she took a big gulp straight out of the bottle.

He smiled and shook his head. "You know, you keep drinkin' like that, Cat, and you're liable to get yourself in a heap o' trouble."

She was already in a heap of trouble. At least while she was drinking, she couldn't be distracted by...

Ohime! Now he'd undone the second button.

She should avert her gaze. She knew that. But her eyes were not cooperating. They kept drifting back to the man who was so brazenly undressing before her.

"So what do they drink in Italy?" he asked as his fingers moved toward the third button.

Forcing her brain to focus, she answered, *"Vino,* wine. My father is known for his wine. The vineyards of Ferrara are...are..." She stuttered, realizing she'd blurted out the name of her home. "Ferrararianna...are the best in the country." She grimaced at her clumsy improvisation. There was no such place as Ferrararianna. Hopefully, he didn't know the regions of Italy.

He paused before the last button. "Well, you may have noticed, whiskey is a mite stronger than wine."

She nodded. That was true. She'd never once choked on a glass of wine, nor had she ever become so giddy on so little.

She gulped as he undid the last button and slid the trousers from his hips. He was still wearing his drawers—white cotton with long legs, tied and fastened with buttons. But to her consternation, they did little to hide what was between his legs. And that part of him seemed somewhat more pronounced than anything that would fit beneath the fig-leaf-covered statues in Rome.

While she tried not to look, he shook out his trousers and hooked them on the bedpost along with the rest of his clothes.

Per carità! She hoped he was finished. Between the whiskey, her own state of undress, and the alluring magnificence of his body...

She set her drink down and tried to walk as casually as possible to the opposite side of the bed. There she knelt, folded her hands, bowed her head, and began to pray.

Mostly she prayed for her own salvation, because she was having the most impure and sinful thoughts. And she didn't think she could entirely blame the whiskey.

Drew stood with his hands on his hips, dumbfounded. Was

she actually saying her prayers? He didn't know much about the religion of his mother, but he was pretty sure working in a bawdy house wasn't on the list of commandments.

While he watched her with curiosity, she genuflected and then started to rise on unsteady limbs. Her eyes widened when she looked at him again, as if she'd prayed he'd be gone and he wasn't.

Placing her palms on the mattress, she pushed herself up. But her camisole tie was under one of her hands, so when she rose, it came untied.

She didn't notice, and for a few seconds, Drew battled with his own morality, debating whether to tell her. Even though he carefully avoided glancing down, he could see the luscious, deep hollow between her breasts and imagine the kisses he could place there.

In the end, his damned conscience guided him. He cleared his throat and nodded to the ties.

She furrowed her brow. She didn't understand.

"Your..." he said, waving a vague hand in the direction of her camisole.

Her frown deepened.

He tapped his own chest.

Finally she got the message. She glanced down and gasped, slamming her hands to her bosom.

"I didn't see nothin'," he assured her, thinking that was the strangest remark he'd ever made in a brothel.

She tried to tie the camisole then, but between her drunken gaze and her fumbling fingers, she made no progress. Then she started giggling.

He couldn't help but grin. Her laughter was as pretty as a music box.

"Do you need some help, ma'am?"

She nodded, still laughing.

Shaking his head, he walked around the end of the bed and

turned her by the shoulders to face him. Then he took the ends of the ribbon laces and looped them into a bow. He'd untied many a camisole, but this was the first time he'd ever laced one up. He was definitely going to lose his reputation as a lady's man if he kept up this kind of behavior.

To make matters worse, he could feel Cat's drunken, sultry smile on him the whole time. And when the backs of his fingers casually brushed the soft flesh of her throat, he felt her breath catch. He probably could have had her wrapped around his little finger with one kiss.

But he wasn't going to. As much as it felt like a curse right about now, he did his thinking with his brain and not his balls. His principles still outweighed his pining.

So, ignoring her languid eyes and her luscious lips, her silky skin and her warm, whiskey-laced breath, he made quick work of the tie and stepped back a pace.

Nonetheless, though he could manage a good poker face, he couldn't say the same for what rose to attention in his drawers.

The little lady took immediate note of his interest, blushed in horror, and practically dove beneath the covers.

While he circled back to his side of the bed, she lay stiffly on her back and pulled the covers up to her chin.

With a self-mocking sigh, he punched his pillow and threw back his half of the covers.

"You do not say your prayers?" she asked in surprise.

He hesitated. He could have explained to her that he wasn't exactly a Christian. His mother followed the Bible. But he'd been raised in the Hupa tradition. His beliefs lay somewhere in between.

He could have explained that. But rather than trying to engage her in a deep philosophical discussion, he decided to follow the path of least resistance.

As he knelt beside the bed, he thought how crazy it was to pray in a brothel.

"Dearly beloved..." he started. No, that wasn't right. "Dear creator..." Close enough. "Thank you kindly for the room and the whiskey...and the lovely lady to share it with. I'm sorry if I've done anything sinful." Lord, that was a long list. "And I pray that you keep us free o' varmints tonight. And please, god, give me strength. Lots o' strength. Amen."

He genuflected, though he was sure he did it backwards. Then he got up and climbed into bed, careful not to touch her.

At first, he stared up at the ceiling. But he could feel her gaze on him, and he took a gander over at her. Her eyes were watering.

"You okay, ma'am?"

Her voice was weepy. "You called me a lovely lady."

"Well, you *are.*"

"Nobody in this country has ever called me that."

That was hard to believe. Her eyes were so wet and wide and inviting, he felt like he might drown in them.

It took all his strength of will to reach over and turn the key of the oil lamp to extinguish the flame.

But with the moonlight streaming through the window, he could still see the shine of her eyes.

"I will try not to steal the covers," she promised.

He smirked, closing his eyes. And he would try not to succumb to her charm.

CHAPTER 9

At least one of Catalina's prayers was answered. Drew was still wearing his undershirt and drawers.

His eyes were closed. Lying on her side, Catalina could look at him freely now. He was truly beautiful. His profile reminded her of the statues she had seen in Firenze. His nose was noble. His chin was strong. His hair fell across his brow in unruly locks. And his lips…they looked so inviting. She licked her own lips, wondering what it would be like to kiss him.

She sighed softly.

Anne and Emily had told her that whiskey made a person drowsy. She'd already been tired from housework. By now, she should be exhausted. Her eyelids did feel heavy, but not with weariness. She was wide awake. Apparently, having a half-naked man beside her made parts of her wake up in ways she had not expected.

As she watched him, his nostrils flared, and his chest rose and fell with his breathing. What would it be like to feel his breath upon her neck? A warm shiver went through her at the thought.

His hands rested idly atop his chest. His fingers were large, but they seemed refined, not brutal. She wondered what he did for a living.

He had said he was not a gunfighter, though he claimed he was good with a gun. A cowboy or a stagecoach driver might be good with a gun, but they would also have callused hands. His hands seemed to be smooth. A bookkeeper or a lawyer would have smooth hands, but they would probably not carry a gun. And he was a few decades too late to be a gold miner.

As she continued to watch him sleep, she saw him swallow. She wondered if he was dreaming. She wondered if he was dreaming of her.

She sighed again. In the morning he would be gone. At first, she had thought that a good thing. Now she was not so sure.

She liked the half-breed. He was funny. He made her laugh. He was charming. And he was courteous.

The men in Italy were courteous, too, but only because she was the daughter of a nobleman. Here, she was just a woman, yet Drew treated her with kindness and respect. He had expressed concern over her drinking. He had told her she was lovely. And he had kept his word not to touch her.

That last was a pity. At least the tipsy part of her thought so.

She let out another long sigh.

Without opening his eyes, Drew said, "I thought we had an agreement—no snorin'."

That made her laugh. "That was not snoring," she said, giving him a chiding rap on the shoulder, absurdly glad he was awake.

"Ow," he complained, turning his head to glare at her with one eye. "*Q'ut!* How do you expect me to get any sleep if you're gonna beat me?"

"Beat you?" She grinned. "I am not beating you." She clucked her tongue. "You Americans are very soft."

He didn't take her bait. "That's right," he agreed, turning his head back and closing his eyes. "So be gentle with me."

She laughed. And then the whiskey and his teasing gave her the courage to do what she shouldn't. She reached out and tickled his ribs.

He yelped in surprise and grabbed her wrist. "Why, you little..."

Still grinning, she squealed in panic and tried to reclaim her arm. But he was holding it fast.

"Where do you think you're goin'?" he asked her.

She could only giggle in answer.

"You think you can just fondle a man without his permission?"

"Fondle? What is fondle?"

His eyes narrowed wickedly. "I'd show you, but unlike a certain little Italian lady, I'm a man of honor."

"A man of honor would let go of me." She tried to wrest her arm free, to no avail.

"I will...if you promise not to do that again."

"Do what?" she asked, all innocence. "This?" She used her other hand to attack his ribs again.

He spasmed and seized that wrist as well. "You are just full o' the devil, aren't you?"

There was something wildly exhilarating about being trapped in his grip. So though she fought against him, her struggles to get away were only halfhearted.

"What am I gonna do with you?"

She knew what she *wanted* him to do with her. Her eyes lowered to his mouth, his beautiful, desirable mouth.

"Oh, no, you don't," he warned her. "Don't you be lookin' at me like that."

"Like what?" she breathed.

71

His eyes grew smoky. She could see he wanted this as much as she did. The thought made her pulse race.

She parted her lips, wordlessly beckoning him closer.

He gathered her wrists in one hand. With the fingers of his other hand, he tilted her chin up.

She shivered in anticipation.

He lowered his gaze to her mouth.

She held her breath. He was going to do it. He was going to kiss her.

Then he snatched his hand suddenly away and began tickling her.

She shrieked, trying to twist loose. Her anger at his trickery was tempered by the fact that she couldn't stop giggling.

"Basta!" she pleaded. *"Basta!"*

He stopped with a scowl. "What did you call me?"

Breathless from laughing, she told him, "I said, stop."

"That's not what I heard."

He resumed tickling her.

She shrieked again. "Stop! *Stop!"*

He did, but he didn't let go of her. "Will you promise to stop pesterin' me?"

"Pestering?" she said, snorting with laughter. "What is this, pestering?"

"See? This is why ladies *sip* whiskey." He shook his head. "This is entirely inappropriate behavior, Miss Cat. You are corned."

"Corned?"

"Completely fuddled."

"Fuddled?" He had such funny words.

"Absolutely roostered."

"I am not a rooster. I am a Cat." She snickered at her own joke.

"Xonilwil."

She wasn't even going to try that one.

"You, ma'am, are as full as a tick."

"A tick!" She knew what a tick was. They were disgusting little bugs. She gave him a pout. "That is not nice."

"Aww, now don't go stickin' your lip out like that. I'm sorry. You've just been goin' at the whiskey pretty hard is all."

A sudden rush of indignation came over her. "You think I am a drunkard?"

He paused uncertainly.

"You do," she said, her eyes welling with tears. She pulled her arms away from him, and this time he let go of her. "I am not a drunkard."

"O' course not," he assured her.

"I am ferfectly pine." She frowned. That hadn't quite come out right.

"Ferfectly," he agreed. "Now how about you go back to your side o' the bed and we get some shut-eye?"

"Shut-eye." She puzzled over that for a moment. "This means sleep?"

"Yep."

She sighed. "I am not sleepy."

"I was afraid o' that."

He rose up on one elbow and looked down at her. His eyes shone in the moonlight. His hair looked lush and inviting. His lips were tempting. He was so beautiful.

"You are so beautiful." She furrowed her brow. Had she said that out loud?

"You should see my brother," he said.

It was an old joke for the twins. He didn't expect her to understand. In fact, he didn't think she could understand much of anything, not in the state she was in. If he'd known how incapable she was of holding her liquor, he might have stopped her sooner.

Now it was up to him to make sure she didn't get herself into trouble.

Actually, she'd taken those words—*you are so beautiful*—right out of his mouth. As he propped himself up, staring down at her, he knew he'd never seen such a breathtaking woman in his life. Her hair spilled like black ink across the white pillow. Her skin, paled by the light of the moon, looked translucent. Her eyes were drowsy with desire, and her lips were parted with longing. She was magnificent.

But one of them had to take control of the situation so it didn't get out of hand. He had no interest in taking advantage of a drunk woman, especially a drunk virgin. The way she was looking at him now—all hot and bothered—it would have been as easy as shooting fish in a barrel.

But that wasn't who Drew was.

"You will give me one kiss?" she asked.

"What?"

"One kiss. You will give me one kiss goodnight? Then I will get the shut-eye."

Was she dickering with him?

"Yeah, I don't think that's a good idea," he told her. The beast between his legs said otherwise, but *it* wasn't in charge.

"It *is* a good idea," she said. "Otherwise, I will be awake all night, wondering what it would be like."

She was a wily one. But he knew where that path led.

"Well, I can tell you what it would be like," he said. "First, you'll just want one kiss. Then, the next thing you know—"

Without warning, she grabbed him by the front of his undershirt and pulled him toward her. Their lips collided.

It was the most unschooled kiss he'd ever received. Her

lips were clamped shut and unmoving. Her eyes were wide open. And since she wasn't sure where to put her nose, it was mashed up against his.

But for some crazy reason, it still made the breath catch in his lungs and the blood rush to his loins.

He couldn't help himself. It was a simple case of action and reaction. Besides, it was only natural to try to fix what she was doing wrong.

So he tipped his head and used his mouth to coax hers open. He nipped gently at her lips, softening the contact, and she sighed against him. The desire behind that sigh was more intoxicating than the whiskey on her breath.

Her hands wandered up his chest, past his neck, to tangle in his hair.

He licked lightly at her mouth, then cradled her head in his hands and deepened the kiss. He let his tongue delve tenderly between her lips, feeling a shiver of lust go through her when her tongue made contact.

He intended to stop then. He'd given her the kiss she wanted. And though he was as randy as a spring bull, he knew when to call it quits.

But that was before the tempting little daughter of Eve tried to climb all over him. She rolled him onto his back and slung her leg over him, right where she shouldn't. Still covering his mouth with eager kisses, she settled her weight on him, and he groaned at the exquisite sensation for a full two seconds before reason intervened.

"All right," he bit out, forcing her off of him and clambering out of the bed. "That's enough o' that."

He spared her one glance. Just as he expected, she looked shocked and bereft. But it couldn't be helped. He was doing this for her own good.

He faced away from her so he could make his case without being moved to pity by the hurt in her eyes...and also so she wouldn't see the ridiculous tent pole holding out the front of his drawers.

"Now, look, Miss Cat, I know you think you're a fancy woman and all. But you just don't have the makin's o' one." He hoped she didn't think that was an insult. "What I mean to say is, you've got a future, somethin' to look forward to, a dream, a *real* dream. You should go after it. But not like this. This ain't right." He spoke over his shoulder. "Look, you can't tell me you came all the way from Italy with a dream in your pocket and stars in your eyes, just to settle for toilin' away in a bawdy house. Have a little patience," he suggested. "Get work someplace else. A nice lady like you shouldn't be sellin' her virginity." He sighed. "Sure, it'll take some time to save up enough money for that sewin' machine o' yours. But in the end, it'll be worth it. You'll still have your self-respect. You'll be able to hold your head up high. And one day," he added, though the words stuck in his craw, "you'll find the right man to love you and care for you, a man who'll be mighty pleased to call you his wife. And you'll be able to come to him, pure and sweet, not tainted by workin' in a place like The Parlor."

She didn't answer him. Maybe he'd gotten his point across. He hoped he hadn't hurt her feelings. But what he'd said was in her best interests. He'd hate to think that after he left, she'd fall prey to some gentleman caller who wasn't so gentlemanly.

He turned back to her, careful to cover his raging erection.

"Understand, Cat?" he said softly.

There was no response.

"Cat?"

He moved closer to the bed.

The little darling was passed out. Her mouth hung open, and her limbs were splayed across most of the bed.

"Shit." He'd wasted a perfectly good speech.

Rolling her onto her side of the bed, he climbed under the covers and turned his back to her. How he'd get to sleep with a stick of wood in his drawers, he didn't know. But at least he'd wake with the knowledge he hadn't compromised the soused little lady.

CHAPTER 10

Catalina was startled awake by the sound of someone bursting in through her bedroom door. She instinctively dove beneath the covers and went still.

It took her a moment to remember the events of the night before, another moment to realize that Drew Hawk was still in her room.

He wasn't in the bed, however. He'd leaped up at once to confront whoever had broken in. She wondered if they were varmints and if he'd shoot them.

It sounded like two men. They were snarling at each other. She couldn't hear exactly what was going on. The voices were muffled. But the men seemed quite upset, and there was some scuffling in the room. She thought she heard them say something about a missing little girl.

Finally, she heard the door close. She threw back the covers.

Before she could even take a breath, in one smooth, lightning-fast move, Drew reached for his gun. He cocked and aimed it at her.

She drew in a sharp breath. In another split-second, he might have pulled the trigger.

But then his shoulders drooped, and he lowered his weapon. He ran a quivering hand through his hair and put the gun back on the night table.

"Sorry, ma'am."

Catalina's heart was still in her throat. She'd never seen anyone so fast with a gun. But Drew looked almost as shaken as she felt.

He sank down onto the bed.

By day, he looked even more captivating. The early morning sun burnished his skin like bronze, gilded his black hair, and lent warmth to his dark eyes.

His lips curved up in a rueful smile.

She recalled kissing those lips. They had been soft and warm, not at all what she'd expected from a hulking half-savage like him.

She also recalled that the kiss had been her idea. Whatever had gotten into her, she had behaved like a wanton last night. And by the bright light of day, the fact that they were sitting alone together in her bedroom in nothing but their undergarments seemed very wrong.

She diverted her gaze and clutched modestly at the front of her camisole. What had she been thinking, drinking so much? Today she had a dry mouth, gritty eyes, and an aching head.

She supposed it could be much worse. He could have taken advantage of her while she was drunk.

She pressed at her throbbing temples.

"Feelin' that whiskey?" he asked.

She nodded.

"They say the best thing is hair o' the dog, but in your case, I'm not so sure that's a good idea."

Catalina shuddered. She did not want to eat dog hair.

Besides, it was not the first time she'd been drunk. Once she had something normal to eat, she'd be fine.

"Who were those men?" she asked. Her voice came out on a croak.

"Just a local rancher and his lapdog," he said.

She frowned. She hadn't heard a dog. "What did they want?"

"It was a case of mistaken identity and a misunderstandin'. I think they were lookin' for Chase. Lots o' folks mistake me for my brother. We're twins."

"Twins?"

"Yep, identical. At least that's what they say. But *I* can tell us apart. So can *he.*" He gave her a wink.

She couldn't help but grin at his absurd logic.

"There's that beautiful smile," he said.

Of course, that made her smile even more.

He was not such bad company, she decided. In fact, a part of her wished he could stay. They could have someone bring them breakfast in bed, and they could spend a leisurely morning, chatting over coffee.

But he must have places to go, and she had things to do.

"Do you know the time?" she asked.

He pulled the pocket watch out of the vest he'd dropped on the floor. "Quarter past eight."

Ahime! She had to get to work. She started to spring from the bed, but was suddenly self-conscious about her lack of attire.

"I'll go first," he offered, "and leave you to your ablutions."

He pulled on his trousers and a clean white shirt from his satchel, slipped on his vest, shoved his feet into his boots, strapped on his gun, and slung his duster over one shoulder.

"This place serve breakfast?" he asked.

She nodded.

"Would you like me to bring you some?" he asked.

For one dreamy moment, she absolutely did want him to bring her breakfast. In Italy, the maid always brought her a *cappuccino* and a *cornetto*. But she was no longer in Italy. She had to fend for herself. Not only that, but it was usually her job to serve coffee and biscuits to the ladies of The Parlor upstairs.

Still, it was a kind gesture. "Thank you, but no. I must begin my work."

"All right, pretty lady. Thank you kindly for the company." He grabbed his hat off of the rack. He hesitated at the door. "Promise me you'll think about another line o' work. Not all men are as gentlemanly as me. A fine woman like you deserves a better life."

Her heart softened at his words. But before she could thank him, he slipped out the door to go down to breakfast.

She hurried into her petticoat and laced up her boots. Then she looked in the mirror. Her hair was a mess. Seizing her hairbrush, she untangled it as best she could, then wound it into a loose bun on top of her head. She splashed water on her face from the basin. Then she slipped her dress on carefully over her head and topped it with a fresh apron.

She glanced at the bed. It should be made before she left the room. As she smoothed the sheets and fluffed the pillows, she couldn't help but notice that his side of the mattress was still warm. She held his pillow up to her face. It smelled like him. She couldn't say how. He didn't wear perfume like her brothers. But there was some masculine scent, like leather and vanilla and sweet smoke, lingering on the linen.

She hugged the pillow to her breast. His words haunted her. *You deserve a better life.* She'd had a better life in Italy, at least when one measured life in wealth and comfort.

And it seemed mad to her that she'd just earned twenty dollars for enjoying a man's company when she was about to scrub and toil all day today for a mere dollar.

But perhaps Drew was right. Perhaps she should not work in such a place.

She tossed the pillow back onto the bed. Then, straightening her shoulders, she went into the hall.

There was the usual flurry of morning activity as the gentlemen callers began to leave the ladies' rooms. But there was a knot of prostitutes at one end of the hall, scowling and whispering behind their hands, glancing up at her.

She sighed. She should be used to their hatred by now. But it was still annoying.

"Is it true?" Anne asked, rushing up and grabbing her elbow.

"What?"

"Did you have a gentleman caller last night?"

Catalina frowned. Anne was right. Rumors flew more swiftly than swifts around The Parlor. "It was not like that."

Emily sidled up beside her, her eyes dancing. "Like what? What did I miss?"

Anne replied, "Catalina had her first gentleman caller."

Emily's smile froze on her face.

Anne continued. "Are you all right, Catalina? Did he hurt you? I swear to god, if he hurt you—"

"He did not hurt me."

Anne and Emily exchanged baffled glances.

Emily cleared her throat. "Have you ever...was this your first...what exactly..."

Anne wasted no words. "Were you a virgin?"

Catalina's eyes went round. "Of course. How can you ask me such a thing?"

"And you're sure he didn't hurt you?" Anne asked. "You can tell me, Catalina. He didn't make you do anything...untoward?"

"No. He just wanted to sleep."

Emily cocked her head. "Sleep?"

Anne looked both ways for eavesdroppers and whispered, "Because I heard he offered you twenty dollars. Nobody—"

"Twenty dollars!" Emily exclaimed, silencing everyone in The Parlor.

Catalina closed her eyes, completely humiliated.

"That's right, girls," Miss Hattie announced as she came ambling down the hallway. "You better keep on your toes, or our sweet Miss Catalina will steal all your regulars."

It was the worst thing she could have said. Most of the ladies hated Catalina already. Now they would be even more envious.

She heard cat-eyed Amanda mutter under her breath, "She musta done somethin' real nasty for that kind o' cash."

The ladies around her agreed.

"Don't pay 'em any mind," Emily told her. "They're just jealous."

Anne asked shyly, "*Did* you do somethin' nasty?"

"No!" she hissed. Then, fed up with the lot of them, she squared her shoulders, picked up her skirts, and went downstairs to start the day's work.

Sitting at breakfast with the other men in the salon, Drew had gone quiet. He stared down at his coffee. He hadn't meant to embarrass Cat. But he was sure she was embarrassed. He could tell by the way she stomped down the stairs and took off for the kitchen with a scowl.

Did everyone know how much he'd paid for her? If they didn't before, they did now. Why had the madam spilled the beans?

The men beside him started talking. And pretty quickly, he learned what Miss Hattie was up to.

The man with the long-handled mustache shook his head. "Twenty dollars. What man in his right mind pays a hooker in this cow town twenty dollars? I mean, she's a pretty thing, sure, but..." He rubbed his whiskers. "For that much gold, she must do somethin' awful special."

Drew tensed his jaw.

The man across from him puffed on his cigar. "Maybe she's one o' them Frenchies. Or maybe she lets you do her in the caboose."

Drew took the last swig of coffee, grinding the grounds between his teeth.

The mustached man said, "For twenty dollars, she'd have to spit-shine my nuts and swallow my wad."

"Maybe she does." The cigar man let out a raunchy chuckle.

"Damn!" The man stroked his mustache in speculation. "You think so?"

"Do you mind?" Drew finally bit out.

The two men glared at him and then exchanged an annoyed look.

The man shifted his cigar to the other side of his mouth. "What's got *your* chaps in a bunch?"

"Nothin'. It just ain't proper conversation."

"Proper conversation?" The cigar man laughed. "You know we're in a brothel, right?"

"Hey," the mustached man said. "You're him, ain't you? You're the one who paid the twenty dollars."

There was no point in denying it. "That's right."

"Holy shit." The man took the cigar out of his mouth and leaned forward in confidence. "So what'd she do for you? Was she worth it?"

"Nothin'." Drew set his coffee cup on the table. "And every penny."

"Nothin'? What do you mean, nothin'?" asked the mustached man.

"I just paid to be in the room with her." He added, "You

want any more than that, it'll cost you fifty." Somehow, the lie just rolled off his tongue like butter.

"Fifty!" boomed the cigar man.

"In fact," Drew added, "she won't even let you leave the lights on unless you give her a hundred."

"What?"

"Jiminy Christmas."

That was an out-and-out fabrication. But Drew couldn't stand the idea of either of these foul-mouthed sons of bitches going up to Cat's room.

In fact, he didn't want *anyone* going up to Cat's room.

It wasn't like he was sweet on her or anything. He just didn't think she should have her virginity taken from her by a random stranger.

How he was going to prevent that, he didn't know. But for the time being, he'd stay in the salon and try to shoo away any interested parties.

It was just as well. He didn't really have anywhere to go. He had to wait for Chase to return from whatever misadventure he'd had. Besides, there was a storm brewing outside. He didn't much feel like getting soaked. He hoped his brother had the sense to get out of the rain.

Eventually, he asked the madam for a poker deck and started up a game of five-card draw.

Even after three hours, the gossip in The Parlor persisted. And like a flaming carriage hooked up to a runaway horse, it spread to the entire town. Men kept coming out of the rain and into the salon, wondering where the twenty-dollar fancy woman was.

The madam wasn't quite as ruthless as Drew had first thought. She didn't mean to sell off Catalina to the highest bidder. But she was clever. Whenever the men would ask after the twenty-dollar hooker, she told them Catalina was all booked up, but they could have one of the other girls for just ten dollars. Drew was pretty sure the prevailing rate in a town like Paradise was no more than two or three dollars. Miss Hattie was making a killing on her fishing scheme, using Cat as bait.

But he didn't expect she'd protect Catalina all day. As soon as Cat finished her chores, Drew was sure the madam would find a gentleman caller for her to entertain for the evening.

That thought left a sour taste in his mouth.

In fact, it affected his poker playing.

He'd lost the last three hands. If he didn't start paying more attention to the game, he'd end up broke, with no place to sleep for the night.

He didn't see Catalina all day, but it didn't surprise him that she'd lie low for a while. He hoped she'd take his advice to heart and change her mind about joining the ranks of Miss Hattie's sporting girls.

Of course, the fact that he'd paid so much for her last night didn't help matters. She might have gotten the notion this was an easy way to make a quick fortune.

He knew otherwise. The ladies who worked in the trade were sometimes mistreated by drunks, ended up in the family way, and were put out to pasture when they lost their looks.

What the hell! Had he just thrown away three of a kind?

He watched as the man across from him happily scraped Drew's money into his pile.

He *had* to concentrate. It didn't look like Chase was coming back any time soon, so Drew might have to fend for himself. It was time to stop daydreaming about that pretty Italian lady and start winning his room for the night.

CHAPTER 11

"SHUT up!" Sheriff Jasper Brown snapped at Harvey as they rode away from the Hupa village. He was trying to think, and his son's yammering wasn't helping.

At first, they'd gotten nothing out of the Injuns. He wasn't surprised. He expected they stuck together like flies on a bloody carcass.

But then he glimpsed the white woman. At least, he *thought* she was white. She was decked out in the same deerskin and beads as the rest of the squaws. But there were strands of blonde hair among the gray, and she had light-colored eyes.

When he asked the chiefs about her, they claimed her name was Mati and that she and her husband, Sakote, had come to them years ago from the Konkow people.

He'd never seen an Injun with pale eyes and fair hair. So he interrogated her.

It turned out if she *had* been white, she'd been taken by Injuns so long ago she could hardly remember how to speak

English. She answered him in broken sentences with her husband glowering on. She must have been damaged in more ways than one. The pitiful woman couldn't seem to remember anything about her folks or where she'd come from.

Jasper shook his head. If a daughter of his had been kidnapped by Injuns, he'd hope she'd have the sense to kill herself.

He asked to see the woman's children. She brought them out. They ranged from fully-grown young squaws to boys who still clung to her skirts. None of them were the poker player.

But now that the sheriff had time to think, he realized the woman just might have an older son who no longer lived in Hupa.

The chiefs had said her husband was originally a member of the Konkow tribe. Most of the natives of that area had been rounded up and marched to Round Valley twenty years ago. If the gambling half-breed knew the law was on his tail and needed to hide out somewhere, his father's reservation was a likely place to go.

It was a good week's ride to Round Valley. It was an even longer trip for the half-breed, traveling on foot. Jasper might be able to catch his quarry before he ever got there. He dug his heels into his horse's flanks and picked up the pace.

"Come on, boys," he said. "We're headin' south."

Catalina had finally convinced Anne and Emily that she hadn't had relations with Drew Hawk. But persuading them wasn't easy, especially once they got a look at him. They couldn't believe a man so young and handsome and virile wouldn't be interested in sex.

She said he'd been interested, but promised he wouldn't touch her.

They arched their brows at her, telling her without words what they thought of men's promises.

After her humiliation this morning, she avoided the salon. She didn't want men staring at her as if she were a two-headed calf. But she couldn't go outdoors. It was raining heavily. So instead, she spent most of the day working in her room.

Jenny, who'd spilled wine one too many times, was relieved of her duties by Miss Hattie. But since the girl was desperate for work, she pleaded with the madam to let her stay on. She planned to try her luck at entertaining gentlemen like the rest of the ladies.

So Catalina was tasked with altering Jenny's yellow silk dress to make it more revealing, more enticing.

Though the work was slow without a sewing machine, it kept her engaged. She salvaged some violet ribbon from one of Miss Hattie's old frocks. This she tacked onto the inside and outside of Jenny's dress in two places so the ruffles could be gathered up and tied in front to reveal her knees. Then she lowered the neckline, sewing a rose crafted of more violet ribbon at the spot between her breasts. She cut off the sleeves at the shoulder and used the extra fabric to make a double flounce, which she attached as a bustle to the back of the dress. Then she sewed the buttons from the sleeves in a cluster onto the last piece of violet ribbon that Jenny could tie around her neck as a choker.

By the time she was done, most of the daylight was gone. But she was happy with the results. Jenny would be the prettiest of the painted ladies.

Someone knocked on the door.

"Come in."

It was Emily. "He's still here. I thought you'd want to know."

"Who?"

"Your gentleman caller."

A silly rush of joy flooded her veins. Drew was still here? Then she frowned. "He's not *my* gentleman caller."

"What if he asks for you again tonight?"

Again, her foolish heart leaped at the thought. "He will not."

"Why else would he still be here?"

"He will go with Mary or Amanda or...or you."

"Me?"

Even as she said it, the thought crushed Catalina.

It shouldn't. It wasn't as if Mr. Hawk belonged to her. Why would he ask for her again when he'd had no satisfaction from her last night?

Emily shook her head. "Naw, I think he wants you again."

She found herself hoping Emily was right. It would break her heart to see him go upstairs with one of the other girls.

And yet she knew that was ridiculous. She hadn't known Drew long enough to give him her heart in the first place.

"What if he offers you another twenty dollars?" Emily asked, her eyes gleaming.

"He will not." She smirked. She doubted he had another twenty dollars. And if he did, he certainly wouldn't waste it. He hadn't gotten his money's worth last night, and he knew it.

"Well, what else is he gonna spend his winnin's on?"

"His winnings?"

"He's been playing five-card draw for the last several hours. Last time I looked, he was up seventeen dollars."

Another knock came on the door.

"Come in," both of them called.

It was Anne. "He's still down there."

Emily said, "She knows. I told her."

"Did you tell her he was winnin'?"

Catalina forced her heart to calm down. She didn't believe in false hope. "Just because he's winning does not mean he wants to *spend* his winnings."

"He's got to spend his money on somethin'," Anne said. "What else would he spend it on?"

This was nonsense. "Food, clothings, a horse, whiskey..."

"She's right," Emily had to admit.

Anne planted her fists on her hips. "Whose side are you on?"

Emily bristled at that.

"All I'm sayin' is," Anne continued, "this could be your regular, Catalina."

Her regular. That was what all the shady ladies longed for—a man they could think of as a husband, a man who would be there for them, as constant as the rising of the sun.

It was a pleasant thought. She could imagine spending every night with Drew Hawk—talking about their childhoods, giggling in their bed, snuggling together under the covers. She would love to be able to look at the pillow beside her and see his beautiful face as he slept.

But as Miss Hattie liked to say, her head was not full of stuffing.

"What will be, will be," she said, shaking out the dress she'd just finished and holding it up in front of her in the mirror.

"Oh, my," Emily crooned. "That's wonderful."

"Is that for Jenny?" Anne asked.

Catalina nodded.

"She'll outshine us all," Emily said.

"Did you figure that out yourself?" Anne asked. "The ribbons and whatnot?"

"Of course."

Anne studied the dress. "Do you think you could do somethin' like that with a few o' *my* old rags?"

Catalina shrugged. "It is possible."

Emily looked longingly at the dress, reaching out to caress the ruffles in the front. "That's real pretty. My frocks could use a freshenin' up too. Would you have time to take a look at 'em? I'd pay you."

It was on the tip of Catalina's tongue to refuse her offer of payment. But then she reconsidered. She'd learned to her chagrin that the twenty dollars she'd earned last night was in fact only half hers. The other half belonged to Miss Hattie. Of course, it made perfect sense. Miss Hattie owned The Parlor, after all, and kept the ladies housed and fed. But it meant that earning enough for her sewing machine would take that much longer.

As for Anne and Emily, when Catalina's business was thriving, she would make special dresses for them for free. But for now, she had to save every penny she could.

"Bring them in," she said. "I will look at them."

The three ladies spent half an hour poring over the dozen dresses between them. Catalina saw a lot of possibilities— ways to make the gowns more stylish, ways to make a more flattering fit, ways to add lace and bows here and there for interest. By the time Anne and Emily left to begin work, their eyes were shining with excitement. Catalina wished she could start on the dresses right away.

But there were other chores to do. She had to wash the dishes from dinner and sweep the floors.

Still, her mind was so full of ideas for making over her friends' gowns that she completely forgot about Drew Hawk.

As she sidled past the ladies strutting on the balcony and started down the stairs, her breath caught at the sight of him, playing cards with three other men at one of the tables. His hair was glossy in the lamplight, and his sleeves were neatly rolled up to his elbows, revealing muscular forearms. He dealt the cards with practiced dexterity. And even though he had a casual look about him, as if he hadn't a care in the world, she could see him studying the other players.

She continued down the stairs, and the motion made him

glance up, twice. The second time, his face broke into a small smile of pleased recognition.

Her heart fluttered. She'd forgotten how appealing he was, with his twinkling eyes and his sly grin.

"Hawk!" one of the other men barked. "Your move."

Drew turned his attention back to the game, and she tried to stop her racing heart. It was no use longing for what she couldn't have. Drew Hawk was not a foolish man. He knew he'd wasted his money last night. He wouldn't do it again. She just hoped, if he was seeking entertainment, he wouldn't choose Anne or Emily. Or Amanda, who was too cruel. Or Mary, who was too pretty for her own good. Or Jenny, who was too young for him. Or...or any of them.

She sighed. What was wrong with her, she didn't know. It wasn't like she owned him. He was a free man. He could spend his money where he liked.

Besides, she had dishes to do.

Chapter 12

Drew almost missed the bald man's tell. He'd allowed himself to be distracted by the beautiful woman coming down the stairs.

She was even more mouthwatering than he remembered. Her hair was mostly up, but a few tempting strands had come loose to tease at her neck. Her lips were slightly parted, and he knew exactly how they tasted. She might be wearing that same faded blue dress, but now he could imagine vividly what was beneath it.

His inattention might well have cost him the game. But the bald man softly cleared his throat, as he had every time he'd been dealt a good hand. Drew folded.

Sure enough, the bald man took everyone else's money, crowing with unsportsmanlike glee. Then he proceeded to count it in front of them.

"Looks like I might have enough to buy me that twenty-dollar whore," he announced.

"She ain't for sale." That rolled off of Drew's tongue, all by itself. He hadn't even known he was going to say it.

"What do you mean?"

"The lady ain't for sale," he repeated.

"Who says?"

"I do."

"What are you, her brother or somethin'?"

"Nope."

"Well, then, mister, I don't think it's up to you." He scraped his chair back and stood, motioning Miss Hattie over.

Drew bit the inside of his cheek. He didn't intend to let the cocky bastard sleep with Cat.

When the madam came to the table, the man said, "I want to buy me that new twenty-dollar ride."

Drew waited for the madam to tell him she wasn't for sale and to offer him another girl for ten, just as she'd been doing all day.

But this time she didn't.

Instead, she glanced once at Drew and then addressed the man. "Is that so? You got that kind o' money?"

Drew's heart shot into his throat. "She ain't for sale."

The bald man grinned. "I got all kinds o' money." He tapped his fingers next to his pile of coins.

Miss Hattie looked impressed. "Well, then, it looks like you're gonna have yourself a—"

"I already bought her." It was the only thing Drew could think to say.

The bald man smirked. "Sure, you did."

"That's right," Drew said, standing, scooping up all his winnings, and dumping them into the madam's hands. "Bought and paid for."

"Now wait just a goldarn minute. I claimed her first."

"No, you didn't."

"I sure as hell did."

"I already put my bid in on her."

"Your bid? A bid ain't worth shit. And besides, you

don't *have* twenty dollars. You lost the last two hands."

He was right. But Drew wasn't going to let him know that. And he dearly hoped the madam wasn't counting his money, because it was definitely shy of twenty dollars.

"Boys, boys." Miss Hattie dropped the coins into her reticule, sidled up to the bald man, and looped her arm around his elbow. "There's no need to fight. We got plenty o' girls. Tell you what, my good man. I've got a couple o' sweet ladies up there who'll do you real good. You can have 'em *both* for twenty dollars."

"Both?" The man frowned. "At the same time?"

The madam cocked her head. "Unless you don't think you can handle 'em both."

The man's eyes gleamed. "Oh, I can handle 'em all right."

Miss Hattie called up to the balcony. "Anne! Emily! Let the nice man see your pretty selves."

Two ladies leaned over the balustrade, showing off their assets.

The bald man nodded and left his stash on the table. "Take it," he said to the madam. Then he bounded up the stairs.

The other two poker players picked up their slim winnings and bid Drew good night.

"Here." Miss Hattie poured a glass of whiskey and handed it to him. "Sit down."

Drew sat down.

The madam sat next to him and murmured, "Now we both know that wasn't twenty dollars."

"I'm good for it, I promise. I'll—"

She interrupted him with a laugh. "Honey, the way I see it, I've already turned a tidy profit from your little extravagant purchase last night. Men came from all over to take a gander at a twenty-dollar hooker. And most of 'em stayed to get half-price entertainment. So I'm not gonna make a fuss if you're a few dollars short."

Drew nodded. The madam was indeed a shrewd businesswoman. Not only had she gotten the bald man's twenty dollars. She'd gotten all of Drew's cash.

He thought she'd probably make a good poker player.

Thankfully, he was a good poker player, too. He was bluffing. That wasn't all of his money. He had a small stash at the bottom of his satchel. But he didn't like to touch it unless it was an emergency.

"Now there's still the matter o' Catalina," Miss Hattie continued. She poured herself a finger of whiskey and tossed it back, then gave her head a shake. "Call me crazy, but I won't make my girls do anything they don't want to. Catalina, she's special. This ain't her regular line o' work. And I got to be frank with you, if she says no, you got to respect that."

"O' course." He lowered his eyes to his whiskey. "I know you prob'ly think I'm a no-count gambler, but my mama taught me a thing or two about women. If Catalina doesn't want me to touch her, I won't."

"As long as we're clear."

"Yep."

"One other thing," she said, putting her hand atop his forearm. "It could get real pricey for you, payin' to keep all the other gents away from her. If you've got that much of a soft spot for the little lady, you might think about makin' an honest woman out of her."

"Whoa, hold on now. I think you've got the wrong idea." Marriage and Drew Hawk were as compatible as oil and vinegar. "I'm a rover. A man like me can't be tied down. Besides, I've only known the lady for a day."

"And yet there's already somethin' goin' on between you two," Miss Hattie said. "I've been around long enough to tell."

He smirked, thinking about the unsatisfied itch below his gun belt. "There's *nothin'* going on between us, believe me."

"Maybe not yet," the madam said, picking up the bottle of

whiskey and standing to leave. "But I think she's taken a shine to you."

He frowned. Lots of women took a shine to him. It usually passed. Once they found out he was a drifter, they let go of him faster than a hot skillet.

The madam waltzed off, and Drew found himself gazing up at Cat's closed door. Of course, the main reason he said he'd bid on her was because it was late and he needed a place to sleep for the night. At least, that's what he told himself.

Still, he had to admit that the notion of spending another night with the lusty Italian beauty was definitely appealing.

"He did?" Catalina asked, drying the last dish in the kitchen. She tried not to let her expression betray the sudden leap of her heart.

"Twenty dollars," Miss Hattie assured her, "same as before."

She didn't know whether to be relieved or apprehensive. She liked the handsome half-breed who made her laugh. But he couldn't be paying her so much coin without an expectation of something more in return.

"Why?" she asked.

Miss Hattie's laugh was like a bark. "Why? Because he's sweet on you. That's why."

"What is this—sweet on you?"

"He's got a hankerin' for you."

"Hankering?"

"A soft spot?"

Catalina shook her head. This American language was very difficult.

Miss Hattie sighed. "I think he likes you."

Catalina scoffed at the idea. Yet part of her hoped it was

true. If Drew Hawk liked her, maybe he would become her regular. Maybe she could buy that sewing machine sooner than she thought.

She put the dish away and hung up the drying cloth.

But even if he liked her, that didn't mean she was going to throw aside her principles.

"I still will not make the sex with him," she said.

"Suit yourself," Miss Hattie replied, "though you could do worse than a man like Mr. Hawk. He's a real gentleman." She leaned closer and whispered. "If you've never had a man in that way before..."

"Of course not."

"Then you'd like a gentleman like him to be your first. Trust me."

Catalina didn't really know what Miss Hattie meant. But she did know that she wasn't going to have sex with a man, no matter how gentlemanly he was, unless they were joined in holy matrimony.

She grabbed the broom from the corner of the kitchen. Miss Hattie took it from her.

"Go on. I'll finish up. He's waitin' in your room."

"Now?" Catalina didn't much care for a man making himself welcome in her bedroom, even if it was Drew. Who knew what he was rifling through?

"Go on, shoo." Miss Hattie practically swept her out of the kitchen with the broom.

At the foot of the stairs, Catalina looked up at her room and gulped. Why she was nervous, she didn't know. She'd already slept with him once, after all.

Maybe it was just that she'd put it behind her and didn't expect to see him after this morning.

She let her eyes drift over to the bottle of whiskey sitting atop the bar. She wondered if she should take a stiff drink to brace herself.

"Per amor del cielo," she muttered. For the love of heaven, she was being ridiculous.

Tonight was no different than last night. She would simply share the bed with him and say farewell in the morning. Besides, she was making ten more dollars.

She climbed the stairs, quickly untying her apron and tucking the stray curls of her hair back into their bun. She hesitated before her door and then straightened her shoulders and turned the doorknob.

Only at the last minute did she realize it was possible he'd taken off his clothes and would greet her in all his naked glory. But it was too late. She'd already opened the door.

He wasn't naked. He was fully dressed. And he was pacing agitatedly across the floor.

She drew her brows together and closed the door behind her. "Something is wrong?"

He stopped pacing and hooked his thumbs into the top of his trousers.

"I want to make one thing clear, Cat," he said. He seemed to struggle with the words, so he resumed pacing. "See, I'm not the marryin' type. I've never been the marryin' type. I'm more of a love 'em and leave 'em kind o' man. It's 'cause o' my profession as a gambler, you see. I've got to keep movin', like a rollin' stone. I don't have time for a...a wife and a bunch o' kids." He stopped and sighed. "So I don't want you to get your hopes up, thinkin' I'm gonna sweep you off your feet, 'cause that's just not me. I'm a freewheelin' tumbleweed. I can't be tied down." He stopped with his arms crossed. "I just think you should know that."

At first, Catalina didn't know whether to be flattered that he was even thinking about marrying her or insulted that he'd already decided against it. She settled on annoyed.

Hiding the sting of rejection, she said offhandedly, "Who

said anything about marriage? I never said I wanted to be married."

"Don't you?"

"Maybe one day...in the future."

"Right." He chewed on his lip for a moment. "How far in the future?"

What did it matter? He obviously did not want to marry her.

"Who can say?" she told him. "Next week, next month, next year."

"Next *week?*"

CHAPTER 13

Drew's heart dropped. He didn't want to get married. But he didn't want *her* to get married either.

It was ludicrous, this sense of possessiveness he felt toward Cat. But he realized he didn't want to share her. Not with the men slobbering over her in the salon. And not with some faceless hero who might show up as early as next week. *Next week?*

Catalina shrugged. "Life is uncertain."

He knew that well enough. He'd built an entire career on a game based on uncertainty. Still, it didn't feel right to gamble with your heart.

"Well," he said, inexplicably disgruntled, "I'm glad that's settled."

It wasn't settled at all, and he wasn't glad. But it was his own fault. He was the one who'd brought it up.

She seemed cool and aloof when she said, "It is the same as before. We will not make the sex."

"Well, o' course not, not if you're gonna be marryin' some Tom, Dick, or Harry next week."

"Who?"

"Never mind." He started getting undressed.

She went to the dresser to take the pins out of her hair. Her gaze was fixed on the marble top of the dresser when she asked him, "Do *you* never intend to marry?"

He'd hung up his vest and was rolling down the sleeves of his shirt. Her words stopped him.

"Sure, some day," he answered carefully. "Just not next week."

She took out the last pin and looked at her reflection, fluffing her hair with her fingers. "I don't think your bride will be happy to know you go to the *bordello.*"

He unbuttoned his shirt. "I don't think your husband will be happy to know you *work* in one."

She gasped. "I am not making the sex with anyone!"

"Neither am I," he said, giving her a sharp look in the mirror.

Then he sighed. Why *had* he forked over another twenty dollars to a woman who didn't want to sleep with him?

Cat began brushing her hair with a vengeance.

It felt like it was going to be a long night.

Last night, she'd hardly been able to take her eyes off of him as he unbuttoned his trousers. Tonight, she ignored him.

He put his gun on the nightstand and hung his pants on the bedpost. He wondered what she'd say if he took off his undershirt and drawers.

In the end, he decided that would only make both of them more miserable. So he slipped between the covers, propping up his pillow and clasping his hands behind his head to watch her.

He swore if she brushed her hair any harder, it would come out by the roots.

But even when she was angry, she really was incredibly alluring. She was far more interesting than the milk-faced maids who fluttered their fans at him on the street and more complex than the fawning ladies who usually worked in a sporting house. She was going to make someone a lucky man...if a man could get close to that kind of fire without getting burned.

The man who married Cat would have to know just how to handle her. He'd have to let her lean on him while making her feel like she was in charge. He'd have to have patience with her skittishness while daring her to break her boundaries. He'd have to lead her into temptation and make her believe it was her idea.

As he watched her at her ablutions, he started thinking it was a shame she didn't want him to "make the sex" with her. He knew he could make her first time special. He knew how to be gentle and sweet and caring.

He would have swept those black curls off the back of her neck and placed a kiss there.

He would have traced every lovely feature of her face with a fingertip.

He would have slipped her dress off of one creamy shoulder, running his tongue lightly along her collar bone.

He would have...

"Do not stare at me like that." It was a breathless plea.

"I can't help it," he said sincerely. "You're the most beautiful woman I've ever laid eyes on."

She didn't believe him. He could tell by the way she lowered her eyes in the mirror and gave a little shake of her head.

"You don't believe me?"

"You are only, what is it when you play cards? Bluffing."

"Bluffin'? No, ma'am. I swear."

Catalina felt the same way about him. But she certainly wasn't going to let him know. Not now. Not since he'd made such a strong argument against any kind of permanent relationship.

She should have known better than to listen to Anne and Emily and Miss Hattie, who had convinced her that Drew might have tender feelings toward her.

He'd made it plain that while he found her pleasing to look at, he wasn't interested in anything lasting.

She told herself that was fine. She needed to focus on her work anyway. Two nights with Drew meant she was closer to affording her sewing machine. She had to look at their time together as a business transaction. He paid her, and she let him share her bed.

He was staring at her again, making her blush. In the mirror, she saw how he caressed her with his eyes. She could feel the warmth of his gaze. It was doing strange things to her insides.

She gulped. She'd washed her face and brushed her hair. Now all she had left was getting out of her clothes.

"I need to undress now," she told him. "You must...close your eyes."

"No."

"What?" She blinked.

"No."

She wheeled around to him. "But you are causing me...great distress."

"Good."

"How can this be good?"

"'Cause you're causin' *me* great distress."

What did he mean by that?

"Look, Cat," he told her, "you said no touchin'. Fine. You said no sex. Fine. So I figure I paid twenty dollars to sit in this bed and watch you undress. And that's what I'm gonna do."

His smug smile was infuriating. His twinkling eyes made

her livid. She hated him for ogling her, even more for being right. He *had* paid a huge sum, and for what?

But the sight of him reclining in her bed, so self-assured, waiting for her, sent a shiver of apprehension through her. She almost wished she'd brought that bottle of whiskey.

"You scared?" he asked, arching a brow.

That did it. Now she was insulted.

"Scared? Never!"

Catalina—who'd defied her father, the lord of Ferrara, left her homeland on her own, and set out all alone to follow her dreams—wasn't afraid of anything.

Determined to prove it, she unbuttoned her dress with furious fingers. She yanked the shoulders down and pulled the sleeves off with such force that she almost ripped the seam. She shoved the dress down until it puddled at her feet. Then she stepped out of it, whipped it up in one hand, gave it a good shake, and draped it across her chair.

If she thought that would wipe the grin from his face, she was wrong. If anything, his eyes sparkled with more amusement than before.

With a frustrated growl, she untied her petticoat and stepped out of that too.

Then, before he could make some self-satisfied remark, she turned down the oil lamp until it guttered out.

But the joke was on her, because the storm had cleared and the full moon shone into the room. He could still see every humiliated inch of her. And she could still see the gleam in his eye.

With an exasperated sigh, she stomped over to her side of the bed, threw back the covers, and got under them before he could ogle her any longer. She flounced onto her side, facing away from him, but not before her foot contacted his briefly.

Her breath caught. His skin had felt warm and smooth, not

at all what she'd expected. But she wasn't going to let that kind of thing happen again.

He flopped over on the bed, dragging most of the covers with him. Her eyes went wide in panic. What if his leg brushed hers?

It didn't. After a moment, she breathed easy again. She closed her eyes, determined to sleep away her conflicted feelings.

But sleep evaded her.

She opened her eyes, glaring at the moon outside the window.

It wasn't the moon's fault. She simply couldn't quiet her brain. She kept thinking about the man lying beside her.

Drew Hawk was surely the most fascinating, irritating man she'd ever met.

She pulled what few covers he'd left her up over her shoulder.

Full of contradictions, Drew could be charming one moment and aggravating the next. He'd cautioned her against pursuing this line of work, and then he'd hired her. He'd claimed she was the most beautiful woman he'd ever seen. And yet he had no interest in pursuing her.

It was baffling.

She squished her pillow into a more comfortable shape, and then lay her head back down.

She began to think about what Miss Hattie had said, about it being good to have a gentleman like Drew for her first experience.

He didn't seem very gentlemanly to her. He was a rogue, a manipulator, a trickster.

She picked up her pillow, flipped it over to the cooler side, gave it a swat, and nestled into it.

She'd watched Drew play cards. He might smile through the whole game, but his strategy was ruthless. She wondered what his strategy was tonight. It seemed to her he had just wasted another twenty dollars.

She released a heavy sigh and burrowed farther under the covers.

Drew startled her. "Hey, Miss Wigglesworth, you plan on settlin' in sometime soon?"

She'd thought he was already asleep. "Well, if you had not stolen all the covers..."

"Did I?" He sounded sincere. "Sorry about that. I'm not used to sharin' a bed."

He reached over the top of her, giving her back her covers. This time his hand grazed her shoulder. She was sure it was an accident. But it still sent a delicious shiver through her.

"There. Better?"

"Yes," she choked out. "Thank you."

Now she *really* couldn't get to sleep. Her shoulder tingled where he'd touched it. If a slight brush could cause such a powerful current...

"How about callin' a truce?" he said.

"A truce?"

"A peace agreement. I'll stop stealin' the covers, and you stop bein' mad at me. Agreed?"

She wasn't mad at him, just disappointed. Who could stay mad at a man who was so charming and handsome and amusing? "Fine."

"A penny for your thoughts," he offered.

"What?"

"I said, a penny for your thoughts."

"You already gave me twenty dollars."

He chuckled.

She didn't see what was so funny.

"For twenty dollars," he said, "I should be allowed to read your mind."

Chapter 14

Catalina bit her lip. She hoped he couldn't read her mind. Her thoughts were going in all sorts of dangerous directions.

"No?" he asked. "All right. I'll tell you mine then. I was just recollectin' the last time I tangled with a *real* wildcat. I was about twelve years old, and my brother Chase and I were headin' to the river to go fishin'."

Catalina tried to imagine what Drew would have looked like as a boy.

"We were almost to the river when we heard a strange sound. We thought it was a baby left on the riverbank, cryin'."

Catalina rolled onto her back, toward him, so she could hear better.

"But it wasn't a baby. It was a *mindich*."

"Min-..."

"*Mindich*. White folks call 'em bobcats."

She repeated the word to herself. "Bobcats."

"It was a little thing, just a kitten really. Poor thing had got stuck in a snare. The noose was wrapped around its back legs, and it couldn't get out. So there it was, squallin' like a colicky baby."

Catalina wasn't sure what a colicky baby was.

"Chase said we should leave it alone. He said it was the will of the Creator. The *mindich* had been led into the trap. Maybe it was supposed to die there, to become food for a *xontehl-taw*."

"What is a—"

"A *xontehl-taw?* It's a coyote. You know coyotes?"

"The animal that looks like a dog." She'd seen one in the canyon on her buggy ride to Paradise.

"That's right. Anyway, I told my brother that if it was the Creator's will that the *mindich* be led into the trap, then it was also his will that we find the *mindich* and rescue him."

Catalina smiled. Drew had been very clever, even as a boy.

"So I pulled out my *yehwilxit*..." He paused. "Funny. When you tell a story from the past, you go back to the language o' the past."

She nodded.

"I pulled out my knife and started to cut the *mindich* loose. But he must have thought I was a *mikyow*, a big bear or somethin'. The little critter started growlin' and attackin' me with his front paws. He got in a couple o' good swats at my arms, drew blood."

She sucked air between her teeth.

"It wasn't so bad," he confessed. "But I sawed through that rope as fast as I could. When I finally cut him free, I thought he'd bound off. But he didn't. He just sat there, starin' at me. Chase whispered somethin' about him bein' a messenger from the spirit world. I think the poor thing was just stunned. Anyway, that little *mindich* sidled up to me, as pretty as you please, plopped down right by my knee, and started purrin'."

Drew laughed low, and the sound of his laughter warmed her like whiskey.

"Did you keep him for a pet?" she asked.

"I thought about it. He let me pet him, and he even licked my knee. But pretty soon we heard a loud yowl. His mama had come lookin' for him, so we left him there and took off."

"Did you ever see him again?"

"Naw."

It must have been interesting growing up in Drew's world. He sounded much nicer than her siblings.

"My brothers used to throw rocks at rabbits," she told him.

"Huntin' 'em, for food?"

"No, for fun."

"Fun?" he scoffed. "Strange kind o' fun. For the Hupa, animals are sacred."

"The only animals that were sacred in my family were pigs."

"Pigs?"

"They were used to hunt the *tartufo.*"

"What's a *tartufo?*"

"You do not know?" Catalina was surprised. Maybe they called them something different in America. "A *tartufo* is a..." She furrowed her brow. She didn't know the English word. How could she explain? "It is a thing you eat."

"Like a chicken?"

She chuckled. "No, it is not an animal."

"It's a plant?"

"Not...exactly."

"So it's a rock then," he surmised. "In Italy they eat rocks."

She laughed. "No."

"No?"

"A *tartufo* is a small, soft thing that you dig out of the ground."

"Ah, a bulb," he said. "My father's people, the Konkow, they used to dig bulbs out o' the ground to eat."

"A bulb. What is this?"

"A bulb? It's like a big round seed that grows into a plant."

"No. A *tartufo* does not grow into a plant."

"But it's under the ground?"

"Yes. It grows under the ground, close to the trees. The female pigs can smell them."

"Now, Miss Cat, I think you're makin' stuff up."

She gasped. Was he accusing her of lying? She elbowed him. "I am telling the truth."

Only then did she see the sparkle of mischief in his eyes. "So let me get this straight. It's somethin' that ain't animal, vegetable, or mineral, hunted by sacred pigs?"

She giggled. It sounded funny when he said it like that. "It is true. And some people believe they make you..." She didn't know the English word. *"Amoroso."*

"Amoroso? Amorous?" He raised both brows.

"I do not believe this."

"Well, I suppose I might eat a rock if it made me amorous." She jostled his shoulder.

He grinned. "So what do they look like, these...*tortugas?'*

"Tartufi. They are lumpy, like soft, brown stones." She hastened to add, "But they are delicious. They are my favorite."

"Uh-huh. And what do they taste like?"

"A sort of dark flavor," she decided, "earthy, like the ground."

"Mmm, sounds tasty," he said with obvious sarcasm.

"They *are* tasty," she insisted, giving him a playful shove. "You will see. I will find you some."

"I don't think we have 'em here."

"No?"

"My father's people ate just about everything it was possible to eat—lichen, bulbs, acorns—and your *tartufo* doesn't sound like anything they ever had."

She sighed. That made her a bit sad. Already she missed the garlic and wine of her country, the pasta and gelato. She missed those familiar flavors almost more than she missed her friends.

"I'll tell you what," Drew said. "If I sniff any out, I'll let you know. I have a nose like a sacred sow."

She grinned. It was nice, talking with Drew like this. She almost forgot they were lying in bed together in their undergarments...

Until he shifted under the covers again and happened to nudge her thigh with his knee. "Sorry."

She blushed. There was an awkward span of silence as she frantically tried to think of something to say. When she finally spoke, it was at the same time as Drew.

"What kind of—" she began.

"What made you decide to—"

"Sorry."

"Go ahead."

She cleared her throat. "What kind of clothings did you wear when you were a boy?" She'd seen drawings of natives with feathered headdresses and buffalo capes.

"Not much," he said with a chuckle. "When the weather was good, I'd just traipse around in a loincloth and moccasins."

Her blush deepened.

"When I was older, I dressed like the rest o' the tribe—a deerskin around my hips and shells around my neck."

"And a shirt?"

"Naw, no shirt."

Catalina's eyes widened. She tried to imagine what he looked like without his shirt. The picture in her mind left her speechless.

"But my mother made us shirts and trousers like the white folks too. We'd wear 'em when we went to town."

"Why?" Catalina asked, though her thoughts were still whirling over the deerskin and shell necklaces.

"She didn't want people teasin' us."

"Teasing you? Why would they tease you?"

"A lot o' folks don't much care for natives. They think we're savages."

"But you are not a savage," she argued.

"No."

"You saved the *mindich*."

"True."

She thought about this for a moment. "Many people are cruel."

"Like your brothers, throwin' rocks at rabbits."

"*Si.* Yes. Your people, they do not throw rocks at animals?"

"Only if they're plannin' to eat 'em," he said with a yawn. "And even then, they thank the animal for givin' up its life."

"That is very kind."

He shrugged. "The animals belong here too."

Catalina thought about that, about belonging. Her brothers obviously didn't think the animals belonged here. In the same way, some white people didn't think the Indians belonged here.

And yet wasn't that all anyone wanted—to belong somewhere?

It was why her uncle had come to America. It was why she had come too.

In Italy, no matter how she'd tried to fit in, she'd never felt like she truly belonged to her entitled family. She couldn't understand wishing to be an idle noblewoman, whose only worth came from marrying well.

Here, in this new country, a woman could start a business, be productive, make a name for herself. Here, Catalina could belong.

She was silent for a long while as she thought more about Drew's people...how they belonged here first, long before the settlers...how they lived in nature and respected the animals...how they wore very little and cared very much. She thought about the food Drew had said his father ate—whatever he could find in his surroundings. And she realized that people like this were worthy of—not ridicule—but great respect.

She decided, "I think I would like to visit Hupa."

But when she turned her head, she saw Drew had already fallen asleep. She carefully draped the covers over his broad shoulder.

Her smile was bittersweet. He had said it himself. He was a love-them-and-leave-them kind of man. In the morning, he would leave her, and she would never get to visit the village of his childhood.

CHAPTER 15

When Drew woke up the next morning, he had to remind himself that he was a love-'em-and-leave-'em kind of man, because the last thing he wanted to do as he gazed down at the sleeping beauty beside him was leave her.

She wasn't only the prettiest lady he'd ever met. She was also bright. And passionate. And innocent. And caring. If he stuck around much longer, he was sure she'd grab on to a piece of his heart. And once she did that, he'd be knocked into a cocked hat for sure.

So before the sun rose, before she could make a bid for his affections with those soulful brown eyes of hers, he slipped quietly out of bed. Stealth was one thing that growing up on a reservation had taught him. While she slumbered on, he managed to dress and steal out the door, bidding her a silent, fond farewell.

He was sure Chase would come back to Paradise today. By now, the rancher would have caught up to him, found out that, no, the big, bad, brooding half-breed had *not* stolen his little girl. Chase would be sober and able to see things more clearly. He might still resent the rancher for keeping their grandmother as a slave. But revenge wasn't in Chase's nature. He might be big and brooding, but he wasn't a violent man.

So Drew let himself out of The Parlor, onto the empty streets of Paradise. The sun was just beginning to lighten the skies, but it would be a while before it pierced the thick pine cover to touch the town. The only shop with any light on at all was the bakery. The smell of baking bread made his mouth water. He wondered if it was too early to buy breakfast—maybe something light and sweet, like a cream puff.

He hoped that by the time the dawn crested the mountain, so would his missing brother.

From the right hand side of the bed, Catalina frowned down at the empty left hand side. She knew she had no right to be disappointed. Drew had made no promises. In fact, he'd made it perfectly clear that he didn't want to be anyone's husband. She should be grateful that he'd kept his word last night and not touched her.

Still, she was saddened to find he'd left. She wished she'd been able to give him a proper goodbye.

But what difference did it make? He was gone. He wasn't coming back.

Still, all the logic and reason in the world didn't keep her from sighing as she dressed. And when there was a knock on the door, it didn't keep her heart from jumping, thinking it might be him.

It wasn't.

"Jenny." Catalina let her in.

The yellow-and-violet gown she'd redesigned for Jenny really did look splendid. But Jenny didn't look well at all. She was pale. Her hair hung over her face. And she wouldn't meet

Catalina's eyes. She was clutching a big bundle of white cotton before her, and she shyly handed it to Catalina.

"Can you...do anything about this?" Jenny asked.

Catalina carefully unfurled the cloth. It was a bedsheet. There was an ugly reddish brown stain in the middle and flecks spattered all over.

Catalina frowned at the marks. It was blood.

"Your monthly courses?" she gently asked.

Jenny shook her head, murmuring, "No. He said that...that always happens your first time."

It took Catalina a moment to understand. Then she gulped. "Are you all right?"

Jenny looked anything but all right as she nodded. She looked as if she might burst into tears.

Inwardly, Catalina was horrified. It looked like a lot of blood. Surely that wasn't right.

But she didn't wish to frighten Jenny. "Do not worry. I will see what I can do."

She gave the girl's shoulder a squeeze of reassurance. But Jenny gave a small gasp of pain.

She released the girl immediately. "Are you sure you're all right?"

"I'm fine." She tried to smile. "He said he wants to see me again." Her voice was soft, and there was a trace of fear in her words.

Catalina wasn't sure what to say. "I have heard it is only the first time that is painful." Even as she reassured the young girl, she thought she was probably the last person who should be giving advice on the subject.

Jenny looked up at her with hope. "Yes?"

It was then Catalina saw that one of her eyes was purple and swollen.

"What happened?" she whispered.

Jenny swallowed. "Nothin'. I just...fell."

Catalina didn't believe her. "That is not from falling. Did your man do this to you?"

Jenny clasped Catalina's hands and made a panicked plea. "Please don't say anything to Miss Hattie. And please don't tell the other girls. I made a whole two dollars last night. I need the job. If I lose this job, I got no place to go. Please, Miss Catalina."

Catalina felt sick to her stomach. But she didn't want to make things worse for Jenny. It was bad enough that she'd lost her virginity, worse that the man who'd taken it had been rough with her. But if Catalina betrayed her trust, it would destroy the girl.

"I will not tell," she reluctantly promised.

"Thank you," Jenny said, her eyes welling with tears, "thank you."

Catalina wondered if she was doing the right thing. No woman should have to endure such pain just to make a living. She only hoped what she'd told the girl was true, that the second time would not be so bad.

Jenny scurried out the door then, and Catalina scowled down at the stained sheet. It seemed like too much blood. And it seemed like two dollars was nowhere near enough for the loss of one's maidenhood.

Twenty dollars was a ridiculous price to pay for a hotel room. If Drew were smart, he'd stay at The Adams, which was only two dollars a night. But then The Adams didn't come with a companionable bedmate. Still, with the day growing longer and Chase nowhere to be found, it was clear Drew was going to have to find lodgings soon.

As he stood on the main street of Paradise, his eyes kept drifting to The Parlor.

Some unsavory character was probably sitting in the salon

right now, drooling over his Cat. It made his stomach churn.

What was wrong with him? It wasn't like he had any say over what she did. He wasn't even going to be in town much longer. And it wasn't like he owned her.

On the other hand, he'd spent forty dollars on the woman. Hell, that was as much as he'd spent on his Colt.

No, he should just let her be and make a clean break of it. He'd managed to avoid a messy goodbye this morning. If he went to see her again, it would only make the leaving that much harder.

But every time he thought about walking through the door of The Adams Hotel, his gaze was drawn back to The Parlor.

"Ling-miwhxiy," he muttered, spitting into the dust. Cursing himself for a fool, he let his feet take him down the boardwalk toward the brothel.

He told himself he was only trying to help her get enough money for that sewing machine she wanted. But even he didn't believe the lie.

He only hoped Lady Luck was with him tonight, because he had just a few hours to earn twenty dollars.

He didn't see Cat. But there was already a game going when he walked into the salon. The three rough-looking gents had the three things Drew always liked to see in players— piles of silver in front of them, an empty chair, and a nearly empty bottle of whiskey.

"Need a fourth?" he asked while the dealer was shuffling.

They eyed him with suspicion.

"You got silver?" the giant with the grizzled beard growled.

"Enough to last a couple hands, I hope," Drew said.

The grizzled one glanced at the other two for their approval. The one chewing tobacco shrugged. The dealer, a brute with a broken nose, hesitated.

"How about I buy the next bottle o' whiskey?" Drew offered.

That got their attention. They kicked out the fourth chair and welcomed him with a nod.

Drew sat down and motioned to one of the girls for whiskey. Then he dug deep in his satchel into his emergency reserves and put the coins on the table.

Miss Hattie herself brought the whiskey and an extra glass.

"Make sure you boys save enough funds for some evenin' entertainment," she said, giving Drew a particularly pointed glare. "We got some real pretty girls available."

The broken-nosed man grumbled, "Jenny's mine."

"Jenny's yours," Miss Hattie agreed, "long as you can pay."

He shoved four silver dollars in her direction. She picked them up and dropped them into the top of her dress.

Then the man shuffled the cards one last time and dealt.

The three men weren't difficult opponents.

The one chewing tobacco was careless with his cards. Every time he turned to use the spittoon, he gave Drew a good look at his hand.

The grizzled giant had a very bad poker face, and it got worse as he drank.

The man with the broken nose had a temper, which made him play badly. He punched the table every time he lost. By the time the whiskey was half gone, he'd lost so many times that one of his knuckles was bleeding.

Drew nursed his drink and cast an occasional glance at the balcony, hoping to see the prize that awaited him if he won enough hands.

It was around the time his winnings had increased to sixteen dollars that the trouble started.

"You got to be cheatin'," the grizzled drunk said as he threw his losing cards into the middle of the table.

"Not me," said Drew.

The second man, who'd already folded, moved his wad of

chewing tobacco into his cheek. "Maybe *you're* just a sore loser."

The drunk glared at the tobacco chewer. They both jumped when the broken-nosed player banged his fist on the table, leaving a bloodstain on the three of diamonds.

"New deck!" he yelled at no one in particular.

Miss Hattie came over quickly, producing a fresh deck of cards. "Trouble, gentlemen?"

"He's cheatin'," the drunk complained, yanking his thumb in Drew's direction.

"Who, Mr. Hawk here?" she asked. "Naw, I think he's a straight-shooter. But mind you, don't get your stash down too low. If your luck don't change, you're gonna want a little consolation."

"I'm not gonna lose," the drunk declared, "now that we have a clean deck."

"Tell you what," scheming Miss Hattie said. "Why don't you reserve your entertainment now, like this gentleman did?" She motioned to the man with the broken nose. "Then you can celebrate your winnin' with the lady...or ladies...of your choice."

"Ladies?" The drunk gave her a stupid grin, as if that had never occurred to him. "How much for two ladies?"

"Well, Anne and Emily, they're a nice pair. For ten dollars, you can have 'em both."

"Ten dollars?" The drunk tried to count his money four times and failed.

"Looks like you're just a bit shy o' resources," Miss Hattie said. "But maybe if you win this next hand..."

"I'm gonna win it," he decided.

The tobacco chewer barked out a laugh.

The broken-nosed man shuffled the cards. Drew thought if anyone was marking cards, it would be him—the man with the bloody knuckles.

At any rate, Drew supposed he should make a point of losing a few rounds, just to keep the peace, even if he was impatient to lay claim to Cat for the evening.

Then he picked up his hand. The man had dealt him three kings...before the draw. He couldn't believe his luck. He couldn't possibly fold now, not with three kings. It would be a disgrace to the game of poker.

CHAPTER 16

When the tobacco chewer leaned over to spit, Drew didn't bother glancing at the man's cards. There was no way he was going to beat three kings.

The drunk straightened with smug optimism. He obviously thought he had a good hand.

The man with the broken nose had gone silent. He must be holding something worthwhile. But Drew was still pretty confident.

They all slid coins into the center.

The drunk took no cards.

The tobacco man took three cards and grimaced in indecision.

Drew took two cards.

The man with the broken nose took just one.

Drew got even luckier on his draw.

The bet was high, and the drunks actually giggled with glee as he doubled it. But Drew didn't think that necessarily meant he had a good hand. The man's judgment might be off.

The tobacco man hemmed and hawed and finally surrendered with a curse and a spit.

Drew glanced at the man with the broken nose, but his countenance was stone cold and unreadable. Drew tossed in his coins.

"Call." The man's bloody fingers shoved his coins into the pile. Then he fanned out his cards. They were all clubs, a flush.

The drunk proudly displayed his three queens, a seven, and a four. "There you go, gentlemen!"

The man with the broken nose growled in his throat. "Flush beats three of a kind, you numbskull."

"What?" the drunk barked. "Since when?"

The tobacco spitter chimed in, "Since always."

"That ain't right," the drunk complained, struggling to his feet and stabbing an angry finger into the table. "Those are three damn queens. I win."

He started to scrape the money toward him. The man with the broken nose hammered his fist down on top of the man's hand so hard that the drunk's knuckles cracked, and he let out a wail.

"Leave it," the brute grumbled.

The incautious drunk came around with his good fist and boxed the brute's ear.

The tobacco spitter tried to intervene. "Hold on now."

But it was too late to avoid a fight. Already the broken-nosed man was turning red, fuming with anger. He reared back his bloody fist and punched forward.

Unfortunately, the tobacco spitter got in the way. When the blow landed on his jaw, his wad sailed out of his mouth and onto the next table.

The drunk made the mistake of laughing. The tobacco spitter, with one hand cradling his jaw, used his free fist to deliver a belly blow that bent the drunk in half and turned his laughter into a groan of pain.

The man with the bloody knuckles started to collect up his winnings. Any other day, Drew would have let him get away with it. The man's eyes were grim and gray, deadly and dangerous.

But at that very moment, Cat appeared on the balcony above. A quick glance told him that she was surprised to see him there. The whistles from the chairs around him told him that he wasn't the only one pleased to see her.

If he collected his rightful earnings, he'd have plenty to pay for Cat. He could give Miss Hattie a nod and be up the stairs in two shakes of a lamb's tail. If he didn't, god only knew which one of Cat's hooting admirers would snatch her up.

"Hold on a minute," Drew said.

The tobacco spitter and the drunk were still shoving at each other. The man's bloody knuckles paused over the coins.

"I believe that's mine."

"What?" the drunk exploded.

"Impossible," said the man with the broken nose.

"It ain't impossible if you're cheatin'," said the drunk. "I told you he was cheatin'."

He tried to give Chase a shove. He missed and knocked over the bottle of whiskey, which poured into the broken-nosed man's lap.

The man stood up at once with a curse. The front of his pants looked as if he hadn't made it to the outhouse in time. He reached across the table and seized the drunk by his shirt, looking like he'd like to murder him.

"Aw, jeeze, mister, I'm real sorry," the drunk whined.

Drew wondered what he was sorrier about, ruining the man's trousers or spilling the rest of the whiskey.

"Well, if you two are gonna fight," the tobacco spitter said, putting his hand atop the pile of coins, "maybe I'd better get this out o' the w-"

Both men turned on him at once. The drunk gave him a hard shove at the same time that the broken-nosed man tried to gut-punch him. When that punch landed on empty air, the man with the broken nose fell onto the table, scattering cards and coins.

Drew had judiciously held on to his cards, and he now scraped his chair back.

When a passing gentleman tried to retrieve a few dropped silver dollars to return them, the tobacco spitter misinterpreted the gesture and pushed him back, into a saloon girl, who gasped as she hit the wall and dropped her tray of wine.

Of course, the gentleman was then obliged to seek retribution for the girl's injury. So as the three poker players fought for possession of the table, he removed his coat, rolled up his sleeves, and prepared for fisticuffs.

The drunk scrambled for a silver dollar on the floor, and the tobacco spitter gave him a kick in the seat of his trousers that sent him careening into the second poker table. He knocked the table over completely, spilling everyone's cards and coins.

The four players shot to their feet in outrage.

It didn't take long for a skirmish to ensue. Boots kicked backsides. Fists hit faces. Bottles broke. Vases of flowers shattered. Men's grunts and cussing were interspersed with ladies' shrieks and gasps as everyone suddenly seemed to have a stake in the fight.

Everyone but Drew. He calmly gathered his full house of kings and deuces into a stack and stuck the cards in his pocket. That way he'd have evidence if there were any doubt he'd won the hand. Then, he carefully began to collect the coin he was owed.

Some of it he managed to pocket before the table hit the floor. Some of it he had to scrounge from underneath the chairs, dodging the boots scuffling all around him. While the chaos ensued, he counted the silver that was owed him, tossing a coin back into the fray when he'd accidentally taken a dollar too much.

Once he collected his allotted winnings, he nodded over the crowd to Miss Hattie, who was standing in the corner, shaking her head at the insanity.

He mouthed "Cat?" to her.

She arched her brow and pointedly held out her hand for payment.

Drew picked his way through the battlefield, stepping over fallen foes, steering clear of flying fists, nudging quarrelers aside, and ducking hurled projectiles.

Miss Hattie gave him a peeved glare when he dropped twenty dollars in coin into her palm.

"Why are you lookin' at me like that?" he asked.

"You gonna pay for the damages?"

"Me? Why? This wasn't my fault."

"The hell it wasn't. If you'd listened to me and done right by Catalina, you wouldn't have had to gamble so's you could meet her price. And if you hadn't have had to gamble, you wouldn't have had to cheat."

"What?" he burst out, dizzied by her logic, offended by her accusation. "I didn't cheat."

She gave him a dubious smirk.

He frowned, injured. "I'm just good at readin' people's tells is all."

"Is that so? Then can you tell what I'm thinkin' right now?"

He could. By the furrow in her brow, her tight jaw, and the tiny tic at the corner of her eye, he could tell she was furious with him. She probably wanted him out of her sight.

He couldn't blame her, even if she was wrong about him cheating. But he didn't want to stand here and argue about it. He wanted to head upstairs to be with his...

He glanced up to find Cat, gripping the banister with pale knuckles and staring at the melée with much the same expression that Miss Hattie wore.

Hell. He was in trouble.

"Go on," Miss Hattie urged, jerking her head toward Cat. "Git."

He was gone and up the stairs before she could finish clucking her tongue.

When Catalina saw the great brawl taking place downstairs, her first reaction was terror.

What was happening? Why were the men fighting? Was Drew hurt?

Only when she saw him wading through the mayhem, unharmed and unruffled, did she breathe a sigh of relief. And once she saw he was safe, then she could afford the luxury of anger.

The men were making a mess out of the salon. The wreckage was all over the floor—broken glass, splintered wood, whiskey, blood, and quite possibly a few teeth. There were gaping rips in the upholstery and the wallpaper. Worse, it didn't look like the fight was going to end any time soon.

And she was going to have to clean it all up.

The fresh bouquets she'd spent an hour arranging were trampled. The carpet she'd just slaved over was ruined. The wood floors would have to be swept and mopped all over again.

Then she saw Miss Hattie taking Drew to task for starting the fight.

Drew was responsible for this?

Her blood began to boil.

When he headed up the stairs as if nothing was wrong, it

was fuel for her rage. She had half a mind to push him back down the stairs after the destruction he'd caused.

Her anger must have shown in her eyes, because he slowed his ascent.

Misunderstanding her ire, he explained, "Aww, don't worry about them, Cat. They're just lettin' off steam."

She folded her arms across her breasts. "And are they going to clean up the mess when they're finished letting off the steam?"

He stopped on the step. Clearly, he hadn't thought of that.

She told him, "Because if I have to clean up this mess, I won't be going to bed tonight."

"What?"

Drew might be handsome and irresistible, but at the moment, his charm was no match for her anger. She dared him with an arched brow.

"Aww, Cat," he reasoned, coming up the last few steps, "can't you leave it till the mornin'? The fightin' could go on for an hour or more."

She sincerely hoped not. At this rate, in an hour, there would be nothing left of The Parlor.

As if to prove her point, someone knocked the shelf behind the bar off the wall, and bottles shattered on the floor with a loud crash.

Drew grimaced and rubbed his chin. "Tell you what. If you leave it till the mornin', I'll help you clean up."

"And how do I know you will not sneak away before I am awake?" she said, adding pointedly, "Like you did this morning?"

"Sneak a-? Shoot, I was only tryin' to spare your feelin's."

She raised her chin in challenge. "Maybe I do not *have* any feelings for you."

"The hell you don't."

"Besides, how do I know you will not try to 'spare my feelings' again?"

"I guess you'll have to take my word on that."

She thinned her lips. She didn't know whether to trust him. But what choice did she have?

There was no point in tidying up until the men were done with their childish horseplay. And she didn't really want to be cleaning the house all night. Drew had paid Miss Hattie for Catalina's company again, and Catalina would be a fool to turn down such easy money. Besides, if he kept his word to help her in the morning, she'd be done in half the time.

"Come on, Cat, what do you say? Shall we get off the balcony before we get hit with a flyin' chair?"

She wasn't happy about this—any of it. In Italy, brawling was done in the streets, where there was nothing to damage. These American men were like animals, destroying the salon. Maybe this was why they called it the "wild" west.

Once they were behind the closed door of her room, the sounds of fighting were muffled, punctuated only occasionally by the thud of a body hitting the wall downstairs and the tinkle of breaking glass.

She wheeled to confront him. "What did you do to start such a fight?"

"Me? Why does everyone keep blamin' *me?*" he said, planting his hands on his hips. "All I did was win the game and...and stake my claim."

"What means this—stake my claim?"

He cleared his throat. "I just demanded what was...what was rightly mine."

"Your winnings?"

"That's right, my winnin's and..." He turned around to unfasten his gun belt and mumbled something she couldn't quite hear.

"What?"

He mumbled it again.

This time she understood him. "What do you mean—'my woman'?" Her heart was beating in an unruly fashion.

He worked his mouth as if he wanted to say something, but couldn't think of the right words. Then he wrapped up his gun belt and placed it on the stand beside the bed.

An awkward silence passed. Catalina wasn't sure if she should be thrilled or appalled that Drew had called her his woman. Then, remembering how he didn't want to make anything permanent between them, she decided she was appalled.

"I am not your woman," she insisted. "You have said so yourself. You are a tumbling rock, remember?"

He gave her a quizzical frown. "You mean a rollin' stone?"

"That is what I said."

He smirked and sat on the bed to pull off his boots. "I know you're not really my woman, Cat. But I just couldn't let one o' those beef-headed no-counts have you. The notion that one o' them might be sleepin' next to you tonight..." He shook his head. "They're just not good enough for a lady like you."

"And you are?" Catalina resisted adding that Drew was certainly possessive for a man who claimed he didn't want to be tied down.

CHAPTER 17

Drew knew he wasn't making any sense.

And there wasn't a damn thing he could do about it.

He felt the way he felt. Something about innocent Catalina brought out the hero in him. He wanted to come to her rescue and keep her out of the villains' clutches.

And yet he couldn't imagine riding into the sunset with her. He was a free spirit, a lone wolf. He'd always been that way.

"Look, I know I'm no prize," he admitted as he pulled off his other boot. "You prob'ly deserve better than me. But at least I'm respectful. I'd never make you do anythin' you didn't want to do. You can't say the same for those men downstairs."

She lowered her eyes and picked a thread from her skirt. He was right, and she knew it

"But tomorrow you will leave, yes?" she said.

He frowned. That was the trouble. That was the part that made no sense. "Maybe. Prob'ly."

She didn't need to put the pieces of the puzzle together for him. It was obvious that after tonight, if he left, he'd have no say whatsoever over who crawled into bed with her. The thought of it made him ill.

The only way he could be sure no one else put their grubby hands on Catalina was if he stuck around. But the lady was damned expensive. He couldn't afford to keep paying her twenty dollars a day. Shit, the gambling men of Paradise couldn't afford to lose that much either.

Frankly, it would be easier—and cheaper—to just marry the lady.

He watched as Cat went to the mirror and began taking the pins out of her hair.

Would it be so bad to be saddled with a wife? He certainly couldn't wish for a prettier one. She was smart and handy, a hard worker. She had a wicked sense of humor and a captivating laugh. And she had a body that made his mouth water.

"Where will you go?" she asked, interrupting his thoughts. She casually ruffled her hair with her fingers to shake loose the seductive black curls.

"When I leave Paradise?"

"*Si,* yes."

"I'm not sure exactly. Where the wind takes me, I guess."

"It is a lonely life, no?"

He shrugged. He never thought of it that way. If he got desperate, towns always had a couple of saloon girls to keep a stranger company. Of course, saloon girls were like tumbleweeds too, wandering across a desert full of men until they found one they could stick to.

Catalina lifted her foot, resting it on the chair in front of the dresser to unlace her boot. Damn, she wasn't even trying to look tempting, and still she managed to make his heart do a flip in his chest.

He'd like to undress her himself. He'd rest her heel on his

thigh, slowly pull loose the laces of her boot, and slide his fingers up her silky calf to slip off the soft leather. Her flimsy stocking would come off next, followed by...

The sound of her boot heel hitting the floor as she dropped it startled him from his daydreaming. She switched legs to remove the other boot.

"I do not think I would like your life," she said. "To have no friends..."

He frowned. "I have friends."

That wasn't precisely true. He had friends he never saw. The people he *did* see were not really his friends. They were card players and bartenders and saloon girls who *pretended* to be his friends.

He'd never really thought about it before. And now that he did, the truth made him uncomfortable.

"What about you?" he challenged. "You left all your friends and family in Italy."

She dropped the second boot on the floor and straightened. Then she began taking off her clothes.

"My friends I miss. But I will stay in Paradise and make new friends."

"What about your family?" He tried to keep his voice steady, which wasn't easy while she was casually unbuttoning her dress.

She shrugged. "The brothers who throw rocks at rabbits? I do not miss them. They are not nice boys."

Drew wasn't really listening. He was distracted by the way the lace of her camisole was peeking out as she continued unbuttoning her bodice. But when her words finally sunk in, he was hit by a surge of inexplicable protectiveness.

"Your brothers, they never hurt *you*, did they?" he demanded, ready to take on the whole Italian army in her defense.

"No."

"Are you sure?"

"Of course. They would not dare. My father would beat them."

He forced his fists to relax. He knew he was overreacting. But he couldn't bear the thought of anyone hurting Catalina.

"What about your folks?" he asked. "Don't you miss 'em?"

"My mother is dead. My father is..." She wrinkled her forehead. *"Prepotente. I do not know the English word."*

"Sick?" he guessed.

"No."

"Missin'?"

"No."

"Meaner than a skilletful o' rattlesnakes?"

She burst into delightful laughter. "No, no, no. He is only very serious. He tries to tell me what I can and cannot do."

"He's bossy."

"Bossy?"

"He gives you orders, and you have to do what he says."

"Sí, exactly. He is bossy."

As Catalina shimmied out of her dress, Drew figured it was a good thing her bossy father lived half a world away. He doubted the man would approve of his daughter working in a whorehouse.

She draped her dress over the chair and began to untie her petticoat. He couldn't help but smile at how used to him she'd become in just a few days. Drew, on the other hand, didn't think he'd ever get used to Catalina's irresistible beauty. She was only half undressed, and already he could feel lust rousing in his trousers.

He sighed, wondering how many nights of unrequited hankering a man could endure.

As Catalina slipped the petticoat from her hips, she could feel

Drew's gaze on her, almost like a caress. It warmed her blood and filled her with a curious longing.

It also filled her with dangerous thoughts...thoughts of defying her father and everything she'd been taught...thoughts of throwing caution to the wind and following her heart...thoughts of listening to Miss Hattie's advice about allowing Drew to be her first lover.

After all, she reasoned, this was the wild West. The rules were different here. That was one of the reasons she'd come to California. Here a penniless immigrant could start her own business. The state was full of spinsters and widows, women who managed ranches, ran brothels, forged their own fortunes...and slept with whomever they chose.

She glanced up at the reflection in the mirror. Behind her, Drew was taking off his shirt. His undershirt did little to hide what was beneath. His shoulders were broad, and his chest was thick with muscle. Her knees grew weak as she imagined running her hands over his smoothly-sculpted contours.

She lowered herself onto the chair and fumbled for her hairbrush, watching him hang his shirt on the bedpost. She gulped and began brushing her hair as he worked on the buttons of his trousers.

When he shoved his trousers down, exposing his drawers, she could plainly see the evidence of his arousal. Rattled, she lost the grip on her brush, and it clattered to the floor.

He looked up sharply, and she ducked her head, feeling the rush of blood to her face.

He snickered and took his trousers off the rest of the way.

"You know, if you keep lookin' at me like that," he warned, "I'm gonna have to start chargin' *you.*"

Mortified, she retrieved her brush.

He hitched his trousers onto the bedpost and threw back the covers, preparing to climb into bed.

Clutching the brush tightly before her, she blurted, "How much?"

He stopped. "Pardon me?"

She swallowed and met his gaze in the mirror. "How much would you charge?"

He paused for a moment and then shook his head with a rueful laugh. "Oh, no, you're not gonna play that game."

She whipped around to look at him over the back of the chair. "What game?"

"Cat and mouse."

"Cat and mouse?"

"Yeah, where the cat teases the mouse and leads him on a merry chase, and then the mouse winds up sorry he didn't just mind his own business?"

She furrowed her brow. "I do not know this game."

"Maybe not, but you learn awful fast." With that, he resumed climbing into bed and pulled the covers up over his tempting body. "Good night, Cat."

Now she was peeved. How dared he dismiss her like that?

She slammed the brush down on top of the dresser. He lifted his head in a questioning glare.

"Now you are turning me down?" she demanded.

He opened his mouth and closed it again. Then he narrowed his eyes. "What exactly are we talkin' about here?"

"We are talking about..." She averted her eyes. "Making the sex."

He let out a forceful breath. "Oh, no, you don't. Not now." He raised a hand as if to ward her off. "We already agreed there was gonna be no touchin'."

"What?" She stormed to her feet. "But you are the one who wanted to make the sex, yes?"

"Well, sure, that first night."

"And now you do not?"

He gave her a sarcastic smirk. "Oh, I don't know. What do *you* think?"

He threw back the covers, just in case she hadn't gotten a good enough look the first time. Glancing at his imposing size, she had a moment of misgiving. But she'd come too far to turn back now.

"I think we should definitely make the sex," she decided.

"Well, I don't." He dragged the covers back over his body.

She stomped her foot. "Why?" she demanded.

"Did you just stomp your foot?"

"I'm angry. I do not see why you will not make the sex with me."

"*Q'ut!*" He threw up his hands in frustration. "You're a virgin."

"I cannot help that." She lowered her eyes and murmured, "Besides, Miss Hattie said I would be lucky to have you for my first."

"Miss Hattie?" He shook his head in disbelief. "And how does *Miss Hattie* know that?"

"She said she can tell."

Drew exhaled and tried to rub the frown from his brow. "The truth is I'm not the kind o' man who goes around plowin' other farmers' fields."

She gave him a quizzical look. "Plowing? Farmers?"

"Look, Cat, you told me you were plannin' on gettin' married...maybe even next week. I don't know how things are in Italy, but in California, it ain't right to make love to another man's wife."

"But I might never get married."

"Oh, you'll get married. A lady as pretty as you?"

"Maybe I do not *want* to get married."

"Well, if you don't want to get married, then why are you so eager to have sex?"

She smugly crossed her arms. "I could ask you the same thing."

Chapter 18

Drew sat forward and pressed hard at his temples. Catalina was taxing his brain. But she had a point. Men were like bees, flitting around from woman to woman, while women were supposed to save themselves for marriage. It didn't exactly make sense.

"Fair enough," he told her. "And I don't have a good answer. That's just the way it is and the way it's always been."

It wasn't up to Drew to change the morals of society. It was hard enough being a half-breed. He didn't need to add seducer of virgins to his list of liabilities.

"So you are turning me down?" she said.

"That's right," he said, though every nerve in his body was screaming at him for it.

"Fine."

"Glad that's settled." He threw back her side of the covers and patted the mattress. "Now why don't you be a good girl and come to bed?"

"If you do not wish to make the sex with me, then maybe I

will go downstairs and find a man who will." She moved toward the door.

"Wait! What?"

She paused.

"You're not serious, are you?"

"I am very serious."

"You're makin' a big mistake, Cat." He couldn't believe she'd actually consider sleeping with one of the rowdy brawlers in the salon. "Did you take a good look at 'em?"

She shrugged. "One of them looked very gentlemanly."

He racked his brain. She must be talking about the man who'd come to the defense of the saloon girl. If that dandy had any experience at all with women, Drew would eat his Stetson.

She took another step toward the door.

"Hold on!"

She hesitated.

She had to be bluffing, didn't she? Just two days ago, she'd blushed to be seen in her underthings. Was she honestly planning to open that door and put herself on display for the whole Parlor?

"I don't think you want to be doin' that," he told her.

"I think I do," she mused. "In fact, I am certain of it. I will just ask Miss Hattie which man she thinks would be the *second* best to—"

"What?" He practically leaped out of the bed. "Are you crazy? You can't go out there and parade yourself in your unmentionables in front of all those men."

She shrugged. "Why not? The other ladies do it all the time."

"You're not the same as the other ladies," he argued as definite panic rose in his chest. "They've got experience. You don't know what you're doin'. They'll eat you alive, Cat."

"I have to learn somehow. And if you are not wishing to

make the sex with me…" She turned again, stepping toward the door.

"Wait!" He bit out the foulest curse he knew under his breath. "Will you just listen to me?"

She turned back and crossed her arms. "I am listening."

He rubbed his palm across his mouth. How could he convince her not to do this? He'd played cards all afternoon, earning enough money so he could claim her for himself and prevent this very thing.

"Look, Cat, I spent my hard-won silver on this room and your company, and I'm not givin' 'em up."

"Miss Hattie will give you back your coin. I am certain one of the other ladies would be happy to—"

"I don't want one o' the other ladies. I want you."

"But that is the point," she said, looking miffed. "You do *not* want me, not in that way."

He couldn't argue with that. It was what he'd said. But it sure as hell wasn't what he meant.

"Cat, you don't know what you're gettin' yourself into. I can't let you throw away somethin' as precious as…as your virginity…to some fumble-fingered roughneck. I just can't let you do it. I *won't* let you do it."

He could almost see steam coming out of her ears.

"You are not my father," she bit out. "You do not get to do the bossy with me. I am my own woman. I will do as I wish."

She wheeled with a sassy flip of her hair. When she reached for the doorknob, he panicked and did the first thing he could think of to keep her from opening the door. He threw a pillow at her.

It hit her square in the back of the head.

She gasped in outrage.

His jaw dropped. Shit, had he actually just thrown a pillow at a woman?

Before he had a chance to say he was sorry, she picked up the pillow and flung it back at him.

He got a face full of cotton before the pillow slid down his chest and onto the floor. Stunned, he bent to retrieve it, formulating an apology in his head. "Aw, Cat, I'm so sor—"

He never got to finish it. Like a mountain lion, Cat charged at him, giving him a hard shove that knocked him backwards onto the bed.

But she wasn't done. She snatched the pillow out of his hands and began battering him with it.

"Wait!"

The pillow hit his shoulder.

"Cat!"

It hit his chin.

"Hold—"

It hit his nose.

He defensively threw his hands up and, after the fourth blow, dug his fingers into the fabric. When she yanked it back for another attack, the seam split.

Downy white feathers spilled forth. Still she continued to pummel him with what was left of the pillow, strewing feathers everywhere.

He sneezed, startling her for an instant, but she immediately resumed her punishment.

He finally grabbed the second pillow from the bed and defended himself. He caught her on the hip, then the shoulder, then the head. Each time she squealed with rage. But still she fought.

"Stop!" he finally commanded. It was clear she wasn't going to win this fight. She was almost out of feathers. "Stop it, Catalina!"

"No!"

She tried to seize his pillow then. For one moment, they

engaged in a fierce tug-of-war. Then the seam on the second pillow burst. Feathers filled the air like a hatching of white moths.

Still stubbornly clinging to the weapon and vying for ownership, they tore the pillow in half, continuing to flail at each other with the scraps of cotton.

Drew finally decided to put an end to the fight, mostly because he knew who was going to have to clean up the room. While she continued to beat at him, he dropped what was left of his half of the pillow and seized her by the wrists.

"Let go of me!" She twisted in his grasp.

"Not unless you promise me you won't go out there."

"Do not bossy me!"

"Fine." He continued to grip her wrists.

Compressing her lips, she reared back her foot. He could see the kick coming. So he hauled her forward, turning her and pinning her on her back to the bed. When she tried to knee him, he threw his leg over hers to hold her still.

She spit out a long string of what he guessed were Italian swear words as she tried to work herself free.

"You are a bad man," she spat.

"Am I?" He leaned in close to her until their faces were almost touching. "Because if you think *I'm* bossy, you don't know anything about men. Those *gentlemen* downstairs? If they had you on your back like this, they'd do whatever they wanted to you, whether you liked it or not. At least you know your virtue's safe with me."

Catalina glared into the dark, burning eyes of her captor. As he loomed over her, she felt anything but safe. She was breathless from the pillow fight. Her blood was running hot. And the pressure of his thigh across hers was doing strange and lovely things to her.

Of course, she'd been bluffing all along. She had no intention of striding out onto the balcony in her camisole and drawers, much less inviting any of the men downstairs to join her in bed.

She'd only wanted to prove to Drew that he *did* feel something for her, even if it was only jealousy.

But things had gotten out of hand. True, he had thrown the first pillow. But she could have laughed it off. Instead, she'd let her temper get the best of her. In a childish fit of fury, she'd escalated the fight.

She should have realized it was a fight she couldn't win. Now she was at his mercy.

Yet that wasn't at all how she felt. She didn't feel threatened in the least. On the contrary, she felt empowered. Though she was trapped like that *mindich* in the snare, her quickening pulse had nothing to do with fear and everything to do with excitement.

She lowered her gaze to his mouth. She wanted to kiss that mouth. And she was feeling bossy enough to do it.

She craned up her head, pressed her lips to his, and stayed there.

He didn't move away. But he didn't respond either. At least, not at first.

But as she pressed softly against him, remembering how he'd taught her, he gradually grew more receptive. She tentatively opened her lips to him.

"Oh, Cat, what are you doin' to me?" he murmured against her mouth.

His words thrilled her. A heady rush of desire coursed through her veins. She might be pinned beneath him, but she felt intoxicated by her own power.

His mouth slanted against hers as he deepened the kiss. When his tongue touched hers, a current of lust sizzled through her like lightning. She moaned as fire seemed to lick her nerves to life, culminating in a bright point of flame between her legs.

His grip loosened around her wrists. But the instant he released her, she reached up to delve her hands into his hair, holding his head still for her eager exploration.

The thick black waves, strewn with white feathers, curled around her fingers as she traced the shells of his ears. Her thumbs rasped over the coarse stubble in the hollows of his cheeks. His breath blew hot across her face as she tasted him again and again.

Then he lowered his body gently to hers, taking her breath away. His hard male body pressed against her like a hot iron on cloth, smoothing away her rough edges and making her feel beautiful. She arched toward him, and he slipped his arm beneath her, pulling her even closer.

The need she felt was stronger than hunger, more intense than thirst. The sharp craving between her thighs transformed into a dull ache in her belly. She wanted him there, deep inside her, filling her.

As if he understood her silent plea, he moved one hand to the very spot of her longing, all the while raining kisses over her cheek and along her neck, nuzzling her ear with sensuous whispers, words she didn't recognize.

His fingers found her through the thin cotton, and she pressed up against his palm, gasping at the divine sensation.

He responded with a soft, rueful chuckle. "Is this what you want?" he murmured.

"*Si,*" she begged. "Yes."

When he slid his fingers away, it was only to untie her drawers and slip his hand inside, against her skin. She held her breath as she felt his warm fingertips glide downward over her abdomen, through her curls, parting her to nestle with reassuring pressure on that throbbing part of her.

"Like this?" he said softly.

She closed her eyes, bit her lip, and nodded.

He began moving his fingers over her flesh with a delicate precision that defied his brutal strength, eliciting a new and strange sensation in her. It seemed as if he summoned forth a goddess hidden within, for Catalina sighed and mewed and purred in a language unfamiliar to her before now.

More and more he gave her, driving her to new heights of passion. And when she didn't think she could reach a higher plane of ecstasy, he murmured tender words in his breathy tongue, sending shivers into her ear.

She squeezed her eyes tightly shut.

She clutched desperately at his shoulders.

A silent scream built inside her.

And then, it was as if her tight corset strings had been cut loose all at once. Crying out in relief at the welcome liberation, she arched and trembled under his touch. He groaned in empathy, and the pressure of his palm was like a soothing final kiss.

She let her eyes drift open. He was gazing down at her.

What she saw in his eyes was impossible to define. They smoldered with yearning, but there was a tenderness cradled within that desire. Sweat beaded his brow. His nostrils flared with arousal. Yet his restraint was clear in the clench of his jaw. And it was this—the gentleness that tempered his lust— that moved her beyond words and made her feel irreversibly connected to him.

Her eyes filled with tears of wonder. Incredible, life-changing words—words she'd never said to a man before— rose to her lips.

Ti amo, I love you.

But just as she would have given voice to them, the loud shatter of a glass bottle against the door split the air, splitting them apart as well.

And the moment vanished.

CHAPTER 19

Hours after Catalina—as content as a kitten with a dish of cream—had drifted off to satiated slumber, Drew still stared up at the ceiling. Not only was his body tormented by frustrated desire, but his mind felt like a battlefield of conflicting notions.

He'd been a "tumbling rock," as Cat had called him, for so many years, it seemed impossible to change. But he couldn't bear the thought of leaving and losing the adorable, maddening Italian lady to anyone else.

Once he was out of the picture, she'd be free to court and kiss and—he thought, grinding his teeth—sleep with whomever she wanted. Would he be able to blithely hit the trail, knowing she might be cozying up to another man?

He rolled toward her, gazing at her moonlit profile. She was beautiful, breathtaking, unforgettable, in spite of the feathers littering her dark hair.

But Drew had met lots of beautiful women.

Cat was more than that. She was brimming with fire

and spirit, ambitious, clever, witty and wise yet sweet and innocent, worldly and full of wonder all at once.

After he'd pleasured her, when she'd looked into his eyes, he'd felt a connection he'd never felt with a woman before.

He didn't want to lose that connection. Damn it, he wanted to feel it again...forever.

The way he saw it, he had three choices.

He could continue fleecing the folks of Paradise for twenty dollars every day and buy Cat's company every night for the rest of his life.

He could steal her away like his ancestors had with women of the neighboring tribes and take her back to Hupa.

Or he could do the right thing and marry her.

Ordinarily when he thought about marriage, it was with a nasty taste in his mouth, as if he were thinking about swallowing a spider.

But this time, the idea seemed as appetizing as a cool swig of manzanita cider—sweet, comforting, and slightly tart.

Marrying Catalina wouldn't signify the end of his journey, after all, but the beginning of a new adventure. And he had to admit it seemed like an adventure worth undertaking.

As he lay basking in the midnight moonlight, listening to the soft sounds of her breathing, he let his brain get used to the idea of having a wife.

He imagined seeing Cat's smile first thing every morning, watching her put on all those intriguing layers of clothing, sitting together at breakfast, sharing a cup of coffee with her.

He imagined coming home in the evening to a cozy house with a white picket fence, swapping stories beside the fire, snuggling with her under the covers and "making the sex."

He imagined having a whole brood of little Hawks that looked just like her, celebrating birthdays and going on picnics and visiting Grandmother Mati and Grandfather Sakote in Hupa.

The more he thought about it, the more he was convinced that maybe it was time. Maybe it wouldn't be so bad to settle down. In fact, after a good hour of pondering, he decided that marrying Miss Catalina would be a change for the better and the best bet he'd ever made.

His mind made up, he smiled over at his dozing bedmate and whispered, "Good night, Mrs. Hawk."

He kissed her temple. She smiled and sighed in her sleep.

Then, filled with new energy and purpose, Drew stole out of bed and quietly dressed. If he wanted to marry this prize of a woman, he had to earn not only her affections, but her trust.

He'd promised her he'd help her clean up the mess downstairs. From the sound of things, the brawl was long over. He might as well get an early start on getting The Parlor back in order.

Catalina was awakened shortly before dawn by a soft knocking on her door. When she opened her eyes in the dim room and saw the empty, feather-littered mattress beside her, she gasped in disappointment. He'd left.

Before her disappointment could bloom into full heartbreak, the knock came again.

"Just a moment," she croaked out.

She climbed out of bed, snatching up her loose drawers before they could slither down to her ankles, and then giving them a hasty tie. She snagged her wrapper from the wardrobe and staggered through a sea of feathers toward the door. The impatient knocking returned as she slipped on the wrapper.

"I'm coming," she muttered with a frown.

When she cracked open the door, Jenny stood there, shaking, her face obscured by her hands and strands of her tangled hair.

Without a word, Catalina immediately widened the door and ushered her in, closing it carefully after her.

Jenny began sobbing at once.

Catalina narrowed her eyes in concern. "What's wrong?"

When Jenny lowered her hands, Catalina could see her swollen, bloody lip and the bruise on her cheekbone.

She gasped in shock, and her gaze was drawn lower, to the tear in the beautiful yellow gown she'd altered for the girl.

She didn't need to ask what had happened. It was obvious. Jenny's client had been rough with her.

Catalina's shock turned rapidly to fury. "Where is he?"

"Gone."

"He cannot do this to you," Catalina growled in frustration, wishing she could wring the bastard's neck.

"He called me bad names," she whimpered, as if that were worse than the beating he'd given her.

Catalina was filled with such rage, she was trembling. But if he was gone, she couldn't do anything to the man who had hurt Jenny now. She had to do what she could to help the poor girl.

"Come." She took Jenny gingerly by the elbow and patted the bed. "Sit here."

Jenny hesitated, furrowing her brow at the mess of feathers. "What happened?"

"Nothing. An accident."

Jenny perched carefully on the edge of the bed. "I'm sorry about the dress. You worked so—"

"It is not important. *You* are what is important, Jenny." She bit back her anger. "It is not all right, what he did."

Jenny lowered her head. "It's on account of I don't know what I'm doin'," she said, sniffling. "I never done this kind o' thing before."

"That makes no difference," Catalina said with fierce conviction. She too was inexperienced, but that didn't excuse a man being rough with a woman. Drew had not been rough with her. "What he did is wrong. If Miss Hattie knew—"

"I don't want Miss Hattie to see me like this."

"She *should* see you," Catalina insisted. "It is not right for a client to beat you."

Jenny clutched at Catalina's hand in desperation. "Please don't tell her. I need this job. I don't want her to find out I don't know how to do it. Please, Catalina, promise me you won't say anything."

Catalina gulped. There was a terrible logic to Jenny's words. And yet the situation was so wrong. She placed a calming hand atop Jenny's and nodded. "You must let me help you." She wasn't sure how she could help, but she couldn't let more harm come to the girl.

"Can you...can you fix this?" She held up the ragged edges of her dress.

"Of course." Catalina could mend the garment. She only wished she could repair Jenny's damaged body and self-worth as easily.

Jenny popped up and began removing the dress. Catalina didn't realize the girl meant for her to start work at once, but she was willing to do what she could to keep Jenny close...and away from whoever had done this to her.

"He is not coming back, is he?" Catalina ventured.

Jenny gulped. "I...don't know."

Catalina fetched her sewing kit. While the two of them sat silently on the bed in their drawers and camisoles, she worked on the torn fabric.

As she stitched, she began thinking about Jenny's situation. Jenny was a timid, earnest, hard-working girl. She should be able to find a way to earn money without working as a soiled dove. She should not be subject to such wretched mistreatment, nor should she be made to feel so insignificant.

Her mind drifted back to the last night. It was horrifying to think that at the very moment Catalina had been enjoying divine pleasure at Drew's hands, Jenny may have been suffering under the bruising blows of her ruthless client. It wasn't right. Jenny deserved better. Catalina had to get her out of this hopeless predicament...before the brute returned, before Miss Hattie saw her, before anyone suspected a thing.

As she tied off the knot and snipped the ends of thread, Catalina came to a decision. She knew she was going to sound *prepotente,* as bossy as her father, but it was for Jenny's own good.

While Jenny slipped her dress back on, Catalina went to her trunk and pulled out the little velvet bag of coins, emptying them into her palm. There was forty dollars there—twenty dollars from Drew for the past two nights and twenty more she'd saved up from housekeeping.

It meant she'd have to do without her sewing machine that much longer. But giving Jenny this money could save the girl's life.

"I want you to take this," she said, pressing the coins into Jenny's palm.

"What? I can't—"

"Take it," she insisted, closing the girl's fingers over the coins. "It is not much, but it will take you as far as Sacramento. And there, you can make yourself a new life."

Jenny's eyes filled with fresh tears. "It's too much. I could never pay you back and—"

"You do not need to pay me back. But if I give you this money, you must make me a promise."

Jenny's chin trembled as she nodded.

"Promise me you will not look for work in a place like this. Even if you have to scrub shirts or wash dishes, find a good job where you are treated with respect."

"But I have no skills," she argued. "I'm...worthless."

"No," Catalina snapped. "You are *not* worthless. The man who did this to you—*he* is worthless. You deserve better than this. And now you will go find it. Go someplace where he will never find you. Promise me."

Jenny's eyes brimmed again, and she nodded.

But at the abrupt knock on the door, the girl jumped up with a wheeze of panic.

Catalina frowned and clenched her fists. If that was Jenny's client looking for her, he'd be sorry he came knocking at Catalina's door.

She stormed to the door and flung it open, primed for a fight.

It was Drew. He looked startled.

"Oh." In the space of an instant, she went from agitation to surprise to relief. And then her heart melted. Drew hadn't left her after all.

"What did I miss?" he asked.

She ushered him in, noting briefly that he'd changed into dark blue trousers with a blue brocade vest. She closed the door behind him.

The instant he laid eyes on Jenny's battered face, his brows came together in a scowl. *"Ling-miwhxiy!"* he cursed. "Who did this?"

Catalina tried to hush him. She didn't want to wake the whole Parlor. But he ignored her. And she had to admit there was something attractive about his righteous indignation. She liked the way he thrust out his chest and towered over them like a menacing storm cloud.

"Where is he?" he demanded. "Where *is* he?"

"Gone," Catalina told him.

He spit out a curse in English that made her blink.

"And I am going to get Jenny away from here," she told him with pride.

"How?"

She didn't want to tell him. She was afraid he'd be disappointed, that he would think she was wasting her sewing machine money on a girl she hardly knew.

But Jenny told him. "Miss Catalina's given me her savin's," she gushed, "so I can get out o' town and find a better life."

It was hard to tell what Drew's scowl meant. "Is that true?"

It was pointless to deny it. So Catalina raised her chin and defended her actions. "It is only money. I will make more."

CHAPTER 20

Drew knew in that instant that he'd made the right decision last night. Catalina was going to make a perfect wife. Not only was she lovely on the outside, but she was beautiful inside as well. The fact that she would sacrifice all she'd saved to come to the rescue of a mistreated waif spoke heaps about her nature.

A lump lodged in his throat as he gazed at his beloved bride-to-be. She possessed a will of iron and a heart of gold. He couldn't ask for a worthier prize.

Now all he had to do was make sure he was deserving of such a prize.

"Was it the man with the broken nose?" he asked Jenny. He remembered the villain from the poker game. "It was, wasn't it?"

Jenny gulped and nodded.

"Do you know where he went?"

She shook her head.

Cat assured him, "It is not your fight, Drew." Then she added a small, pointed poke at him. "Especially since you are going to be moving on."

"Any time a man mistreats a woman, it's my fight," he told her. "And about my movin' on, I've been thinkin' about that."

"Have you?" Her face she kept carefully neutral, but he could see she was holding her breath.

He wouldn't say any more about it than that, at least not until he scraped together enough money to buy her a proper wedding ring.

"So where are you headed?" he asked Jenny.

Jenny looked in question at Catalina. "Sacramento?"

Cat nodded.

"That's good," he agreed. It was far enough away to be safe. And it was easy to disappear in a big town like Sacramento, where nobody looked too closely into a person's background. She could, as Cat said, make a new beginning. "What do you need me to do?"

Cat looked askance at the battered girl. "Can you pack your trunks right now?"

"I don't have a trunk. I don't have much of anything, to be honest, just this dress and a few sundries."

"If you hurry," Catalina said, "you can catch the morning stage to Chico and go from there.

Jenny's eyes said she was afraid.

Catalina narrowed her gaze. "I will fashion a hat for you so no one will see your face, yes?"

The girl nodded.

Drew felt useless as Catalina made plans for Jenny's escape. But he had to admire her resourcefulness, especially watching her transform an ordinary basket into a hat.

First, she broke off the basket handle. Then she cut a swath of cloth from the underskirt of the girl's dress. Placing the basket at an angle atop Jenny's head, she wrapped the sheer yellow fabric around the basket, pulling part of it down to create a veil of sorts. Then she clipped the purple rose from the front of the girl's dress, wrapping the ends of the ribbon around the hat to hold it in place.

Satisfied with that, she helped Jenny get dressed, untying the ribbons that normally hitched it up above her knees so that the skirts fell at a respectable length. She retied the outside ribbons at the front and cut off the inside ribbons, weaving them together into an insert, which she basted into the indecently low neckline of the gown.

It was genius.

No wonder Cat wanted to be a clothing designer. She had a real gift for it. If she could do that with odds and ends of cloth, a needle and thread, and her two hands, what could she do with real material and a sewing machine? Her talent made him even more determined to help her get out of The Parlor and buy her the sewing machine she wanted.

Within a matter of minutes, Jenny had gathered her meager belongings. Catalina tried unsuccessfully to pick all the feathers from Jenny's dress, and then kissed her on both cheeks, bidding her goodbye and good fortune. Then Drew escorted her to The Adams Hotel, where the stage was due to arrive.

Catalina dusted off her hands. At least one problem was solved today. But there was still the feathery mess of her room. And she didn't even want to think about the carnage downstairs.

At least Drew was still in Paradise, she thought as she secured her petticoat. Finding him gone this morning, she'd feared his lusty behavior last night had been a gesture of farewell.

She ran her hands over her shoulders, remembering his velvety touch on her skin and his sultry whispers against her hair.

It was obvious that Drew coveted her. He couldn't stand the thought of another man laying a finger on her. If only he could see how much he needed her, maybe he wouldn't be in such a hurry to run away.

But the day was rapidly approaching. She couldn't afford the luxury of a leisurely morning. She'd just lost all her money, after all, and was starting over again with her job as a housekeeper. So she hastily dressed, planning to clean The Parlor before she began to attack her feather-infested bedroom.

When she opened the door, she was glad to see the bottle that had struck it in the middle of the night had been swept up. But when she stepped out onto the balcony, the sight below took her breath away.

The salon was spotless.

To be sure, there were fewer chairs, and a table was missing. Portions of the carpet were torn, and in some places, the wallpaper was beyond repair.

But all the glass and splinters of wood had been swept away. The counters, tabletops, and mirror gleamed. The wooden floors were scrubbed. Even the one unbroken vase that remained had been filled with blooms. True, there were a few weeds tucked in among them. But there was no question in Catalina's mind that this was the work of kindhearted Drew.

Moved to a watery smile by his generosity, she pressed a hand to her breast. Such generosity deserved a kind gesture in return.

She knew what he would like, what would make him most happy, what would make him glad that he had stayed in Paradise.

She would show him the kind of pleasure he had given her last night. She would confer with the other ladies to discover the best method. And then she would give him a night to remember.

Drew eyed the silver star peeking out from under the coat of the man across the table from him. Normally, he didn't like playing poker with lawmen. Sore losers were bad enough. But when their right hand was holding bad cards and their left was the strong arm of the law, it was a dangerous combination.

Still, today it was worth the risk. He needed to win enough money, not only to buy Cat's company tonight, but also for the wedding ring he planned to give her tomorrow.

Fortunately, though he still didn't believe it was his fault, he'd worked off what Miss Hattie felt he owed for the damages to the salon by cleaning up the mess. To be honest, the grateful embrace and gushing thanks from Cat had been far more valuable to him than Miss Hattie's dismissal of his debt.

Besides, Sheriff Campbell seemed like a decent sort. He was a bit tipsy for this early in the day. But he was a good enough fellow, and his tells were easy to spot. Every time he was dealt a favorable hand, he straightened visibly in his chair. And every time he bluffed, his eye twitched.

The other two players were only slightly more challenging.

Ed sniffed when he was holding winning cards. And Greg stroked his bushy beard when he had a good hand.

Halfway through the day, the good sheriff was soused enough to start waxing poetic about his lady love. According to Campbell, the sun rose and set on his Maggie Ellen, and he intended to marry her one day soon, as soon as he had the funds to buy a nice place with a proper yard and a pretty little chicken coop.

Drew feared that might take a while at the rate the sheriff was losing money. But though Drew was careful not to let the pot get too high, there was no hiding the fact that he was slowly robbing the sheriff of his bank.

In order to keep Ed and Greg in the game, Drew made it

worth their while, losing just often enough to make them happy.

Meanwhile, every time Miss Hattie came by with refills of whiskey for the sheriff, she gave Drew a pointed look of warning. He returned her look with a subtle nod, letting her know he was well aware he was going up against a man with the power to string him up if he didn't like the look of his cards.

Dollar by patient dollar, Drew managed to move the pile of coins to his side of the table. By mid-afternoon, he had almost enough to pay for Catalina. But by late afternoon, he could tell that Ed and Greg were growing bored of the game.

If he was lucky, he could get to the jeweler's shop before it closed. First, however, he'd have to place one last big wager...and win.

An opportunity arose three hands later. After the draw, Ed sniffed, Greg stroked his beard, and the sheriff sat up straight. By the signs, all three of them thought they had winning cards. But when Drew glimpsed the four handsome jacks sitting shoulder to shoulder in his hand, he knew this was his chance.

He tossed out a modest bet of a half-dollar.

Overconfident, the other two met his bet, and Greg raised it by another half-dollar. Twice more the wager circled, until the pot was over fifteen dollars and Ed needed to add three dollars to call.

Ed couldn't spare it, so he folded.

Sheriff Campbell tossed back a shot of whiskey, exhaled, and then pushed his last eight dollars into the middle of the table.

"All in," he said with a grin of self-assurance, "for Maggie Ellen."

Greg cussed and folded.

Drew stared at the pile—twenty-three dollars—then

glanced up at the sheriff. Of course, there was always a slim chance that Campbell was holding four aces or a straight flush. Hell, he might have a royal flush.

Still, he was fairly certain the sheriff's confidence came not from his hand, but from the whiskey—that and his desire to buy a dream house for his Maggie Ellen.

If Drew was wrong, if he lost, he wouldn't have enough to buy Cat or the ring. If he won, he'd have enough for Cat, the ring, and a decent supper to boot.

With a calm expression that revealed none of the turmoil he was feeling, he met the bet.

The sheriff gleefully laid out his cards. "Who's the gamblin' fool now, Maggie Ellen?" he crowed.

It was a full house—three queens and two tens.

The sheriff rubbed his hands together, ready to gather up his winnings.

If Drew hadn't needed that cash so badly, he would have made the wise choice of laying his cards face down and letting the man with the silver star take home the pot. He didn't need a sheriff mad at him.

But he couldn't go another day without Cat. Just leaving her this morning—with her eyes full of passion, her hair full of feathers, and her camisole full of temptation—had been painful. Half his brain was riled up with delicious thoughts of what he'd like to do to her, and the other half was tormented by the fear that someone else might get there before him.

So instead of taking the easy way out, Drew fanned his cards on the table.

Ed gave a surprised whoop.

Greg shook his head.

Sheriff Campbell sat stunned.

Drew knew how to win gracefully. He didn't immediately collect his winnings. Instead, he gave a low whistle. "Damn, Sheriff, you almost had me. Well played."

"That can't be," the sheriff said, crestfallen.

Drew placed one hand on his holstered Colt. He wouldn't draw it, not on a lawman. But it gave him some comfort to know it was there in case things got dangerous.

Ed and Greg exchanged a look that said they were done playing poker. As they scraped their chairs back, the sheriff frowned down at his cards.

"I'm gonna lose her," he mumbled. "I'm gonna lose my Maggie Ellen." He compressed his lips and picked up his whiskey glass, putting it back down when he saw it was empty. Drew could see he was trying not to blubber. "She said she's got no use for a man who's up to his eyeballs in gamblin' debt."

Drew quietly gathered his winnings. "Listen, Sheriff, I don't want you to go nary cent, especially 'cause o' your Maggie Ellen." He pushed a couple of silver dollars to the man's side of the table.

The sheriff stood up, knocking his chair on its hind legs and weaving a bit. "Dammit! I don't need your charity."

Ed and Greg grabbed the sheriff's arms to steady him, but he shook off their help.

The three managed to find their way out of the salon without incident, and Drew finally took his hand off of his pistol. But no sooner had they left than Miss Hattie waltzed up with her hand out.

He shook his head. She knew him too well. He dutifully handed over twenty dollars, and she tucked it into her bodice.

But instead of leaving the table, she leaned forward. "You got any idea what happened to my girl?"

"Your girl?" He started gathering up the cards.

"Jenny?"

He didn't hesitate. He didn't even blink. "Jenny? Not sure I know which one she—"

"The hell you don't. I saw you leavin' the salon with her

this mornin'." She clucked her tongue. "No wonder you're such a good gambler. You got one hell of a bluff."

He started to explain, but she held up a hand.

"I don't want to hear any lies, Mr. Hawk. But I want you to know one thing. You do wrong by my girls, and you'll be out on your ass." She jabbed a finger at his chest. "If Jenny doesn't come home tonight, I'm gonna take it out o' your wallet. And if I find out you've been playin' false with that little Italian girl who's sweet on you, I'm gonna take it out o' your hide."

He quirked up one corner of his lip. So Miss Hattie thought Cat was sweet on him? That was good news. He didn't want to waste his money on a ring, only to have Cat turn him down.

Miss Hattie shook her head. "You won't be smilin' when the sheriff loses his girl 'cause o' you."

"Me? Why are you always blamin' *me* for everything? It's not my fault the sheriff's a gamblin' fool."

Her answer was a silent glare as she picked up the whiskey glasses from the table.

Drew pocketed what was left of his coin and headed out to buy the prettiest wedding ring twenty dollars could buy.

CHAPTER 21

By the end of the day, Catalina was so confused by the conflicting information she'd received from her friends that she decided she might not be capable of pleasuring Drew after all.

Anne had told her to use both hands.

Emily had said she really only needed one.

Anne had insisted most men liked it rough and fast.

Emily argued, saying long and slow was the best.

Anne had given her a small tin of lard mixed with peppermint oil.

Emily had brought her lavender-scented lanolin.

In the end, she'd thanked them and sat in her room with both potions in her hands, wondering if she should just ask Drew which he preferred.

When he finally knocked on the door, she felt sudden misgiving about the whole idea. It sounded so complicated and specific. She didn't even know if she could remember everything they'd told her. What if she did something wrong? What if she hurt him?

Deciding it was better to forget the whole thing, she quickly ditched the tins under her repaired pillow. Then, with a determined toss of her head, she answered the door.

Drew looked almost as anxious as she felt.

"Miss Cat," he said with a nod of his head.

"Mr. Hawk."

She closed the door behind him. He looked very handsome in blue. She wanted to tell him so, but the words stuck in her throat. There was an awkward silence between them and then an awkward conversation.

"The room cleaned up nice," he said.

She forced a smile and picked up her pillow to show him. "I sewed the feathers back in." Then she glanced down in horror at the tins she'd unwittingly revealed. She quickly thrust the pillow back onto the bed.

He didn't seem to notice. He was busy tangling with his duster, trying to get it to stay on the coat hook.

"How was your day?" she asked, wincing as she realized what an inane question it was.

"Fine," he replied, sounding just as inane. "I won a decent chunk off of the town sheriff."

"Did you?" Of course he had. Otherwise, he wouldn't have been able to pay Miss Hattie for her company.

"Look, Cat, there's somethin' I need to say." He licked his lips, took a deep breath and blew it out.

She didn't want to hear what he had to say. By the look in his eyes, it wasn't going to be good.

Though she hated to admit it, she'd grown very attached to Drew Hawk, probably too attached, considering she'd come here to pursue her dream of designing, not find a husband.

But her heart didn't care why she'd come. And now it beat fast, afraid Drew was going to say something unpleasant, like he hadn't paid Miss Hattie, and he didn't plan to spend the night.

Then again, he'd taken off his duster. He must not plan to leave right away.

"Shall I order whiskey?" she said brightly, hoping to delay his news.

"No. No whiskey." Then he reconsidered. "Yeah, let's get a bottle. Why not?"

She went to the door, her mind spinning with dire possibilities.

He was leaving.

He didn't care for her.

He'd had a change of heart.

Now that he'd sampled her wares, he was no longer interested in the conquest.

Whatever it was, she told herself, she'd face it bravely.

When she called down from the balcony for the whiskey, her voice cracked.

By the time she came back to the room, he was pacing back and forth. "This ain't easy," he confided.

She wanted to put her hands over her ears. She didn't want to hear all his stupid excuses again. She didn't want to hear how he couldn't be tied down or that a nice girl like her would find somebody else.

If she could distract him, maybe she wouldn't have to hear it.

"We can wait until the whiskey is here," she suggested. "Why don't you take off your gun?"

If she could get him to linger a little longer, maybe she could convince him to stay.

He unbuckled his gun belt and set his pistol on the night table.

Frantic for something to say, Catalina asked, "So...what do you think will become of Jenny?"

"I'm sure she'll land on her feet...thanks to you."

"Land on her feet?"

He smiled. "Yeah, like a cat."

"Ah." She traced the edge of her dresser with a finger. "I wonder what kind of work she will find."

"In Sacramento? It's a big city."

"Maybe she'll find work in a good household. Or a shop. Or a laundry."

"Or maybe she'll find herself a man, settle down, and, you know, get married...or somethin'.'"

Drew winced inwardly at his broad and awkward hint. He was going about this all wrong. He had an important question to ask Cat—the most important question he'd ever asked anyone in his life. And at the moment, he was as tongue-tied as a gambler caught with an ace up his sleeve.

What if she turned him down? What if, like Sheriff Campbell's Maggie Ellen, Cat decided she didn't want to marry a gambler? What if she felt ashamed by what he'd done to her last night and didn't want to be with him anymore?

No, he wouldn't believe that. He just needed to set the proper tone for the conversation. Once they got out of their clothes, once they had a sip of whiskey and climbed under the covers, she'd melt into the warm and welcoming Cat he knew.

Then he'd ask her to be his wife.

He was sure she'd say yes.

Pretty sure.

Miss Hattie came to the door with the whiskey and two glasses. But before she handed them off to Cat, she said, "You haven't seen Jenny, have you? She snuck off with *some man* this mornin', up to who-knows-what, and I ain't seen her since."

Drew narrowed his eyes at the madam. Was she seriously accusing

Drew of hanky-panky with Jenny? Did she think Drew would double-cross Catalina like that?

Fortunately, Cat was quick on her feet. She came to his defense.

"I hope it was not the man who bought Jenny last night," she said, "because he hurt her."

"What?" Miss Hattie looked genuinely shocked.

"He cut her lip and bruised her cheek," Cat said. "If that is the man who took Jenny, then we must pray for her welfare."

Miss Hattie gave Drew a sidelong glance.

He told her pointedly, "And if someone *else* took her, I'm thinkin' they prob'ly put her on a stage to someplace safe."

Miss Hattie nodded. Her reply was notably humbled. "Well, if that's the case, then I owe that man an apology."

Drew gave her a subtle nod, and Miss Hattie excused herself.

Once the madam was gone, Cat poured them both a glass of whiskey.

Drew downed it all at once and blew out a steadying breath.

He didn't know why he had such a case of the jitters. People got married all the time. His own parents had been married. Marriage never killed anyone. Why he was so nervous, he couldn't say. But he had to calm down before he blurted out something stupid. "Think Miss Hattie'll ever get married?" Like that.

"Miss Hattie?" she said, raising her brows. "Who knows?" She held out the bottle to refill his glass. "Life is uncertain."

He took a slow and cautious sip of whiskey, stalling for time. "I suppose a woman like her with a business and all might not think she needs a man."

Damn it all! What was he doing? If he weren't careful, he'd undermine all the arguments for wedding him.

"She *doesn't* need a man," Cat said with a measure of pride.

Then she lifted a suggestive brow. "The question is does she *want* a man?"

He studied her face. "And do you think she does?" He hardly realized he was holding his breath for her answer.

"It's hard to tell," she answered carefully. "I am certain it depends upon the man."

Why did it suddenly feel like they were gunfighters circling each other with their fingers twitching above their holsters, each one waiting for the other to draw?

Worse, Drew didn't feel like he was getting any closer to asking his question or getting his answer. As crass as it sounded, he knew he would be much more comfortable if they were both wearing less clothing.

"Shall we get undressed?"

Shit, that sounded like an invitation to tea. What was wrong with him? What had happened to his slick, smooth-talking way with women?

She answered with more enthusiasm than he expected. "Yes."

Maybe he hadn't lost his touch after all. He set down his whiskey. By the time he got the buttons undone on his shirt, she was already down to her camisole and drawers. Things were looking up.

He hooked his shirt over the bedpost. She stretched her arms above her head and let out a blatantly phony yawn. Then she slipped hastily beneath the covers. Now they were getting somewhere.

But he got in such a big hurry to catch up that, purely out of habit, he whipped off his undershirt. He would have stripped out of his drawers too, except for the gasp from Catalina.

Thankfully, it wasn't a gasp of horror. In fact, she looked pleasantly impressed as her gaze fell to his bare chest. Her jaw loosened. Her eyelids lowered. Her eyes smoldered with desire.

Pretending modesty, he clutched his undershirt to his chest in one fist.

"Would you prefer I..."

"No," she was quick to reply. "No. It is fine."

Drew smiled to himself. He could tell it was more than fine. Cat liked the look of him. Nothing could have made him happier. He hung the undershirt on the bedpost too.

When he turned back, the breath stuck in his throat. Cat was toying with the ties of her camisole.

Afraid to breathe, he watched as she slowly pulled loose the bow and let the lacy edges part.

She was too shy to look him in the eye. But she managed to transcend her modesty to reveal her lovely cleavage.

When her fingers hesitated in uncertainty, he moved to intercept her.

"May I?" he asked.

She swallowed visibly, but let him finish the task for her. When he removed her camisole and laid eyes on the beautiful twins of her breasts, the blood surged to his loins so fast that he nearly groaned at the sensation.

But she didn't stop there. She tugged on the tie of her drawers. This time she looked into his eyes, as if seeking his permission.

He was too amazed and aroused to speak. All he could do was send a silent message of approval with his eyes.

She lifted her hips and slipped the drawers down, bending her knees to slide them off of her ankles.

He let his eyes feast on her divine body. Her skin was the color of honey, smooth and unblemished except for that adorable mole beside her mouth and a matching dot high on her thigh. Her curves were as graceful as the river that wound through Hupa. And the fine black curls that hid her woman's flower looked soft and inviting.

He remembered how warm and wet she'd been last night,

how she'd moved beneath him, responding to his touch. He grew as hard as iron with the memory.

"May I?" she whispered.

At first he didn't understand. Then she reached for the top of his drawers. There was no question what she intended.

He almost told her no. *Hell* no. After all, she was a virgin. She may have never seen a man in this state. He didn't want to frighten her. And it wasn't like he could make it go away with a snap of his fingers.

But several days of abstinence was definitely affecting his judgment.

"Are you sure?" he croaked.

She nodded.

Still he hesitated. Once he did this, there was no going back. It wasn't a matter of control. He'd been subject to temptation before. But he didn't want to do anything with Catalina until he was sure she'd say yes to his proposal of marriage.

Where had he put the ring?

It was in the pocket of his trousers. Before things went any further, he'd just fetch it out, put it on her finger, and ask her if she'd be his wife.

Then he felt her hands on him. As her fingers worked on the buttons of his drawers, her palm brushed his hard length.

He sucked a breath between his teeth, forgetting all about the ring.

He wasn't sure what she intended. At least, he wasn't sure until he lifted his hips to let her drag down his drawers, dislodging his pillow, and discovered two strange little tins cached there.

"What's this?" he murmured.

She blushed. "It is to thank you for...for last night."

His brow creased as he tried to make sense out of what she was saying.

"Anne and Emily gave them to me," she explained. "I have not done this before. They said it would make it more...pleasurable...for you." She rested her palm on his thigh, and a warm current of lust flooded his loins. "Which would you prefer—the peppermint or the lavender?"

He barely had time to whisper, "Lady's choice."

Then all rational thought was drowned in a sea of pleasant sensations as she showed him what her shady lady friends had taught her.

A quarter of an hour later, he lay splayed across the mattress, grinning and satiated, reeking of peppermint, lavender, and sex.

Under his guidance, Cat had given him an exhilarating journey and a rewarding completion. He'd never felt so incredibly adored and beloved, so worshipped. Her love warmed him, making him feel free and magnificent and all-powerful.

In another moment, he told himself, he'd return her affections and bring her to her own brilliant ecstasy. Then he'd cradle her in the afterglow of their lovemaking, slip the wedding ring gently on her finger, and ask for her hand in marriage.

Unfortunately, his good intentions came to nothing.

Blissfully satiated and drowsy, he slipped off into a deep sleep.

When he woke alone in the morning, it was to the sound of loud cursing coming from downstairs.

His eyes went wide. That was one very angry woman. And she was cursing in a language he was beginning to recognize.

Lickety-split, he pulled on his trousers and grabbed his Colt.

CHAPTER 22

Catalina thought it was probably a good thing she didn't have a gun. She would have shot the broken-nosed *bastardo* where he stood. And then the sheriff of Paradise would have hanged her for murder.

As it was, Catalina was being restrained by Miss Hattie, who had a steely grip on her arms.

"Where is she?" the brute demanded again, growling like a pig hunting for *tartufi*. "Where's my Jenny?"

"She is not yours, you *figlio di puttana!*" Catalina yelled at him.

"Hush!" Miss Hattie hissed.

The madam might share Catalina's sentiments, but she never liked to anger customers, no matter how rude they were.

"Now, mister, to be fair," Miss Hattie said in diplomatic tones, "the last time you visited us, you got a little rough with Jenny."

"She's mine!" he bellowed. "Where is she?"

"Gone where you will never find her, *bruto!*" Catalina spat.

Miss Hattie gave Catalina's arms a jerk. "She ain't here, mister. You're gonna have to mosey along."

Catalina was incredulous. "You will just let him go? After what he did to Jenny?"

"I didn't do nothin' to Jenny," the man said. "If she said I did, she's lyin'."

"I saw her!" Catalina shouted. "You ripped her dress. You cut her lip. You striked her in the face."

Miss Hattie intervened. "You should prob'ly just get out o' town before word starts spreadin'."

"Jenny belongs to me," the man insisted. "I had her first."

Catalina bit the words out between her teeth. "Yes, you had her first. I saw the sheets. You hurt her so badly, there was blood everywhere."

Miss Hattie flinched at this revelation.

The man spat on the floor. "Don't you know nothin', whore? That's just the way it is." Then he yelled, "Now tell me where Jenny is! Jenny!"

His roar brought the upstairs ladies drifting timidly out of their bedrooms.

Then the man whipped aside his coat and pulled out a pistol. He shook it toward the balcony. "Jenny? Where are you, girl?"

He fired off a shot at the ceiling, chipping the plaster and setting off a spate of shrieks.

"Jenny! I know you're here!"

He fired again, clipping the wood railing of the balcony and sending the ladies diving for the floor.

"Someone better tell me where she is," he threatened, "or I'm gonna start shootin' whores—startin' with this one."

Suddenly, Catalina found herself staring down the barrel of his gun.

In the next instant, before she could even gasp, there was a loud crack.

For a split second, Catalina thought she'd been shot.

But then she saw the pistol fly out of his grip into pieces and hit the wall as if by magic. He recoiled and cursed in pain, shaking his hand.

From upstairs, she heard Drew's familiar voice. "You'd best get the hell out o' Paradise before I get a bead on somethin' more than your trigger finger."

Miss Hattie loosened her hold. Catalina turned to see shirtless Drew coming down the stairs with his Colt drawn.

The broken-nosed brute must have recognized him. "This ain't your business, Hawk," he grumbled. "I got no quarrel with a fellow gambler."

"Well, I got a quarrel with men who pick on ladies half their size."

"Hell, I didn't pick on her."

Catalina itched to slap the brute's face. But Drew was still holding a gun on the man. She knew better than to get between him and his target.

The broken-nosed man groused to Drew as if he thought he'd found a kindred spirit. "You know how it is. You got to teach a woman from the start, break her in right."

Catalina felt her blood rising. She heard the soft whimpering of the women upstairs, who were still cowering on the floor.

"Is that so?" Drew purred, coming down the last step.

"Sure," the man said. "Otherwise, they're never gonna know who's boss."

Drew lowered his gun, but continued advancing on the man. "Gotta show 'em the ropes?"

"Yeah."

He ambled forward. "Give 'em a swat now and then when they get out o' line?"

"Yeah."

He stepped closer. "A little...love tap?"

"Y—"

Drew raised the butt of his pistol and cracked it hard against the man's forehead. "Like that?"

The man staggered back. A lump was already rising on his brow. "What the hell?"

Drew shrugged. "Just lettin' you know who's in charge."

Catalina fought the urge to cheer him on. Miss Hattie might have to be diplomatic. But Drew had no such need. And the fact that he was coming to the defense of women everywhere made her giddy with pride.

Then the man shook off the cobwebs and barreled back up to Drew. "You're playin' a dangerous game, half-breed."

"Name-callin'? Really?" Drew said, shaking his head. "That's a mite cowardly."

The man threw a punch. Drew ducked under it. The man stumbled forward under his own momentum. A light shove by Drew sent him crashing, chin-first, into a card table.

Red-faced, the man struggled to his feet, as mad as a raging bear. "Get your hands off me!"

"Is that what Jenny said?" Drew demanded.

"You don't know shit!" The man was foaming at the mouth.

Against Catalina's wishes, Drew set aside his gun and turned to face the brute with his arms wide.

"Come on," he urged. "Show me who's boss."

Catalina's heart stuck in her throat. Drew was every bit as big as the broken-nosed villain. But he was probably not as ruthless or underhanded. The bullies in Italy didn't believe in fair fights. They would knife a man in the back and kick him when he lay bleeding on the ground. Drew had said he was good with a gun, and by what she'd just seen, he was telling the truth. Why wasn't he using his pistol now?

Afraid for Drew's life, while the men were warily circling each other, Catalina slipped over to the table and rested her hand on his pistol. She didn't intend to fire it. But if Drew wasn't going to use it, at least she could keep it out of the hands of the bad man.

Like a bull stamping its hoof in a show of threat, the brute wrenched a chair out of the way.

Drew stood his ground, beckoning the man forward with a flip of his fingers.

With a low growl, the man lunged toward Drew.

Catalina's breath caught. But at the last minute, Drew sidestepped. The man missed him by inches and went crashing into the wall.

When he whipped around in fury, Drew was ready for him.

"Best stay back, ladies," he murmured.

Miss Hattie grabbed Catalina by the elbow, dragging her back to a safer spot under the balcony. Catalina hid the pistol in the folds of her skirt.

The bully punched one scarred and meaty fist into his palm in threat. To Catalina's anxious eyes, that fist looked twice the size of her head. If the brute thought what he'd done to Jenny had been love taps, what damage could he inflict upon Drew?

The man hurled himself forward again. This time his fist grazed Drew's cheek. When Drew dropped abruptly to the ground, Catalina gasped, afraid he'd been felled.

But Drew was clever. He was using the man's own force against him. The brute had thrown all of his weight into his attack. So when Drew knocked the man's feet out from under him, his knees hit the floor with a great thud.

He howled in pain and rage.

Drew wiped his scraped cheek with his thumb. It hadn't even drawn blood.

"That's for what you did to Jenny," he bit out.

"*Si!*" Catalina chimed in.

"It ain't near what I'm gonna do to you!" the man declared as he staggered to his feet.

"No!" Catalina cried. "Get your dirty hands off of—"

Miss Hattie elbowed her. "Hush."

Drew shook his head, but prepared for another attack.

Catalina couldn't bear to watch, but she couldn't stand to look away. So she peered through squinted eyes.

The man was limping now as he made his way toward Drew. His eyes were full of bloodlust. His fists clenched and unclenched. Spittle hung from his sneering lip.

With his right fist, he threw a hard punch at Drew's head.

Drew dodged aside and caught the clout in his palm. But he wasn't ready for the second punch.

The man's left fist caught his ribs. It was a glancing blow, but it was enough to make Drew grimace and grunt in pain.

Catalina squeaked in fear.

The bully laughed in victory as Drew clutched at his bruised ribs.

"Nobody pushes me around!" the brute roared. "Not you!" He stabbed a finger at Drew. "Not her!" He pointed at Miss Hattie. Then he narrowed his eyes at Catalina. "And not some filthy, foul-mouthed, foreign fu—"

His tirade was interrupted by a gruesome crack as Drew's fist broke his nose, not for the first time.

"No one..." Drew spat, seizing the brute by the front of his shirt. "...talks like that..." He pummeled the man again, bloodying his lip. "...about the woman..." His next blow sent two teeth flying out of the brute's mouth. "...I intend to marry!"

His final punch hit the point of the man's chin. The brute went instantly silent. His eyes rolled back in his head, and he hit the floor like a felled tree, with a thundering thud.

Someone fired a gun.

Beside Catalina's foot, a great hole had suddenly appeared in the wooden floor.

She gasped. Then she looked at her hand. The pistol was smoking.

She looked up at Drew. He was staring at her with a strange expression, like a combination of wariness and horror.

He held out his hand. "You want to hand that over, nice and careful, Cat?"

She nodded, lifting it up by the stock with two fingers to hand it to Drew.

She let out a shuddering breath. She hadn't realized how terrified she'd been.

Above her, the ladies started murmuring softly in wonder. Miss Hattie swept out from behind her to peer down at the wreckage of a man laid out like a corpse on her salon floor.

Suddenly, Catalina frowned.

"Wait," she said, glancing at Drew, who was cradling his battered ribs. "What did you just say?"

"I said, do you want to hand over the—"

"No, before that."

"Oh. That."

While the ladies hushed and leaned over the balcony, Drew set down the gun and dug in his pocket.

He pulled forth something and went down on one knee before her.

"Miss Cat, Catalina..."

Her eyes welled with happy tears as she pressed one trembling hand to her bosom. She was so moved that she gave him her real name. "Catalina Palatino Prosperi Valentini di Ferrara."

He gave her a lopsided grin. "Miss Cat Etcetera...will you do me the honor of givin' me your hand in marriage?"

"Mr. Drew Hawk," she breathed. "I will give you my hands and my arms and my feet and my legs..."

"All right, that's quite enough givin' in public," Miss Hattie scolded.

The ladies squealed and cheered in delight.

Drew slipped a beautiful ring on her finger. The band was of simple gold filigree, and the brilliant diamond in the middle twinkled through the blur of tears in her eyes.

"I suppose you'll be wantin' Cat for the night," Miss Hattie quipped.

"Yes, ma'am."

Catalina frowned at the madam. "You will not make him pay for me."

"For you? No. But I'm still chargin' him two dollars for the room."

Drew patted his pockets. Then he crouched beside the man he'd knocked unconscious, who lay snuffling through his broken nose. He dug in the man's pockets and handed Miss Hattie two silver dollars.

"You'll prob'ly want to get the sheriff," Drew told her. "When this fool wakes up, he's gonna be madder than a hornet."

"You got that right," Miss Hattie said. Then she added, "Look, in light of everything that's happened, I'm gonna let you two have the day off alone. Think of it as a honeymoon. But bright and early tomorrow, Miss Catalina, I expect you to report for work...as my new saloon girl. You've got a raise. The pay is a dollar and a half a day."

"Oh, thank you, Miss Hattie," Catalina gushed.

Then Drew retrieved his gun, looped his arm through Catalina's, and led her back up the stairs.

When he closed the bedroom door behind them, he sagged against it. Catalina realized he'd been more injured than he let on. His chest was red where the brute had struck him.

"You're hurt," she accused.

"It's just a bruise."

"Let me see." She took his hand, pulling him toward the bed.

He followed her willingly and sat on the edge of the mattress. "You were pretty brave out there."

"Not as brave as you."

She gazed into his dark and sparkling eyes. They were full of pride and love and something else...

Lust.

Santo cielo, how could Drew think of sex at a time like this?

"You know," he murmured, lifting a hand to cup her cheek, "I'm not hurt from the waist down."

Despite her worry about his ribs, she couldn't resist smiling at his teasing words. And the sight of his bare chest, sleek and golden and full of muscle, sent a thrill through her that made every nerve tingle.

CHAPTER 23

Drew's ribs might be cracked, but by nightfall, he was feeling no pain. His talented little bride-to-be had not only seen to all his hurts, but most of his itches too.

She'd traced his every contour with her delicate fingers, kissing every place her fingertips touched. She'd whispered Italian syllables in his ear and sighed against his throat. She'd caressed him boldly, yet blushed as he slipped her camisole from her shoulders.

He'd repaid her in kind. He'd run the back of his knuckles across her sweet flesh. He'd breathed endearments in his native language softly across her face. He'd bathed her like a cat, running his tongue over every inch of her until she arched and purred in ecstasy.

The madam had brought them a tray of food halfway through the day, muttering that newlyweds needed to keep up their strength. They'd fed each other apples. Cat had nibbled on cheese from his fingers, and he'd slurped berry pie off of her lovely stomach.

They'd spent all day exploring, learning, reveling in each new discovery.

They currently lounged across the linens without a stitch of clothing. In fact, the only thing his lovely bride-to-be was wearing was the filigree wedding ring that made her his.

Their limbs were entwined like the roots of a tree. Her long golden legs wrapped around his, and her precious little toes peeped out from between the arches of his feet. Her hips made a sinewy curve in contrast to the angular jut of his. He blew a gentle breath across her rounded breasts. She squirmed, stiffening in sweet response. The beast nestled among his black curls roused as well.

He gazed down at their clasped hands, at how perfectly they fit together. He had no doubt the rest of them would fit as well. But that was the one feat they hadn't yet attempted.

Inspired to perform the final act that would make their union complete, Drew initiated a bold seduction. He slipped his fingers between Cat's thighs and stroked her to life.

She moaned and turned toward him with her eyes closed and a languorous smile on her lips.

He grew instantly hard. Disentangling from her legs, he levered up on one arm and moved over her. Tenderly, he nudged her knees apart and urged her thighs to open.

But when he pressed against her, begging entrance, she pushed at his shoulders.

"No," she protested.

He frowned. "No?"

"No."

His jaw tensed. "But we're gonna be married."

Si, but we are not yet married."

For an instant, he felt like an upset little boy who'd had his peppermint stick snatched away.

But in the next moment, he realized he couldn't gamble with her affections. They had their whole lives ahead of them.

It wasn't worth risking her love to seduce his bride before she was ready.

With a resigned sigh, he rocked off of her.

"When we are properly married, then I will give you everything, *mio caro,*" she told him, "I promise."

He nodded. She wasn't being unreasonable. But he wasn't feeling reasonable, not at all. He was feeling achy with lust.

"So when do you want to get married?" he asked her, hoping his voice didn't reveal his impatience.

She ran a pensive palm low across his belly, which didn't help matters any. He closed his eyes with painful yearning.

"First I must make a suitable wedding gown," she said.

"Hell, you don't need a weddin' gown," he told her. "I'd marry you in rags."

"Do not be silly," she told him. "I am a dressmaker. How will it look for a dressmaker not to have a proper wedding gown?"

He grunted.

"The other ladies will need dresses as well," she said.

He scowled. Other ladies? What other ladies?

She added, "Then there will be the men's suits to order."

"Men's suits? Now hold on a minute. What men?"

"You, your brother, your father..."

He smirked. Drew's father hadn't worn a suit since the day a bunch of white miners had forced him into a shotgun wedding.

"All that sewin'—how much time are we talkin' about?" he asked her. "A day or two? A week?"

Her laughter would have been charming if it hadn't jangled his nerves.

"Are you so impatient, my husband?" she chided.

Yes, as a matter of fact, he was.

She tapped her lip as she considered his question. "If I can get a sewing machine, I can order the fabric, design the clothings, and make them in...no more than a month, I would guess."

"A month!"

He didn't mean for it to come out like that, so abrupt and outraged. But damn it, he didn't want to wait that long to make love to her. It was ridiculous.

He loved her. She loved him. Why couldn't they just speak some words in front of a preacher and be done with it?

But Catalina bristled at his words. She moved her hand away and rolled onto her back. "If you do not think I am worth waiting for..."

"No, it ain't that, not at all," he was quick to assure her. "It's just, well, in Hupa, when a man finds a woman he fancies, he just brings her folks a deer and moves in with her."

"A deer?"

"Yeah, to prove he can provide for her."

She smiled at that. "You do not have to bring me a deer."

"Well, that's good to know. But honestly, I don't know if I can stand it..." He ran the back of his finger along her arm, making her shiver. "Sleepin' next to you every night..." He lifted her hand and kissed the tips of her fingers. "Tempted by all that delicious flesh..." He slipped her thumb into his mouth and gave it a gentle, sensual suck before he released it. "The feel of you...the taste of you..." He moved her hand down until her palm rested against his chest. "Can you feel how my heart beats for you? I can hardly resist you, Cat."

Her eyes were smoldering. He had her wrapped around his finger now. It was just a matter of getting her to say the word "yes."

"That is why," she murmured, "we should not sleep together."

He blinked. "What?" That wasn't the "yes" he was expecting.

"Until the wedding, I think it will be best if we do not sleep together."

"Why not?" He didn't mean it to come out so much like a petulant whine.

"Because it *is* too tempting."

He couldn't very well argue with her. He'd just told her that himself. That clever Cat had managed to hang him with his own noose. He muttered a very foul Hupa curse under his breath.

"Besides," she added softly, "I need to be sure that you are loving me for myself and not just for making the sex."

"Really?" Now he was getting a mite peeved. He crossed his arms. "That's interestin'. Because I seem to recall you didn't care all that much before. I seem to recall you threatenin' to go downstairs to find a gentleman to 'make the sex' with you. I don't think you were all that interested in a man lovin' you for yourself."

She at least had the grace to blush with guilt.

But in the next moment, she looked up at him with her big, brown, irresistible eyes, and he knew he'd already lost the argument. "It is not the same, because you I love with my *heart.*" She lowered her gaze. "I do not want you to love me and leave me."

He melted. Then he scowled. Love her and leave her? Why would she think that?

Why *wouldn't* she think that? Ever since he'd met her, he'd done nothing but tell her that he wasn't ready to settle down, that he was a rolling stone, a drifter, a free spirit.

He supposed it would take time to convince her—and maybe even himself—that he could change his ways. Until then, he guessed he'd have to play by her rules.

It wouldn't be easy.

He nodded. Then he sat up, wincing once as his ribs complained. "Well then, if I'm not beddin' down with my bride-to-be tonight, where am I supposed to sleep?"

She shrugged. "In Jenny's room?"

He grunted. Cat sure seemed to have everything figured out nice and neat. He might as well put on his trousers, since nothing was going to come of his attempts to seduce his lovely bride.

Satisfied she'd made a wise decision, Catalina turned down the oil lamp and snuggled under the covers...alone.

An hour later, she was still awake. Her bed felt big and empty without Drew in it. All night, she kept waking up and missing Drew. She missed talking and laughing with him. She missed listening to his deep breathing. She missed watching him as he slept. She missed the heat of his body beside her.

By the end of her restless night, she woke in a bad temper. It didn't seem like she was testing the strength of Drew's love as much as she was torturing herself.

With a sigh of self-pity, she dressed in her favorite gown of rich red silk in preparation for her new job. To her surprise, Drew was already downstairs and playing poker. She smoothed her skirts and crossed to the balcony railing to peer down at him.

Her heart swelled as she gazed down at the handsome gambler in his well-tailored brown suit. She knew his coal-black hair was softer than it looked. His tawny skin was warm and supple. His broad shoulders were impossible to span with her fingers. And she remembered that when she rested her head on his flat stomach, she could hear the strong beat of his heart.

She sighed, wondering if she could wait so long to make the sex with him.

As if he heard her sigh, he raised his eyes briefly and then lifted his entire head to gaze at her. A smile of appreciation graced his lips as he let his eyes rove over her from head to toe.

She lifted her hand and let her fingers tease at the edge of her neckline.

He narrowed his eyes and ran his tongue across his lower lip.

Then the player next to him gave him a nudge of his elbow.

Catalina grinned. She shouldn't distract him from his game. After all, the sooner he won, the sooner they could afford a wedding.

Still, she swayed a bit when she came down the stairs, lifting her scarlet skirts enough to give Drew a glimpse of her ankles.

All day long, they carried on a silent flirtation.

When she visited his table to refresh the gamblers' whiskey, she gave him a tiny peek at the top of her bosom.

When he caught her sauntering past the bar, he gave her a sly wink.

Halfway through the day, she brought a plate of fried chicken for the players, taunting Drew by suggestively licking the grease from her fingers.

While she stood beside him, he sneaked his hand beneath her skirts, sensually stroking the back of her knee.

Her eyes half closed at the heavenly sensation.

He gave her a knowing grin.

Then she pointedly arched a brow at the swelling in his lap.

He answered her sassiness by surreptitiously pinching her bottom.

She squeaked in surprise, blushing when the other players gaped at her, and then gave Drew a scolding shake of her head.

By nightfall, Catalina was aching for him. When he knocked on her door, she practically dragged him into her bedroom.

They didn't even make it to the bed.

Drew rained kisses all over her face and neck and shoulders.

She clawed at the buttons of his shirt.

He slipped his fingers down the front of her dress, and she sobbed, puckering instantly at his touch.

She thrust her fingers into his lush hair and feasted on his mouth.

He rubbed his hand firmly over the front of her skirts, delving between her legs.

She moaned, pressing her palm hard against his trousers.

He answered with a groan, backing her against the wall.

But deep in her heart, she knew she dared go no further. Their passion was like a wildfire, burning out of control. If she continued, there would be no stopping.

She couldn't give him what he wanted, what they both wanted. Not yet. Not until she was sure he was hers for good.

So she rested one hand on his shoulder and murmured, "We must not."

"Aw, Cat, don't tease me."

"I do not mean to, truly."

He let out a breath that was half a sigh, half a growl. Then he backed away, running both hands through his hair.

"I'm sorry," she said softly, then gave him a hopeful smile. "I promise it will be worth the wait."

He nodded, then mumbled, "If my balls don't turn blue and fall off first."

He adjusted his trousers, trying to hide the bulge there, and put his hand on the doorknob.

Then, remembering, he dug in his pocket and tossed a pouch of coins onto the bed. "Twenty-four dollars. That should move the weddin' date up a bit." He gave her one last longing look. "Good night, Cat."

CHAPTER 24

Catalina felt terribly guilty. Perhaps she should not have tormented Drew so. But it was just as much torment for her.

Before, when she'd thought of losing her maidenhood to him, it had seemed like a thing to check off her list of accomplishments.

But now she was gambling with her heart. She had fallen in love with Drew. And until she was sure he could be trusted to keep his promise to stay with her, she didn't dare raise the stakes.

She fell asleep—miserable, lonely, and unrequited— realizing she was in a prison of her own making and not knowing what to do about it.

It was still dark when she abruptly awakened out of a deep sleep.

She threw back the covers and sat up. The moonlight was streaming in through the window, making a pale rectangle on the bed. Outside, crickets whirred softly in the summery night. The air was still.

But something was wrong. She didn't know what it was or how she knew. But she definitely felt that something was wrong.

She climbed out of bed, slipped on her wrapper, and quietly opened her door.

Voices were coming from Drew's room.

One was Drew's.

The other belonged to a woman.

Catalina's heart wrenched, even though she knew she was jumping to hasty conclusions. It might be Miss Hattie. It might be Anne or Emily. There was no reason to believe she wasn't hearing an innocent conversation between Drew and one of the ladies of The Parlor...even if it was behind his closed door.

She couldn't make out the words. But as she strained to hear, she realized it wasn't Miss Hattie or Anne or Emily. She didn't recognize the woman's voice.

Against her will, her eyes filled slowly with tears of hurt. Her throat began to ache with a trapped sob.

It would be naïve to deny that Drew had betrayed her.

He hadn't been able to wait until they were married.

He'd taken another woman to his bed, right under Catalina's nose.

She told herself this was why she'd made him wait. This was why she hadn't made the sex with him. He might make promises with his words. But they were promises his body could not keep.

Still, knowing she'd been right didn't stop the heartrending pain of his infidelity.

It wasn't fair.

Catalina had slept with Drew. She'd kissed him. She'd shared secrets with him. They had been intimate. She'd given him her attention, her time, her heart.

He owed her his loyalty.

As Catalina continued to listen to the voices, chatting casually back and forth while she stood in her doorway in misery, her sorrow evolved rapidly into anger.

It *wasn't* fair.

Drew had been so possessive of her—burning with jealousy at the thought that another man might have her. Did he truly expect her to feel any differently? Did he believe she would willingly share him with another woman?

It was more than heartbreaking. It was infuriating.

She drew her brows together, glancing at her nightstand. Drew had left his forty-five there. For one melodramatic moment, she imagined exacting revenge. She could use the pistol on the man-stealing *puttana* in Drew's room...and then perhaps on Drew.

Of course, she'd never do such a thing—not really. She might be furious, but she wasn't a killer. She'd never even used a gun, except for the accidental shot she'd fired into the floor of the salon.

Nonetheless, she couldn't just retreat to her room to lick her wounds like a kicked hound. She had to do *something.* She quietly closed her door, shimmied back into her red dress, and swept her hair into a hasty knot.

In the moonlight, the revolver on the nightstand gleamed up at her. Even if she didn't mean to use it, it wouldn't hurt to have the weapon in her hand. It made her feel more powerful.

The gun seemed cold against her palm, but no colder than her heart.

Taking a shaky breath, she opened the door and stole onto the dimly lit balcony. Then, gripping the pistol in both hands, she approached Drew's room.

She pressed her ear to the door. There was no sound.

For a crazy moment, she wondered if she'd dreamed the whole thing, *hoped* she'd dreamed the whole thing.

She carefully turned the doorknob and pushed the

door open. By the moonlight, she could see that Drew wasn't sleeping with another woman. He wasn't even in his room.

She furrowed her brows. Where had he gone?

The floor beside the bed, where he would have left his boots for the night, was empty. But when she rested her palm atop the rumpled sheets, they were still warm.

Then she heard a noise in the hallway.

Holding the gun in front of her, she crept toward the door. When she got to the doorway, she saw a shadow fall across the balcony.

She lunged out.

Someone gasped.

Startled, Catalina almost pulled the trigger.

It was Miss Hattie.

Catalina managed to steady her hands, but she didn't lower the gun.

"Where is he?" she demanded, sure Miss Hattie must know.

"Who?" Miss Hattie choked out.

"You know who."

"Put the gun away, and I'll tell you."

"Tell me, and I will not shoot you."

Miss Hattie's brows shot up. But she complied, with the warning, "You ain't gonna like it."

Catalina gulped. But she had to know the truth, no matter how painful. "Tell me."

"A young blonde lady came for him. I think she was the daughter o' one o' the ranchers here. She said it was a...a family matter."

"Family? What family?"

Miss Hattie grimaced. "I got a notion she might have been in the family way."

"What does this mean—in the family way?"

"Expectin' a baby."

"A baby? But what does that have to do with..."

A horrible thought came into Catalina's head, and she knew at once what Miss Hattie was trying to tell her.

"No!" she cried, full of disbelief and hurt and anger all at once.

Miss Hattie was shaking her head. "Never trust a gambler. I should have known better. And I should have warned you."

"It cannot be true," Catalina insisted. "He said he was going to marry me. He gave me a ring."

But even as she said the words, they sounded hollow and meaningless.

"I'm so sorry, Catalina."

Miss Hattie's pity made Catalina's heart ache. But she wouldn't cry. She wouldn't give Drew the satisfaction. "Where did they go?"

"It might be best to just let the bastard go," Miss Hattie advised. "A man like that ain't worth cryin' over. He certainly ain't worth wastin' a bullet."

"Where did they go?" she repeated.

The madam bit the corner of her lip and eyed the gun uncertainly. "Now you don't want to be doin' anything foolish."

Catalina's eyes flattened. "Tell me."

"You don't want to be shootin' him, Catalina," she warned. "They'll hang you. It don't matter how bad a man he is."

Catalina was growing impatient. "And will they hang me if I shoot *you?*" She arched her brow at the madam.

Miss Hattie swallowed, glanced again at the gun, and reconsidered. "They said somethin' about the jail."

"The jail?" Catalina scowled. Why would they be going to the jail? "You are certain?"

"That's what she said. She meant to take him to the jail."

Then the jail was where Catalina would go.

She swept past the madam and headed down the stairs.

Standing half-naked outside the jail in the middle of the night, Drew decided this was the most reckless thing he'd ever done. And for Drew, that was saying a lot.

His twin, Chase, had definitely gotten himself into a heap of trouble. He'd been arrested by Sheriff Campbell and wound up in the town jail. And now it was up to Drew to spring him, no matter what ridiculous lengths he was going to have to go to to do it.

He just wished he hadn't been so careless, leaving his gun in Cat's room. He was fine running around the woods in nothing but his drawers. It wasn't so different from the way he'd dressed as a youth in Hupa. But he felt naked without his forty-five.

From what Drew had been able to decipher of what he'd heard so far, a lot had happened in the past few days. While Drew was preoccupied with the beautiful Catalina, Chase had gone to exact revenge on Samuel Parker, the Paradise rancher who'd enslaved their grandmother.

When Chase had left The Parlor that night, Drew assumed his brother was too liquored up to even find the ranch. But not only had he found it. He'd managed to break into the ranch house, kidnap the rancher's daughter, and ride off with her to parts unknown.

That was the "little girl" Samuel Parker and his obnoxious accomplice had been looking for when they'd burst into Drew's room that first morning.

Only it had turned out she wasn't so little.

Claire Parker was definitely full-grown. His brother must have appreciated that fact too. In just a few short days, he'd managed to fall in love with his pretty little captive.

The crazy thing was she loved Chase back, even though he'd abducted her and dragged her all over kingdom come.

But the girl's father had finally hunted her down and intended to bring Chase to justice for kidnapping...and probably worse. Hell, if Sheriff Campbell had been the one to haul him in, he'd probably mistake Chase for Drew and add cheating at cards to his list of crimes.

The sweet little blonde had sneaked away in the middle of the night. She'd come looking for Drew, calling herself "Chase's woman" and begging for his help in springing Chase out of jail.

How could he turn her down, especially when she looked as helpless as a lamb and when her big green eyes started filling with tears?

He was just glad Catalina wasn't awake when he left with the woman. He'd have a devil of a time explaining who she was and what he was about to do.

As it turned out, Claire Parker wasn't quite as sweet and innocent as she appeared. Chase must have told her his twin brother was a dead-eye gunslinger. She fully expected Drew to behave like a dime novel hero and rescue Chase by shooting his way out of jail.

But though Drew was good with a gun, he didn't like wasting ammunition. Besides, he didn't want to disappoint the lady, but his brother Chase was the one in the white hat. Drew was nobody's hero.

CHAPTER 25

As Catalina swept down the dark, deserted streets of Paradise toward the jail, she bit her lip, holding back the tears that wanted to spill over her lashes.

Could it be true? Could Drew have a wife? Was she carrying his child?

It was too painful to think about.

She couldn't be angry with the lady. After all, she could have been an innocent like Catalina. Drew Hawk could have used his charm on her. He may have seduced her into sleeping with him, never imagining there would be a baby.

On the other hand, she might be his legal wife. Perhaps Drew had overlooked that tiny detail in his quest to bed Catalina.

Either way, she knew she couldn't shoot the woman. None of this was her fault. Drew, however...

She furrowed her brow. She couldn't shoot him either, no matter what she tried to tell herself. But at least she could take control of the situation. The pistol would give Catalina courage when she felt like she was about to fall apart.

The last thing Catalina expected to find when she reached the jail and let herself in through the unguarded door was a lady handcuffed to the bars of the jail cell.

It had to be the woman who had taken Drew.

Catalina's heart sank as she saw how lovely and delicate she was, like a fair-haired, sweet-faced cherub in a painting. She had sun-kissed skin, eyes as green as emeralds, and short hair like a sunlit wheat field.

How could Drew *not* be attracted to her? She was as beautiful as a summer day.

In fact, the only flaw Catalina could see was that she was dressed in an ugly brown gown that did nothing for her features or her figure. But then, what would Drew care? He'd probably have her out of her clothes in the blink of an eye.

Despite the pain wrenching at her heart, Catalina swung the forty-five around. "Where is he? I know he came here."

The woman pretended she didn't know who Catalina meant.

"Are you his wife?" Catalina asked, choking on the words, dreading the answer.

"Whose wife? And will you please put down that—"

"Drew's."

"Drew's? No!"

She might not be his wife. But she might be promised to him. "His, what-you-call-it, financier?"

"Fiancée? No. Who are you?"

So the woman wasn't his wife and wasn't his fiancée. She should be relieved. But she was more confused than anything. Who was the woman then? "But you came to the jail with Drew, yes?"

"Yes, but—"

Catalina brandished the pistol. "What have you done with him?"

"Nothing. I haven't... Will you please put down that gun?"

She lifted her cuffed hand. "I can't do you any harm. Who are you anyway?"

Since the woman obviously had no hold on Drew, Catalina would tell her in no uncertain terms. She lowered the pistol. "I am Drew Hawk's lady."

The woman gave her a look full of doubt, a look that incensed Catalina. How dare this ragged woman in an atrocious, drab dress that wasn't even buttoned properly question her word?

"What's your name?" the woman asked.

She drew herself up proudly and lied. "Catalina Isabella Anna Maria Borghese d'Agostino."

The woman looked suitably impressed.

Then Catalina's gaze fell to the floor.

"*Santo cielo!* Those are Drew's clothings! What are you doing with them?" She pointed the gun at the blonde again. "What have you done with him, you...bad lady?"

"Nothing! And stop calling me names."

Catalina would do more than call her names. "If you've done anything to him..."

"Absolutely not."

"Then why do you have his clothings?" And if his shirt and trousers were here, what was he wearing?

The woman blushed. "He...forgot them."

"You are a liar."

"Don't call me—"

"Drew would not forget his clothings."

"He was in a hurry."

"A hurry?"

"He was running away."

Catalina's breath caught, and she felt a twinge in her heart. "Running away? What means this—running away?" She was afraid she knew exactly what it meant. The truth settled like a weight on her chest.

But after a moment, the woman answered carefully. "He wasn't running away from *you*." To Catalina's surprise, there was a glimmer of compassion in the woman's eyes. She didn't want to dissolve into tears of relief in front of the woman. So she muttered with false bravado, "Of course not. He would be a fool to do so."

Then, grateful for the woman's reassurance, she lowered the gun and glanced at the handcuff on her wrist. "Who did that to you? Not Drew?"

"No."

"You cannot get free?"

"No, I can't. But maybe you can help me. Maybe we can help each other."

"Why should I help you?" Catalina asked. "You took Drew away from me."

"I did not...that is...it was his idea to... All right, I did talk him into coming. But I didn't think there would be trouble. I only wanted him to help Chase."

"Chase. His brother?"

"Yes. I'm Chase's woman. My name is Claire. Claire Parker."

"Claire Parker." Where had she heard that name before? All at once, she remembered. Claire was the name of the kidnapped daughter the men had been looking for when they burst into Drew's room that morning. It made sense now. They must have mistaken Drew for his twin brother, Chase. "The rancher's...*little girl?*"

"Yes."

Catalina arched a brow. Claire Parker was definitely *not* a little girl. But then she supposed all fathers thought their daughters were little girls. Hers certainly did.

If, as Claire Parker claimed, she was "Chase's woman," then Catalina decided she was probably no threat. In fact, she might prove helpful.

"Do you think you can get me out of these?" Claire asked, holding up the handcuffs.

As a girl, Catalina had learned how to pick a lock with a sewing needle. She'd done it all the time to get back her dolls when her brothers locked them up in their trunks. In a pinch, a hairpin would work. She set down the gun, pulled the pin out of her hair, and set to work on the shackles.

Meanwhile, Claire told her the story of what had happened after Chase had stolen her from her home. They had had a few rough days of wandering in the wilderness. But it seemed the woman had fallen hopelessly in love with her captor.

Catalina couldn't say she was surprised. If Chase was anything like Drew, his charm was probably impossible to resist.

Unfortunately, Claire's father had finally managed to track the couple down. He'd had Chase arrested and intended to put him on trial for kidnapping.

Claire had come to The Parlor to ask for Drew's help in freeing his twin brother, with whom she intended to run away.

The romantic story served to restore Catalina's faith in Drew. He hadn't been untrue to her after all. He didn't intend to abandon her. He was a good man. He'd only gone to help his brother. Everything was going to be all right.

Then her glance fell on Drew's gun.

She bit her lip.

Drew was unarmed.

Chase probably didn't have a weapon either.

That meant it would be up to the two ladies to work together to save them. She hoped Claire was up to the challenge.

After many attempts and much cursing, Catalina managed to pick the lock and free Claire. Then Chase's woman and

Drew's lady stole off into the night, two fierce allies determined to find and rescue their half-breed heroes.

Drew hadn't played the two-spirit game since he and Chase were boys. He hoped he wasn't too rusty.

Since neither of the brothers had weapons—Chase didn't care for guns and Drew had left his in Catalina's room—they would have to rely on their wits.

Fortunately, Drew's wits were as sharp as those of *Xontehl-taw,* Trickster Coyote. He'd already lured the jailer away so Claire Parker could let Chase out of the cell. The look on the jailer's face when he saw the man he believed was his prisoner suddenly outside the jail was almost comical. It would have been funnier if the man hadn't been waving around a loaded Remington as he pursued Drew.

He'd given Claire specific instructions. Still, he wasn't convinced Chase's little Calamity Jane of a sweetheart would follow them. If things went as planned, once Chase was free, he was to strip down to his drawers so the brothers would look exactly alike. Then he'd head south and meet up with Drew in the woods for the two-spirit game.

The game was a ruse Drew and Chase had invented to pull on visiting tribes when they lived in Hupa.

In some tribal communities, twins were considered a terrible curse. When twins were born, often one or both infants would be killed, sometimes along with their mother. This was so for the Konkow, his father's people, which was why their parents had fled to Hupa shortly after Drew and Chase were born.

Instead of fighting against the superstitious nature of the tribes, whenever there was a gathering, Chase and Drew would simply pretend to be one person. It became a source of great amusement for Drew to be able to magically appear in two places almost simultaneously. Chase wasn't quite as fond of the game, mostly because he was usually the one forced to hide while Drew explained to the wide-eyed girls of the visiting tribes that he was endowed with two spirits.

They hadn't used the ruse in years. Never had they attempted to carry it off while being pursued by a gunman. Worse, the jailer seemed a little trigger-happy. So Drew figured the best strategy was to draw the man's fire and empty his revolver before Chase got there.

His tactic of rustling bushes and throwing rocks to spook the jailer into shooting was working well until after the fourth shot, when Drew heard his brother arrive.

To distract the jailer, Drew immediately let out an eerie moan and streaked across the clearing.

An instant later, Chase echoed the sound from the opposite side.

To the panicked jailer, spinning back and forth, it likely appeared that his prey was either possessed of incredible speed...or he was a ghost.

Concealed behind a manzanita, Drew suddenly felt a sharp punch to his gut, followed at once by the close crack of gunfire.

Xongquot! Had Chase thrown a rock at him? That only worked when you threw them *away* from where you wanted someone to shoot. He grimaced from the impact, limping through the brush. Damn, his blacksmith brother sure had an arm on him. That was going to leave a mark.

Soon after, the jailer fired his last bullet.

While the man reloaded, Drew crossed the south side of the clearing with a moan that was only half simulated. The place beneath his ribs where Chase had hit him with the rock hurt like the devil, making it hard to walk upright.

Chase moaned in answer from the north side, startling the jailer.

Drew rattled the bushes, peering over them, then ducking down.

Chase imitated his moves.

Then they got close enough to the jailer to brush past him and lunge toward him in quick succession, finally frightening the poor man so much that he dropped his gun and, with a shriek, ran back in the direction of the jail.

It was then Drew started to feel the burning. When he lifted his fingers to the place he'd been struck, they came back bloody.

Ling-miwhxiy. Son of a bitch.

His brother hadn't hit him with a rock.

He'd been shot.

He tensed his jaw. Damn it all. What could he do now?

He didn't want Chase to worry about him. Chase was a wanted man. He needed to get out of Paradise.

So when Chase came up with a companionable chuckle, Drew kept to the shadows and forced a weak smile to his lips. "Remember the last time we played that?"

Chase grinned. "It was for those two young Yurok girls who were visiting."

Drew's stomach felt like a burning arrow was lodged in it. "Sure scared them," he said tightly.

"Scared them enough to earn us a whipping from their father."

Drew broke out in a cold sweat. He didn't know how much longer he could stay on his feet. "He should have been grateful," he joked, fighting to keep his voice steady. "One of those girls was tryin' to get me to share her blanket."

Chase laughed.

Drew staggered back a step and waved down the trail. "Go on now. Git. I don't think the jailer's gonna make trouble. Go grab your girl and skedaddle."

Chase smiled. "What do you think of her?"

"Who?" He wiped his brow with the back of one shaky forearm. "Calamity?"

Drew should have known he couldn't fool his twin for long.

Chase narrowed his eyes. "Are you all right?"

Drew smirked. "Sure. Right as rain." He faltered forward. "I just..."

Then the world went black.

CHAPTER 26

At the sound of gunfire, Catalina's heart jabbed against her ribs with bruising force. And though desperation made her determined to protect Drew with the forty-five if need be, she was relieved when Claire took the gun from her. After all, Claire was a Californian. She was probably as handy with a gun as Catalina was with a sewing machine.

After the sixth gunshot, there was silence. Then, suddenly, someone was running toward them through the brush. Catalina pulled Claire out of the way just in time.

"Spooks!" the jailer cried as he thrashed past them. "There's spooks in the woods!" And then he vanished into the trees.

Once he was gone, a sudden, certain misgiving filled Catalina.

Something was wrong with Drew. He was in trouble.

She hurtled down the path, hampered by her voluminous skirts, trailed by Claire.

When they finally broke into the clearing and saw Drew lying on the ground, still and silent, her worst fears were realized. Kneeling beside him with guilt written all over his face was a man who looked almost exactly like Drew—almost, but not quite.

"You!" she demanded, rushing up to him. "What did you do? What did you do to my Drew?"

When he didn't answer right away, she responded with all the pent-up rage and grief of a woman in love. She punched Chase in the nose, sending him sprawling.

Then she heard a click. She'd forgotten about Claire and the forty-five.

"Get away from him!" Claire cried.

But Catalina was too concerned for Drew to pay heed to the blonde lady's warnings. She dropped to her knees at Drew's side.

He was bleeding.

He'd been shot in the chest.

She wailed, holding Drew's hand to her breast. "Do not leave me, *mio caro*. Do not leave me. You promised, Drew."

He roused with a faint murmur. "Cat?"

"You promised. Remember?" she said, her throat aching with tears. "You promised to buy me tonight."

"Sure." He tried to sit up, but fresh blood seeped from his wound.

"Don't try to move," Drew's twin told him, groaning from the blow Catalina had given him. He struggled back onto his feet and then waggled demanding fingers at Catalina. "Your petticoats, quick. Give me your petticoats."

"What!" Catalina wouldn't hesitate to punch him again for his rudeness. She suspected now that Chase was nothing like his brother.

"To stop the bleeding," he explained.

Finally understanding, she nodded and began ripping up her petticoats.

Together, the three of them managed to stanch the flow of blood and bind the wound.

When they stole back to Paradise through the moonlit forest, it was in solemn silence.

Drew's brother carried him up to his room at The Parlor. Claire stayed close by her man, obviously ill-at-ease in the bawdy house. And Catalina hovered over her beloved Drew while the madam quietly summoned the doctor.

It took three slugs of whiskey, a belt between Drew's teeth, and his blacksmith brother to hold him down. Catalina had to bite back sobs of despair through the whole ordeal. But the doctor finally managed to dig out the bullet. Fortunately, it hadn't done too much damage.

After a secure bandaging and a dose of laudanum, Drew drifted off to sleep. Then Catalina began shaking and couldn't stop. Now that he was safe, the terror of what had happened hit her all at once. What if the bullet had hit him an inch to the left? What if she and Claire hadn't managed to stop the bleeding? What if she'd never left her room to find Drew? What if she'd slept through it all?

She gave Chase and Claire her room while she stayed with Drew in his. She didn't sleep much. She was too worried about her husband-to-be, whose golden skin had turned to a deathly ashen shade.

When she finally managed to close her eyes, it was near dawn. But no sooner had her head hit the pillow when her slumber was interrupted by the sound of the door bursting open. When she woke, she was staring down the barrel of a rifle.

Too exhausted to feel fear, she charged from the bed to confront the intruder and defend Drew.

But when the distinguished, white-haired man with the rifle saw Catalina, he apologized. He'd apparently come to the wrong room.

"Who is it, Cat?" Drew mumbled from the bed.

Before she could answer, the man scowled at Drew and

spoke to him in a nasty snarl. "Well, I see you're showing your true colors, Mr. Wolf."

Catalina frowned. Mr. Wolf? The man had mistaken Drew for his twin brother.

"I can't say I'm surprised," he continued. "But I *am* disappointed. You could have at least waited till you left town to take up with..." Instead of speaking the slur, he gave Catalina a look of contempt.

Instantly furious, she bit out, "How dare you! Can you not see he's hurt?"

"Cat," Drew called weakly, "who are you talkin' to?"

Her heart melted at the vulnerability in Drew's voice. She hurried to his side. "Don't worry, *caro mio.* I will make him go away."

Before she could consider how she was going to do that, the door swung open, and in walked Claire with breakfast. She froze when she saw the intruder.

"Father!"

"Claire?"

Catalina wasn't sure how Claire was going to explain things to her father. But while she made several attempts, Catalina studied the old gentleman.

So this was the rancher who Drew claimed had enslaved his grandmother. Samuel Parker was clearly upset, but he didn't seem like a cruel man. And he seemed very out of sorts to be found in such an establishment.

Halfway through the discussion, Catalina realized Claire was letting her father believe that Drew was Chase. Samuel Parker probably didn't even know Chase had a twin brother.

Catalina wasn't sure this was the best course of action. What if Samuel Parker decided to put Drew in jail, thinking he was Chase?

When Claire tried to convince her father that the man in the bed was Chase, running her fingers through Drew's hair and kissing his brow, Catalina made fists of her hands and choked back an outraged outburst of jealousy.

But when the rancher casually asked if the half-breed was going to live, Catalina could bear no more of the pretense, asking how he could ask such a thing. She rushed to the bed to take Drew's hand in reassurance. *"Va tutto bene."*

"Father, this is Chase's...sister," Claire said, "from Hupa."

Catalina didn't protest too much at that introduction. After all, it was partially true. She was going to be Chase's sister-in-law soon.

What surprised Catalina was that Claire agreed to leave The Parlor and return home with her father, on the condition that he wouldn't tell the sheriff where Chase was.

Catalina was impressed by her cleverness. If Claire loved Chase as much as Catalina loved Drew, it was an enormous sacrifice to leave him, she knew. So when Claire murmured, "Please take care of...Chase...for me," Catalina nodded in understanding.

It was almost an hour after Claire and her father left that the real Chase came staggering into the room, wrapped in a sheet.

He wanted to know where Claire was. He wasn't happy when Catalina told him she'd returned to her ranch. But he had to agree it was a good plan, at least for the time being.

Catalina could tell Chase truly cared about the woman he'd kidnapped. He was an intensely serious man, as one might expect in a person seeking vengeance. She sensed he was just as intensely serious about his feelings for Claire. She didn't think he was dangerous, however, just determined, a bit overbearing, and somewhat lacking in charm.

In other words, he was nothing like his twin.

Catalina dipped her lace handkerchief in the basin of water again and dabbed tenderly at Drew's brow.

"How is he?" Chase asked.

She wished she could tell. The doctor hadn't been in yet this morning, and Drew had barely been conscious. She was naturally worried about him.

Still, she supposed there was no shortage of devoted caretakers at The Parlor. Here, Drew was a hero. For Miss Hattie, he'd brought in business. For Jenny, he'd given her a new life. He'd come to the rescue of the rest of the ladies against a gunman. And for Catalina...

"Listen, ma'am," Chase murmured, obviously ill-at-ease. "I don't know what my brother told you, but he's not the marrying kind of man. I'm sure he paid you well for your services and probably enjoyed them too. But if you're looking for him to put a ring on your finger, I don't think that's going to happen. I'm sorry to have to break it to you this way, but..."

Catalina thought nothing could make her laugh this morning. But Chase's assumption that Catalina was a prostitute and his delusions about his own brother were highly amusing.

With a smug smile, she flashed her engagement ring at him.

He didn't believe her.

Even after she finally managed to convince him the ring had indeed come from Drew, he shook his head.

"My brother is a love-them-and-leave them kind of man."

Catalina frowned. He apparently couldn't imagine that Drew was capable of change.

Thinking she didn't understand his English, he tried, "A rolling stone? A tumbleweed? One that doesn't put down roots?"

Roots? She hadn't heard that one before.

Chase sighed. "My brother is the kind of man who will give a woman a kiss and then vanish into the night."

"Oh, that he does," she agreed with a nod. "But he always comes back in the morning."

The week-long ride from Hupa to Round Valley had only sharpened the edge of Sheriff Jasper Brown's ire. He'd been so sure he'd be able to track down the half-breed who'd killed Billy before he made it this far.

But there was no sign of the villain. The man had paid for no lodging, stolen no horses. He hadn't even stopped at any of the saloons along the way.

He supposed any other man would have given up. His own damn sons had started whining about turning tail and going home.

But Jasper wasn't about to wave the white flag. The South had made that mistake. To his mind, Lee's men should have fought until every damn soldier lay on the battlefield, dead.

Because the South had knuckled under, Jasper was forced to live in the world they'd left, a world full of damn Yankees, freed slaves, and uppity Injuns.

Today, however, proved to be his lucky day. To his surprise, he got a piece of useful information from Round Valley.

A scowling Konkow named Hintsuli came forward, identifying himself as the brother of Sakote, the Injun with the white wife Jasper had met in Hupa. He claimed his people had been marched from their homes and that their father, a great chief, had starved himself to death on the way. He went on to say their mother had been left behind, enslaved by a rancher in Paradise, and that she had died only last month.

Jasper didn't give a shit about the Injun's parents. Hell, his own parents weren't around anymore. He *was* interested, however, in the place Hintsuli called home. Maybe Hintsuli's half-breed nephew had sought refuge there, in the place he was born.

It was a long shot and another week-long ride. But at least, he thought with a grim chuckle, he didn't have to march on foot along the route like the Injuns had. He had a horse, food, water, and a silver star.

Chapter 27

For Drew, two days passed as a blurry memory.

He remembered playing the two-spirit game in the dark, getting shot, blacking out. He drifted in and out of consciousness, only to wake to the agony of a doctor rooting around under his ribs, in an exhaustive search for the bullet lodged there.

After that, the doctor gave him something bitter to drink, and he fell into a deep sleep.

It felt almost like the journeys he'd taken in the *takiwh,* sweat lodge, as a youth in Hupa. He went to the spirit world, communicated with animals, understood the world's mysteries, spoke in strange tongues.

Most of it was otherworldly, a figment of his drugged brain. But some of it was real, he was sure.

He remembered his brother bending close, speaking in their native tongue and in tones of concern.

He remembered Miss Hattie tucking covers around him.

He remembered a distant conversation between a blonde angel and her white-haired, rifle-toting father.

He remembered the murmurs of pity and the sweet perfume of ladies who visited him.

And always he remembered Cat hovering near. He caught glimpses of her red-rimmed eyes, the tangled black ribbons of her hair, her rumpled scarlet dress. She stayed by his side, easing his fever, giving him sips of water and spoonfuls of soup, speaking soft and soothing Italian words into his ear like a medicine woman's incantation.

Suddenly one morning, he opened his eyes, clear-headed, feeling strong, and hungry as a horse. His wound still throbbed, but he could tell it was healing. Soon he'd be able to leave The Parlor.

Somehow, he'd find a way to sneak Chase and his ladylove safely out of town. Then he'd have to figure out what to do about Catalina.

He obviously couldn't stay in Paradise. It wasn't safe for him here. With Chase gone, sooner or later, someone would claim that Drew was Claire Parker's abductor, and he'd have no way of proving he wasn't. The only ones who even knew the twins existed were the shady ladies of The Parlor. And their word was probably worth about as much as a half-breed's.

So until he figured out what to do, Drew guessed his best move was to bluff.

It wasn't so bad pretending he was still too weak to move. The bed was comfortable, and the food was decent. Beautiful women came to his room, cooing over him and catering to his every need. Cat kept him company, feeding him, mopping his brow, doting on him as if he were a helpless child. He could hardly complain.

But he knew for Chase, being confined to The Parlor was torture.

His brother missed his little Calamity Jane something fierce. Samuel Parker's ranch might be just down the road a piece, but it probably felt like it was a world away.

According to Chase, Claire had a fiancé who was bound and determined to regain her affections. And despite Claire's devotion, the knowledge that someone else was out there, vying for the woman he loved, had to be gnawing at Chase and setting him off-kilter.

His normally levelheaded brother was growing short-tempered. Helpless and frustrated, Chase snapped and snarled at everyone, reminding Drew of the *mindich*, bobcat, they'd found in that snare long ago. He lashed out at even those unfortunates who tried to give him a hand.

But when he started grousing at Catalina, Drew realized it was time to goad his brother out of The Parlor and off to the Parker Ranch.

It was a risk. Chase was now a wanted man. If anyone spotted him, he'd be reported to the sheriff and put back in jail.

But under cover of the night, Chase could be as stealthy as a *minim-millediliw*, mountain lion. So if he could convince his brother that Claire was worth fighting for, maybe he'd find the happiness Drew had found with Cat.

It wasn't difficult. Drew tossed out a few good-natured taunts and snuggled up with his own beautiful bride-to-be to remind Chase of what he was missing. Cat convinced him it would be romantic for Chase to kidnap his bride again in the middle of the night. By nightfall, Chase still wasn't sure what he intended or whether he was doing the right thing, but he was on his way to the ranch and his sweetheart.

Lady Luck must have gone with him. As it turned out, Chase arrived just in the nick of time.

Sometime after midnight, Miss Hattie started knocking on doors, waking everyone in The Parlor. She said she had something to tell them, and it couldn't wait till morning.

When all the ladies had gathered in Drew's room, she told them there had been a fire at the Parker Ranch.

Drew's heart dropped. "My brother..."

"Chase?" Cat reached for Drew's hand.

"He's fine," Miss Hattie assured them. "A bit smoky, but fine." She clucked her tongue. "He's actually a hero."

The ladies softly gasped. But that didn't surprise Drew. Chase had a good heart and a strong back.

"What happened?" he asked.

"What about his lady?" Cat breathed. "What about Claire?"

For an instant, an almost imperceptible shudder went through Miss Hattie. Then she pursed her lips and said, "She's sufferin', but she's gonna be fine."

The other ladies murmured in worry.

Miss Hattie held up a hand for silence. "Claire almost..." She stopped, choking on the words. "She got caught in the fire. Thank heavens, Chase managed to pull her out in time."

There was a collective sigh of relief.

But Drew wasn't going to be satisfied until he heard the whole story. Forgetting he was supposed to be incapacitated, he pushed himself up until he was sitting upright in the bed.

"How did the fire start?" he demanded. "Who was there?"

While everyone listened intently, Miss Hattie related what she knew, which was sketchy.

It appeared that Claire's ex-fiancé had something to do with it. Once he found out that Claire had her heart set on another man—Chase Wolf—he decided if he couldn't have Claire, no one could. He'd settle for inheriting the ranch without her help.

"It looks like the son of a bitch might have set the barn on fire," Miss Hattie ground out, "with Claire in it."

Gasps sucked all the air out of the room.

Miss Hattie shook her head. "It was pure good luck your brother showed up in time to save her."

Drew exchanged a meaningful glance with Claire. If they hadn't convinced Chase to go to the Parker Ranch when they did, Claire might be dead now.

"What happened to her fiancé?" Cat asked. The fire of revenge burned hot in her eyes. Drew reminded himself never to get on Cat's bad side.

"The sheriff arrested Frank," Miss Hattie told them. "He'll be tried tomorrow, prob'ly hanged soon after."

Catalina hoped so. When she thought of sweet Claire, trapped in a burning barn, it made her feel sick.

"Where are they now?" Drew wanted to know. "Chase and Claire?"

"Recoverin' at the ranch," Miss Hattie said. "Thank goodness it was only the barn and not the main house."

"I have to see him," he said, throwing off his covers. "I have to see my brother."

Catalina knew he wouldn't believe Chase was safe until he saw him with his own eyes. But that was impossible.

"You can't," she said, throwing the covers back on again. "You're hurt."

He threw them off once more. "Not so hurt I can't see my own brother."

Miss Hattie shook her head. "Even if you could, it ain't safe. Nobody except Claire and The Parlor know there are two of you. If you're spotted, it won't be long before everyone in Paradise knows you're twins. You'll put yourself and your brother in danger of arrest all over again."

"We won't be spotted."

Miss Hattie clucked her tongue. "One six-foot half-breed is hard enough to hide, but two?"

Drew's shoulders slumped. He knew she was right.

Claire made up her mind. "I'll go," she offered.

"I can't let you do that," Drew said. "He's *my* brother."

"And he will soon be mine," she argued. "I'm glad to go."

"But it's the middle o' the night, Cat. You can't go alone."

"I'll go with her," Miss Hattie offered.

Drew looked at them both, rubbing the back of his neck, and then nodded. "All right. Fine. Tell him...tell him our grandmother's spirit will help Claire." He pulled the covers back up. "And you ladies be careful out there."

Claire would be very careful. She wasn't terribly afraid of the wild animals. But she'd seen enough of the wild California men to know they were a dangerous breed.

She was no fool. After quickly dressing in her cocoa-and-cream dress and jacket, she returned to Drew's room. As she gave him a tender kiss on the brow, she reached for the nightstand and slipped his pistol into her purse.

Nothing could prepare Catalina for the grim sight of the Parker barn. Like the cast-off gown of some daughter of Satan, the structure slumped haphazardly in shades of burnt black and scorched gray, trimmed in shimmering coals of devilish red.

Men still doused the timbers with buckets of water to knock down the embers. Every splash sent up a hiss, like the sound of an iron on wet cloth.

Catalina held her sleeve across her face, wincing at the stench of smoke that permeated the air.

When they approached the ranch house, Miss Hattie hung back. She didn't want the presence of the town madam to stain the upstanding Parker name.

Though this saddened Catalina, she understood. She'd felt the same way when she'd started working at The Parlor. She couldn't have her reputation tarnished by her association with such an establishment. Yet how quickly her opinion had changed once she got to know the women there. Miss Hattie might be the proprietress of a *bordello,* but her heart was in the right place.

Though Claire's weary-eyed father, Samuel Parker, willingly let Catalina in to Claire's bedroom, she felt like an intruder on the intimate scene.

A candle flickered beside the bed. Chase sat beside Claire, cradling her hand. His black hair was full of ash, his eyes were bleary, and there were smudges of soot on his skin and clothing.

"How is she?" Catalina ventured.

Chase's lips tightened. It was clear he didn't want to get his hopes up. But he was also determined to do everything in his power to save the woman he loved. "She'll live." It sounded more like a vow than a prediction.

Though he didn't invite Catalina closer, she drew near, gazing down at Claire. The frail blonde woman looked even more like a child. It was clear Chase had painstakingly washed her face, but charcoal dust still clung to her hair and powdered the pillow.

Moved to pity, Catalina reached out and gently took Claire's other hand. It felt small and limp, like one of the baby bunnies her brothers had killed.

"Is there anything I can do?" she murmured.

"Not much."

She nodded. "Oh," she remembered, "Drew asked me to tell you that your grandmother's spirit will help."

He gave her a half-smile. "You can tell him our grandmother's spirit has already helped."

Catalina didn't ask what he meant by that. She'd learned that, unlike Drew, Chase was a man of few words, most of them cryptic. So when he started talking again, half to her, half to himself, she was astonished.

"You know, you and Drew ought to get hitched...right away."

She waited.

"When something like this happens…" He swallowed. "It shows you what's important. I was wrong, thinking I could avenge my grandmother's death. There was nothing to avenge. All along, she was where she was supposed to be."

Catalina nodded.

He shook his head. "And Claire, trying so hard to make her father happy…she never should have taken up with that no-count Frank."

Claire's hand twitched in Catalina's hand. But when Catalina looked at her, she was fast asleep, probably dreaming. Catalina hoped she wasn't having nightmares about what had happened.

"What I'm trying to say is…" he said, scowling. "Strike while the iron is hot." Before she could decipher what Drew's blacksmith brother meant, he added, "Don't wait until it's too late, until you almost lose…" He stopped as emotion choked him.

Catalina's eyes filled with tears. She knew how he felt. She'd felt that way when Drew had been shot—as if her heart had been crushed by a great fist. That first night, she would have made a deal with the devil to get rid of the pain.

Chase loved Claire so much. Just as he'd pulled Claire from the inferno, Catalina was sure that if the worst happened, if somehow Claire was taken from him, he'd follow her into the very fires of hell and drag her back.

Love was all-powerful, she realized. And time was precious. In the blink of an eye, life could be snatched away.

Claire was probably going to live. She and Chase would wed, make a home, fill it with children.

But what if it hadn't gone that way?

She bit her lip, watching as a rogue tear dropped from Chase's cheek onto Claire's hand.

Chase was right. She had to seize the day.

Chapter 28

By the time Catalina and the madam returned to The Parlor, Miss Hattie was flushed and out of breath.

"Honestly, Cat." Miss Hattie huffed and puffed as she staggered through the front door. "I don't know why...you're in such a...an all-fired hurry."

"I must iron the clothings while they are hot," she explained. She wasn't sure that was quite how Chase had said it, but it made sense to her.

While Miss Hattie puzzled over her words, she picked up her skirts and swept past the madam, up the stairs.

Drew wasn't asleep. When she walked in, she could see worry etched into his brow.

He sat up. "How are they?"

"Good. They are good." She set her purse on the nightstand and started unbuttoning her jacket.

"What did Chase say?"

"He said your grandmother's spirit was there." She wrenched off her jacket with unaccustomed haste, dropping it on the stool.

"That's good. That's good." Drew seemed distracted as he thought things over. "Yoema was a great healer. If Chase can feel her there..."

Catalina sat on the edge of the bed and began unlacing her boots. One of the laces tangled and knotted. With a quiet curse, she wrenched the boot off her foot, breaking the lace.

"You all right?" Drew asked.

"Yes, fine." She was *very* fine. She felt finer than she'd felt in a long time. She knew she was doing the right thing.

He moved over in the bed to make room for her. "Was Claire awake? Did you get to talk to her?"

Catalina kicked off her second boot, tugged off her stockings, and then stood to untie her skirt. "No. She was asleep."

"Prob'ly tuckered out. She's had a rough couple o' weeks."

She pulled off her skirt and flung it aside. Then she started on her bustle.

Drew frowned at her rumpled clothing. "Is somethin' wrong?"

"No. Something is very right."

Normally she folded her clothes neatly, careful of each crease. But for some reason, that didn't seem important right now. She tossed her bustle over her shoulder. Then she started on her corset.

Drew was still reflecting on what had happened. "If her fiancé was responsible, I hope they do hang him—the sooner, the better. Any man who'd do that kind o' thing..."

Per amor di cielo! Catalina cursed. She'd never noticed before how many laces there were on a corset. It was ridiculous. At this rate, it would take her half the night to get undressed.

"You need some help with that?" Drew asked.

"Please."

She sat beside him, and he went to work on the laces. She

wanted to believe he was so adept at it because of his nimble card-dealing fingers. But she was afraid it was because he'd had a lot of practice with corsets. He managed to finish the task in less than a minute.

As she freed herself from the contraption, Drew looked thoughtfully down at his hands in his lap. "If anythin' like that ever happened to you, Cat, I just don't know what I'd do."

A lump wedged in her throat as she warped the corset between her hands. "That is why we must…" She paused. She didn't want to say it wrong. "In Italy we have a saying—*carpe diem*. It means 'seize the day.' It is to say we must not waste a moment." She set the corset aside. "Life is…uncertain. It is a candle that can be blown out so quickly. None of us can know how much time we have left."

Drew was staring at her. His eyes softened as his gaze traced the contours of her camisole and drawers. "What are you tryin' to say, Cat?"

She took a steadying breath as she pulled loose the bow at the top of her camisole. "I think you know."

One part of Drew's body knew for certain exactly what she meant. It began to harden and throb with longing.

"Are you sure?" he managed to croak as the straps of her camisole dipped low on her shoulders.

"Yes."

His heart leaped.

It wasn't going to be easy. He was gunshot, and his muscles weren't acting the way they should. But somehow he'd make it good for Cat.

"Let me do that," he whispered.

He beckoned her close, slipping the camisole down to reveal her breasts. Threading his fingers through her hair, he brought her mouth to his and kissed her with sweet patience.

She sighed softly against his cheek.

His hand drifted down until the backs of his knuckles grazed her nipple. At her quick intake of breath, he cupped her breast, weighing it in his palm.

He grasped the back of her head then and moved his mouth away to murmur against her ear.

"You're sure?" he asked her again.

She nodded.

He moved his hand to her other breast and lifted it. Then he lowered his head and gave her warm flesh a tender kiss.

She tipped her head back and closed her eyes, enjoying his attentions. He bathed her thoroughly, caressing and licking and suckling at her breasts until she clawed eager fingers into his shoulders.

He moved up then to nuzzle her neck. She gasped and shivered as he nibbled at the sensitive place beneath her ear. He took her lobe lightly between his teeth. When he ran his tongue around the delicate crevices of her ear, she squealed deep in her throat and squeezed at his shoulders.

His body reacted with bold fervency. He freed one hand to untie his drawers and lifted his hips enough to drag them out from under his buttocks.

When she unexpectedly seized him in her palm, he groaned. Then he chuckled. "Slow down, Cat. We got all night."

"I do not want to take all night."

He grinned. Neither did he. But that wasn't the right way to treat a lady—especially not her first time. So he gently disengaged from her.

"Why don't you lie back?" he said. "Let me look at you."

She pulled the camisole over her head and hauled off her drawers, dropping them on the floor. Then she stretched out on top of the covers, awaiting his pleasure.

For a moment, he only caressed her with his eyes. How breathtaking she was—this woman who was going to be his wife. Her skin was smooth and tawny, and her curls were soft and black. Her voluptuous breasts narrowed into a trim waist, flaring again into hips that seemed to undulate as she gazed up at him with longing.

Resting on one elbow, he let his free hand explore her. He stroked her lovely curves. He coiled his fingers in her silky locks. He brushed her blushing cheek with his thumb and then pressed a kiss to the adorable dot beside her lips.

She opened her mouth, inviting his kiss. He willingly accepted, dancing lightly across her lips at first, then delving deeply with his tongue, tasting the honey of her desire.

She seized the back of his neck and arched eagerly against him. He sucked in a quick breath as her ribs grazed his bandaged wound.

When her eyes flew open and she tried to apologize, he hushed her.

"It's all right, darlin'. I'll be careful for both of us, all right?"

He hoped he could be careful. He had a feeling that once things got going, someone could stick a white-hot poker in his wound, and he wouldn't feel it. But he needed to be careful for Catalina's sake. The last thing he wanted to do was to hurt her.

The last thing Catalina wanted to do was to hurt Drew. Perhaps it would be best if she lay quiet.

She closed her eyes and tried to be very still. It wasn't easy. It seemed each touch of his finger changed her skin somehow, the way the brush of a hand could change the color of velvet.

She drifted in a sensual haze while he caressed her with the delicacy of a sheer lawn petticoat. When his fingers slipped slyly between her thighs, she squeezed her eyes shut, shivering at the delicious invasion.

His breath was ragged against her ear when he whispered one last time, "You're certain?"

She nodded. She'd never been more sure of anything in her life. There was an aching deep within her, a craving in her body as well as her soul. She wanted to join with him, not just for physical relief, but to be intimately bound to him.

He retrieved one of the feather pillows and tucked it under her hips, coaxing her thighs apart.

For a moment, she felt too vulnerable, too exposed. Her face warmed as she experienced a moment of doubt and an overwhelming urge to slam her legs together again.

But she realized she trusted Drew. He'd asked her to be his wife. He loved her. He would do nothing to harm her.

Careful of his wound, Drew eased on top of her then, supporting his weight on one forearm as he settled his legs between hers. She felt his hard length pulsing against her.

"I don't mean to hurt you," he murmured, "but it might sting, just for a bit."

She opened her eyes to look at him. She'd heard all about it from the ladies at The Parlor. And she could see in his dark and caring eyes that he was trying to temper his own passion for the sake of her comfort. That moved her beyond words. No pain could diminish her joy at becoming one with him.

"I understand," she whispered.

He aroused her then with deft fingers until she was desperate and sobbing with need. By the time he entered her, the pinch of pain was no more than the brief poke of a sewing needle.

As he hovered over her with a soft apology, she relaxed under him. Already the sting was subsiding, and a compelling urgency was taking its place.

He moved within slowly, still guarding his injury, and she moaned at the strange fullness inside her. His leisurely, languorous motions incited her to greater heights. Soon, despite her intentions to lie quiet, she was responding to his movement, twisting and arching to match him, thrust for thrust.

His growls of passion fueled her own, sending her spiraling upward. She clenched her fists in the bedclothes and rocked her head across the pillow. It felt like she was dancing in a full and beautiful dress of shimmering silk. As they spun together, faster and faster, it was as if the folds of cloth compressed, hugging her tightly, so tightly she couldn't breathe. And then, as if he'd suddenly set her free with a great cry, she swirled away in an exuberant explosion of skirts, twirling and twirling until the music stopped and she slowed to a gentle turn.

He covered her face with breathless kisses until she was laughing with relief and amusement. Then, though she made a mew of protest, he cautiously withdrew, collapsing on his back with a pleased grin on his face.

She couldn't help but smile back.

Then he furrowed his brow in concern. "I didn't hurt you too badly?"

She shook her head, deciding, "Making the sex? I think this is even better than eating *tartufi.*"

He arched a sarcastic brow at her. "Better than chewin' on a soft brown lump that pigs dig up from under the ground? I'm flattered."

She gave him a playful shove.

They clasped hands, and as they lounged on the bed, staring up at the ceiling, Catalina thought she'd never been happier.

"I am glad we seized the day," she said.

"Me too."

"I would like to seize every day."

He chuckled. "I don't think you can afford it."

She blinked. "What?"

"The way I figure, you owe me twenty dollars for makin' the sex with you."

"What?" She swatted his shoulder. She could see by the sparkle in his eyes that he was teasing her.

"I hear that's the goin' rate," he said.

"If I had twenty dollars a day, I would definitely spend it on you, Mr. Drew Hawk."

He took a deep breath full of pride and satisfaction. "And I'd gladly do your biddin', Mrs. Catalina Hawk."

Catalina Hawk. She grinned. It was such a short name. But she liked the sound of it. She closed her eyes, repeating it over and over in her mind.

It was only after Drew's hand went limp in hers and he began drawing in the deep breath of sleep that Catalina realized there might be a consequence to their lovemaking.

They might have made a baby.

She bit her lip. The idea of having Drew's baby thrilled her. Yet it was too soon. She hadn't even gotten her dress design business started.

And she had wedding gowns to make—for herself and the ladies of The Parlor. After all, they couldn't possibly go to Catalina's wedding in their scanty saloon dresses.

It surprised her that she wanted them to come. But they were her friends. It didn't matter that they were fallen women. Besides, she supposed she was fallen now too.

She drifted off, wondering how she could possibly get a dozen gowns made before she started growing round with child.

CHAPTER 29

Cat must have let him sleep in. When Drew woke to the rough knock on the door, followed by his brother forcing his way in, Cat was no longer beside him in the bed, and the sun was already streaming in through the curtains.

He supposed he should be glad. He didn't particularly want Chase running his greedy eyes all over his beautiful bride-to-be in her altogether.

Still, he was groggy and mildly irritated, until he saw his brother's grim face and remembered the fire.

"Claire?" he asked in concern.

"Better," Chase said, closing the door behind him.

"They hang the varmint that did it?"

"Yep." Chase rubbed his hand across his chin. "But I think we've got more trouble."

That got his attention. "What kind o' trouble?"

"After the hanging, Sheriff Campbell stopped by the ranch. He said he wanted to see how Claire was and to let me know I was off the hook."

"That's good."

Chase grimaced. "Not quite. He also said something about losing his girl and how he wanted the chance to win her back." He tossed up his hands at that. "Damn it, Drew! What kind of stakes are you playing for these days?"

"Aww, hell," Drew said. "He didn't wager his sweetheart. He only lost his girl 'cause she didn't like him gamblin'." He added with a sniff, "Mostly she didn't like him losin'."

Chase grunted. "Well, anyway, he thought I was you."

"So what'd you tell him?"

"Nothing. I didn't get the chance."

Drew shrugged. "I'll take care of it."

"That's just the thing," Chase told him. "It's too late. When the sheriff started jawing about poker, Mr. Parker said, 'You'll have to play his brother then, because this man isn't the gambler.'"

"Shit. How'd he find out?"

Chase looked disappointed. "Claire might have told him. Anyway, it won't be long before the whole town knows we're twins. I just thought, you know, you might want to make a quick getaway."

Drew scowled. Why should *he* have to be the one to leave Paradise? Why couldn't his brother take his bride and move out of town? It was on the tip of his tongue to say so.

But then he reconsidered.

"Wait." Drew rubbed at the crease between his brows. "The sheriff doesn't hold you responsible any more for what happened to Claire, right?"

"Right."

"And her father's grateful to you for savin' her life?"

"Yep."

"And nobody cares that you busted out o' jail?"

"Nope."

"Then what does it matter if they know we're twins?"

Chase let out a resigned sigh. "Well, I figure you must have gotten into trouble with the law for something." He straightened with noble purpose. "So since you made the sacrifice for me, I'm offering to cover for you."

Drew was simultaneously honored and annoyed. "You know, I'm not *always* gettin' into trouble."

Chase raised a brow at that.

"I've done nothin' wrong," Drew insisted.

"You're telling me you're holed up in a cathouse, gambling with lawmen, and you're not in trouble?"

Drew smirked. "That's right."

"Huh."

Whether Chase believed him or not remained to be seen. But now that he'd delivered his message, Chase figured his duty was done. With a nod of his head, he said goodbye and turned tail to get back to his ladylove.

The news was actually a relief to Drew, now that he thought about it. White folks didn't have the same superstitions as natives about twins, so he didn't have to worry about people thinking the brothers were bad luck. And if all was forgiven—hell, his kidnapping brother had turned himself into a local hero—then both of them could walk freely through town.

He thought again about the beautiful woman who had shared her body with him last night, the woman who would shortly become his wife. Now the clock was ticking. If they were going to start enjoying each other's company on a regular basis, Cat could very well get pregnant.

They had to get married sooner rather than later.

And since Cat was so set on making her own dresses for the wedding, he had to find a way to get her that sewing machine she wanted. But how?

He could raise the stakes in poker. But he'd almost bled the town dry. And he didn't dare win another cent off of the sheriff.

What did he have that was worth selling?

All of a sudden, it dawned on him. He could sell his Colt forty-five. Sure, he'd had that gun by his side for seven years, and there was nothing like a pistol to keep a poker game honest. But if Drew was going to stay put in Paradise, he wouldn't be gambling much anymore. He'd have to find himself a proper job. So he might as well sell the piece and order that sewing machine for Cat.

He glanced over at the nightstand. His gun wasn't there.

He narrowed his eyes. Then his lip curled up in a smile. Maybe in their wild coupling last night, they'd knocked it from the nightstand.

He looked down at the floor. Nothing was there.

Throwing the covers back, he climbed out and searched behind the nightstand and under the bed. He lifted up the pillows. He looked in his boots. He rummaged through the sheets.

Nothing.

What the hell had happened to his forty-five?

While he was standing nude with his hands on his hips, the door opened, and Cat peeked in.

Her jaw dropped, but then she gave him a devilish grin and closed the door behind her, leaning against it with lust in her eyes.

He couldn't help but be captivated.

He meant to ask her about his revolver, but promptly forgot.

Then, after they spent a delicious half-hour seizing the day by reliving the entertainment of the night before, Drew changed his mind about selling his weapon.

He realized that Cat considered him her gunfighting protector. Without his gun, she might think he couldn't defend her properly. The truth was it *had* come in handy a few times in the last month.

He'd find the piece eventually. He must have left it downstairs or something.

As he cradled her in his arms, smiling at the rumpled dress with its bustle twisted to one side—the dress she was in too big a hurry to remove, he decided he'd just have to earn his money the way he always had—at the poker table.

By late afternoon, Drew was up and around. He was already in a foursome and up by three dollars when Sheriff Campbell waltzed in.

"Twins," he said, shaking his head at Drew. "Well, I'll be." Then he rubbed his hands together. "Any o' you boys headin' out?"

All three players were willing to surrender their spot, considering it was the sheriff asking.

But Drew shook his head. "Look, Sheriff, I don't want any trouble. I don't want to cross the law. And I don't want to take any more of your hard-earned money."

The sheriff snorted at that. "That's hogslop. You just don't want me to win my money back...or my Maggie Ellen."

"Now, Sheriff," Drew tried to explain, "that ain't it at all. There's no one wants your girl to come back to you more than me."

"But you're refusin' to play me."

Drew grimaced. "It's just the principle of the—"

"Fine," the sheriff snapped, jamming his hat down onto his head. "But I've got my eyes on you—you *and* your twin brother." Then, making sure it was loud enough for the whole Parlor to hear, he said, "I guess I'll just be takin' my business to The Pair-o-Dice Saloon from now on."

Then he left in a huff, slamming the door of The Parlor behind him.

Though things were far from perfect, most nights, Catalina

hummed happily as she carried the tray of whiskey glasses through the salon. She didn't mind her job, especially since the regulars understood that she belonged to Drew.

Men rarely accosted her as she weaved in and out of the crowd, delivering drinks. When new visitors arrived, Miss Hattie was quick to inform them that unless they wanted to tangle with the hulking half-breed at the poker table, they'd best leave the Italian lady alone.

But even making a dollar and a half a day and sharing a room with Drew, she wasn't able to put much aside for her sewing machine. And the way they'd been seizing the days this last week, it was inevitable that she would find herself with child soon.

So far, she was safe. She'd just started her monthly courses this morning.

Meanwhile, in every spare moment, Catalina had been sketching out designs for dresses. The English Queen Victoria had made white wedding gowns popular, so that was what she envisioned for herself. She sketched out pearl buttons and lace trim with taffeta bows along the draped overskirt.

For the ladies of The Parlor, she imagined gowns in a rainbow of colors, each dress matched perfectly to the lady who wore it. For Anne, she drew a smart ensemble of vivid green with lighter green inserts and trim. For Emily, she created a stunning design in royal and sky blue stripes. Mary's dress had pastel pink ruffles and deep rose piping. The other dresses of dove gray, goldenrod, plum, and creamy beige were adorned with unique features like ribbon roses and side-swept swags, lace insets and bell sleeves. For Miss Hattie, Catalina designed a simple but elegant emerald gown with a jacket in dark teal to set off her brilliant red hair.

Catalina's fingers itched to bring the gowns to life. It was one thing to draw them on paper, quite another to see them realized. But it was anyone's guess as to when that would be possible.

Fortunately, Drew had been winning at cards. He'd won thirty-seven dollars this week. If Lady Luck stayed with him, they might be able to afford a sewing machine in a few weeks. If he had a few bad games, it might be months.

Then she glanced over at her handsome husband-to-be, who was carefully studying the other three players for what he called their "tells," the little secret gestures they made when they had good or bad cards. Her heart melted.

She decided that, even if he lost tonight, even if they couldn't afford a sewing machine for months, even if she had to wear a wedding dress with a gigantic waist to cover her condition, she would be happy. Lady Luck was definitely on her side.

CHAPTER 30

Sheriff Jasper Brown was feeling lucky as he rode into the town of Paradise near sunset. He knew he was close to his quarry, and he could almost taste the acrid fire of revenge.

Then again, that might just be the charred ruin of the barn he smelled as he and his sons rode toward Paradise. A large wooden sign over the entrance proclaimed the place THE PARKER RANCH.

Another few miles, and they hit the center of town. It appeared the evening was just getting started for the drinking men.

Paradise was off the beaten track as far as towns went. But it was a decent place with plenty of orchards and shops, churches and hotels. Best of all, by the tinny music and chatter he could hear coming out the doors, it had several saloons.

He reined up at the first establishment he saw, The Red Dog Saloon, and tied the horses to the hitching post. With his boys flanking him, he went through the open door, bellied up to the bar, and ordered three sarsaparillas.

"Aww, Pa," Harvey complained.

"Make mine with a shot o' whiskey," Jim told the bartender.

Jasper grabbed the bartender's arm before he could comply and shook his head. "We're gonna keep our wits about us, boys."

He had a feeling tonight was going to be the showdown. This was the end of his journey. If he didn't find his man here, he'd never find him. But he sure didn't need his boys half-drunk when it came time to settle the score.

While he waited for the sarsaparillas, he scoured the room. A piano player made a racket in the corner while a skinny kid scratched on a violin, making a noise that sounded like a cat in heat. There were only two card games going—both games of faro. He studied the faces of the players. None of them were the half-breed.

Once he got his drink, he told the boys to circulate while he had a little chat with the bartender. They immediately started cozying up to the saloon girls.

"I'm lookin' for a good game o' five-card draw," he said, carefully concealing his star. For this bit of ugly business, he'd just as soon not be known as a lawman. Unless his credentials came in handy, he planned to slip in and out of town with no fuss. "You get that in here?"

The bartender popped the cork back into a bottle of whiskey. "Faro's the favorite here. You might try down the street at the Pair-o-Dice."

Jasper nodded and took a sip. For an instant, he forgot it was sarsaparilla and flinched at the syrupy sweet taste.

The bartender continued pouring drinks while Jasper perused the saloon. The men were mostly white, but since the area had been settled during the Gold Rush, a lot of immigrants had infested the town.

Jasper took another slug of sarsaparilla. "You got any half-breeds come through?"

"Half-breeds?" the bartender said, wiping a spill off the bar. "Sure."

"Got any here now?" Every town had a couple drifters.

The bartender, misunderstanding him, took a gander around the room and gestured to a man playing faro. "Joe there is half-Mexican." He smirked, nodding to an exotic-looking lady beside the piano. "And the lady grabbin' your son's crotch is half-Chinese."

Jasper narrowed his eyes to slits. He'd talk to Jim about his taste in women later. "Any half-Injuns?"

The bartender shrugged. "Robert might be a quarter-Injun, not sure about that. He's the one on the fiddle."

Jasper decided he was getting nowhere at The Red Dog. So he drained his glass and rounded up his sons.

The Pair-o-Dice was a few doors down. This saloon had a lady barkeep and four games going. There was a woman warbling "Silver Threads Among the Gold" into the room, but only one of the dance hall girls had a partner, a grizzled old gent. As Jasper's gaze roved over the room, it landed on a player with a silver star on his vest. It appeared the town sheriff was sitting at one of the tables, playing five-card draw.

Jasper scratched at his cheek. Maybe he'd try a different strategy since the local lawman was a gambler.

He told his boys to buy themselves a couple of dances. Then he watched the poker game till it was over. When the players slid their chairs back, he approached the sheriff with his friendliest smile.

"Howdy, Sheriff," he said, flashing his own badge. "Good to see one o' my fellow lawmen havin' a little fun at the card table. Can I buy you a drink?"

"Can't say no to that," the sheriff replied. "I'm drinkin' bourbon."

"Bourbon it is." He waved to the barkeep. Then he extended his hand and said, "I'm Sheriff Jasper Brown o' Shasta."

"Pleased to meet you." The sheriff shook his hand. "You're a long way from home."

"Yeah, well, I'm a gamblin' man, but where I'm from, the locals frown on their sheriff playin' cards."

"You don't say." He clucked his tongue. "Folks here don't seem to care. I'm Sheriff Ernie Campbell, by the way."

"Ernie," he said, handing the man his bourbon when it arrived. "You seem like a smart, trustworthy fellow. Can I confide in you?"

"Yes, sir."

"I've been trackin' a particular poker player, a man they say is unbeatable."

"Is that so?"

"I figure an eagle-eyed sheriff like you is bound to notice a stranger in town."

"A stranger like you?" he said with a wink.

"That's right, Ernie. That's right." He clapped the man on the back. "At any rate, this man I'm lookin' for is a...a half-breed. You wouldn't know of anyone like that come through here lately?"

"A half-breed? Hell, we got two of 'em in town. And yeah, one of 'em is a poker player. In fact," he said, gulping down a swallow of bourbon with a grimace, "he took me for a bundle. After he was done fleecin' me, my Maggie Ellen wouldn't have anything to do with me." He sadly shook his head.

"So where does he play, this half-breed?"

"At The Parlor, just down the street."

"Would he be there now?"

"Prob'ly," the sheriff said. "His bride-to-be is workin' there. But I'd be careful. He'll steal you blind."

Jasper spent a few more minutes in mindless chitchat with the sheriff, just for appearance's sake. Then he interrupted the dances, much to his protesting sons' chagrin, and headed out the door with them to The Parlor.

When they entered the salon, the two boys gave a low whistle, impressed with the rich décor and quality "merchandise."

While Harvey stared in slack-jawed awe at the ladies preening on the balcony, Jim waved to one of the girls, and she lifted up her skirts in return.

"Can I get one o' them, Pa? Can I? I won't take long, I promise."

Jasper figured he was probably right. The state the boy was in, it'd be all over before he even got his drawers halfway down.

"Sure. Just don't pick up any bugs and don't give her any bastards."

"I want two whores," Jim decided. "Can I have two?"

"Don't be an idjit."

He summoned the madam and gave her enough money for one apiece.

She eyed the boys and said, "You'll have to hand over your guns, just for the safety o' my girls. You can have 'em back after."

The boys unbuckled their gun belts and gave them to the madam. Then he watched in relief as they clambered up the stairs, as excited as toddlers with a new puppy.

"I'm lookin' for someone," he told the madam. "The sheriff told me he frequents your place."

"Did he?" She crossed her arms. "Well, I'm not in the habit o' disclosin' who does and doesn't come to my establishment. It's a matter o' discretion."

Jasper itched to show her his badge, slam her up against the wall, and demand to know where the half-breed was. But he knew he'd get more flies with honey than vinegar. So he bit the bullet and gave her a wide, innocent smile.

"Oh, it's nothin' nefarious, ma'am," he assured her. "I'm just lookin' for a good game o' poker. The sheriff said there was a half-breed in town who—"

"A half-breed?" The woman's face tensed slightly. Something rang a bell with her. Then, just as slick as a hawker of patent medicine, she clammed up and played stupid. "I wouldn't know nothin' about half-breeds. Don't allow 'em in my place."

"Is that right?" Jasper grinned. He had a feeling she'd allow a monkey in her place if it could come up with the funds. "That's interestin', 'cause the sheriff said this is where he usually plays."

The madam's eyes were as cold as steel as she answered, "Well, the sheriff must be mistaken."

He knew she was lying. They both knew. But it had taken Jasper several days to come this far. He didn't mind waiting another couple of hours. Sooner or later, he had a feeling his man would show up. His boys were upstairs entertaining themselves anyway. He'd just sit here, have a sarsaparilla, and wait it out.

Unless they were ordering a drink, Catalina usually paid no heed to the conversations of the men who came into The Parlor. Most of their exchanges with Miss Hattie had to do with perversions she didn't want to hear about. But the word "half-breed" had caught her ear. From behind the bar, she glanced up.

The man was as big as a bear. His beige duster strained at the shoulders and looked like it couldn't be buttoned over his girth. His brown trousers were dusty and flecked with horsehair from a recent ride. His black vest was undone, and beneath it, his faded blue shirt was stained. Catalina guessed he was either a bachelor or a widower. No woman she knew would let her husband out of the house looking like that.

She poured a glass of claret and put it on a tray beside the two bourbons. She wondered if the man was inquiring about Drew. Maybe he was a poker player. Then she smiled to herself. Maybe Drew could win enough money off of him to buy her a sewing machine, and she'd make the bear a proper set of clothes.

She poured whiskey into the last glass and glanced up at Miss Hattie. The madam looked alarmed. Catalina had never seen her look like that. What was wrong? The bottle clinked against the glass as Catalina corked it with nervous hands.

With a furtive glance at the newcomer, who sat by himself, she delivered the drinks to the table of card players adjacent. Then she approached the stranger.

"Care for a drink?" she asked.

"Sarsaparilla, if you've got it."

Catalina blinked. Usually only the ladies drank sarsaparilla. But she smiled and nodded. She'd worked in the brothel long enough that not much surprised her.

As she went to fetch the sarsaparilla, Miss Hattie gave her a grim and pointed look. Catalina frowned. She knew the madam was trying to give her a warning, but about what? So far, the man had only asked for a drink. What harm could there be in that?

But when Catalina returned and set his glass on the table, he seized her wrist. She gasped with a start. It wasn't a painful grip, and he smiled, running his thumb across the back of her knuckles and across her wedding ring as if in friendship.

Catalina tried not to shudder with distaste. If Miss Hattie hadn't given her that look of warning, and if she hadn't heard that the man was looking for a half-breed, she would have wrenched her hand away at once and clobbered him with the tray.

But she sensed this was not a man to anger. So she clenched her teeth and gave him a smile in return. "Something is wrong?"

"You been workin' here a while?"

"*Si,* yes." Maybe he had mistaken her for one of the sporting ladies. She would set him straight. "But I only serve the drinks and—"

"So you know who comes and goes."

He released her hand.

She resisted the urge to wipe it on her skirts.

He took a sip of sarsaparilla.

She wasn't sure how to answer him. "Many men come and go." She shrugged. "After a while, they all look—"

"Ah, but this one you'd remember. A half-breed? Tall? Dark? Handsome?"

Catalina could tell by the sneer in his voice that he meant harm to Drew—or maybe Chase. That was why Miss Hattie had warned her away.

Fortunately, Drew was safe upstairs in their room, taking a bath. He probably wouldn't be down for another hour. With any luck, the stranger would be gone by then.

She made a point of looking the man in the eye as she lied. "I do not think I know this man."

The stranger smiled, sat back in his chair, and took another drink. His eyes glittered in amusement over the top of his glass. But he said no more.

With a nod of her head, Catalina picked up the tray and returned to the bar. She exchanged a wary glance with Miss Hattie, but then the madam was suddenly distracted by a customer.

Catalina was tempted to run up to the room to warn Drew

that someone was looking for him. But that would likely lead the stranger right to him.

So instead, with as much nonchalance as possible, she filled a tray of glasses with sarsaparilla. Then, grabbing her purse, she ambled up the stairs with the refreshment for the ladies on the balcony. From here, she could keep her eye on the man. If anything happened, she'd be ready.

CHAPTER 31

Jasper swirled the sarsaparilla in his glass. He'd come to the right place. These ladies knew something about the half-breed.

They weren't going to give him up easily. They were protecting him, probably because, as the town sheriff had told him, one of the girls was the filthy redskin's bride. He'd bet it was that foreign lady. She was wearing a wedding ring.

The little miss should be grateful, Jasper decided. He'd come to save her from the shame of having a half-breed husband.

In actual fact, if it were up to Jasper, he'd geld them all. The damned mixed bloods were polluting the white race.

Jasper washed away the bitter taste of injustice with another drink.

He was a patient man. He'd sit here sipping sarsaparilla all night if he had to. Sooner or later, his quarry would show up. He was sure of it.

No sooner did he settle in for a long wait than a plump little auburn-haired tart sidled up to him. She was so friendly that if he hadn't moved his leg out of her way at the last instant, he was sure she would have perched herself on his knee.

"What's *your* name, darlin'?" he asked.

"Amanda," she cooed. Then she glanced conspiratorially around the room and bent close. Her eyes glittering, she whispered, "I've got somethin' you want."

That might be true. She had mischief in her eyes and a little extra meat on her bones. But his flag had only been able to fly at half-staff since his wife passed. Besides, he was on duty.

"Not now, ma'am," he said.

Undeterred, she toyed with the buttons on his shirt and murmured, "I know where the half-breed is."

His eyes widened. Now he was getting somewhere. "Is that so? And are you gonna tell me?"

She gave him a simpering smile. "How much is it worth to you?"

He grabbed her forearm and flattened his eyes. He hated uppity women. Peeling back his duster, he showed her the butt of his revolver. "How about you tell me, and I don't shoot you in the face?"

She squeaked in panic, then started stumbling over her words, which came out thin and whispery. "He's...he's...he's...up-, upstairs."

"Which room?"

"The...the s-, second one on the...on the right."

He glanced over her head, locating the second room. "Thank you kindly, ma'am." He let go of her arm, and her knees buckled. Catching herself on the chair, she limped off.

Jasper finished off his glass and wiped his mouth with the back of his sleeve. He gave his pistol a pat, even though he knew it was there...and loaded. Then, keeping an eye on the second story room, he eased away from the table, stood up, and headed for the stairs.

He was met at the foot of the stairs by the madam.

"You ain't goin' up there," she said. "Not without payin' me first."

He knew better. The madam wasn't going to let him up there at any price. So he played his trump card. Hooking his thumb in the lapel of his duster, he pulled it back to show her his badge.

Her face fell. He could see she still wanted to block his way. But she was smart enough to realize the madam of a whorehouse didn't dare tangle with the law.

Still, the glimmer in her eye told him she wasn't quite done fighting. She opened her mouth to shout out a warning.

Fortunately, he caught it in time. He drew his six-gun and shoved it into her stomach. She choked back her cry.

"Out o' my way," he mumbled. "And if you don't want your girls shot, you'll keep quiet."

She faltered back against the stair rail and let him pass.

He took his time climbing the stairs, keeping his gun under the flap of his duster. After all, there was no reason to get anyone else involved. Men were still drinking and playing cards. The ladies on the balcony were still displaying their wares. Hell, his own boys were in one of these rooms, getting their pistols polished. He'd just settle the score behind closed doors.

Jasper figured the half-breed was probably knocking boots with one of the shady ladies. So when he forced open the door and found the man alone in a tub, he was taken aback for a moment.

The half-breed dove for the nightstand, and Jasper raised his pistol.

But the half-breed's hands came up empty. Whatever he was looking for wasn't there. He spat out what Jasper assumed was an Injun curse. Then, raising his hands and hanging his head, he stepped from the tub, naked and dripping.

Jasper could have shot him right then. He should have. But even though he'd spent days on the trail, hunting the man responsible for his son's death, there was something about shooting anyone that naked and helpless that made him hesitate.

That moment of hesitation cost him everything. He took a step into the room. In the next instant, he heard the unmistakable click of a gun cocking behind his head.

"Stop."

He froze. It was a woman. He wasn't afraid of a woman.

Catalina wasn't afraid of the big bear. She had Drew's gun in her hand. She might not have shot a man before. But she had shot a hole in the floor. She knew what to do.

Behind her, sensing danger, the ladies retreated to the safety of their rooms with soft cries of dismay.

Catalina's hand was steadier than she expected. But determination did that to a person. And she was quite determined that the big, bad man would not shoot her beloved.

"Cat, no!"

From around the man's big shoulder, she could see Drew. He was still wet from his bath and completely nude. He had his hands above his head and a look of desperation on his face.

"Put the gun down, Cat!"

She hesitated. He shouldn't talk to her like that. Now her hands were quivering and indecisive. Still, she didn't lower her weapon.

"Cat, he's a lawman, a sheriff. You can't shoot him. They'll hang you."

She blinked in surprise. A sheriff? What did a sheriff want with Drew?

"That's right, ma'am," the stranger murmured. "So you'd best..."

She jabbed the back of his head with the barrel. "I do not care if he is the *Duca di Spoleto*," she bit out. "I came halfway around the world to find you, Drew Hawk, and I am not about to let you get shot again. One bullet in your body this month is enough."

Drew's gaze softened just enough to let her know that her words had moved him.

Then, to her surprise, the sheriff started chuckling. "Oh, I don't mean to shoot him, ma'am. Is that what you thought?"

Catalina swallowed. She knew better than to trust him, even if he was a man of the law. Men often said one thing and did another.

"No," the sheriff said, "I'm just here to collect him so's he can have a fair trial, that's all."

Catalina tightened her grip. "A fair trial?" she challenged. "For a half-breed? There's no such thing as a—"

Before she could brace herself, the man's hand came around and seized the barrel of the pistol, wrenching it aside. The reflexive shot she fired missed his head and hit the wall. And then he ripped the gun out of her grip.

"Cat!" Drew's voice rang out over the suddenly silent salon.

The brute wheeled and gave her a hard shove. Her spine struck the balcony railing with paralyzing force and bent her backward. Everyone on the ground floor gasped. Then he took aim.

She heard the shot. But she didn't feel it.

Time seemed to slow to a crawl. She blinked once, and it felt like it took forever.

Drew had told her what it was like to be hit by a bullet. At first there was no pain. Later, he said, the burning had come.

She was numb. There was a queer ringing in her ears, and beneath that sound, she could hear her own heart beating.

That was good, wasn't it? Her heart was still beating. But for how long? She was afraid to look down, to see where the bullet had hit her, afraid of the blood and the hole that might look jagged and empty, like the hole she'd shot in the floor.

But as her eyes remained fixed on the ominous gray barrel bearing down on her, she saw it begin to waver. Then she moved her focus beyond the pistol to the stranger's face.

He blinked twice, looking puzzled. Then, as the barrel began to droop, his arm lowered, and she saw his throat.

At first, to Catalina's eyes, he appeared to be wearing a brilliant red silk poppy on a lady's choker. After a moment, she realized it wasn't silk at all. It was blood.

She hadn't been shot. He had.

The pistol fell slowly from his fingers, seeming to float through the air. He moved his hands to his throat, trying to stop the deadly flow. But ribbons of red streamed through his knuckles as he opened his mouth in a silent scream.

Slowly, gradually, he sank to the floor, smearing the wall behind him with stripes of his blood.

As if from very far away, she heard Miss Hattie's voice. "Catalina! Catalina! Are you all right?"

Clinging to the balcony railing, Catalina turned in the direction of the voice. It felt like she was moving through molasses. Miss Hattie stood below her on the stairs. She was holding a pistol.

"Cat!" Drew called.

Slowly, Catalina looked back over her shoulder. He was standing in the doorway. He wasn't wearing a stitch of clothing. For an absurd moment, she wondered why he didn't go put some trousers on. After all, the door was wide open.

It was the real and naked relief in Drew's eyes that finally woke her up and brought her out of the lethargic fog. And when he rushed over to her, stepping over the body...

She lowered her eyes to the ground for only an instant...and wished she hadn't.

She started wheezing in horror.

The man lay twitching on the floor. Blood gurgled out of his throat. His face was red and sweaty. His hands clawed at his chest. And his eyes were glassy with disbelief.

And then Drew was there to block it all, taking her in his arms, burying her head against his chest.

"It's all right now, Cat. Don't think about it. Everything's gonna be all right."

At first, she couldn't stop shivering. Even when he stroked her hair and murmured soothing words in his breathy native tongue, she kept trembling, unable to piece together what had just happened.

"It's all over now, Cat," he whispered. "You're safe. He can't hurt you. He can't hurt anyone."

Eventually, her heart slowed, and she could breathe without rasping.

Downstairs, the men started up their quiet conversation again, speculating over who had been shot and why.

Miss Hattie summed it up for them, showing them her pistol. "Out-o'-towner messin' with my girls."

They seemed to believe that explanation and went back to playing cards.

One by one, the upstairs doors opened, with the ladies and their clients tenuously peeking out to see if it was safe. A few of the ladies ogled Drew.

Catalina, struck by a sudden wave of possessiveness, pushed him back inside the room. He obliged her by putting on his trousers.

Miss Hattie swept along the balcony and knocked on Mary's door. "Young man, you'd best come out."

A moment later, a bearded man emerged with a frown, pulling up his suspenders. His frown dissolved when he saw the grisly remains of the sheriff.

"Pa!" he yelped. "What happened? Who did this?"

Then he banged hard on Sophie's door. "Harvey! Get out here!"

Harvey came out boiling mad, buttoning his trousers. "What do you..." His face crumpled when the first man pointed to the body. "No. Oh no."

Miss Hattie showed them the pistol. "Now you listen, boys. Your daddy did somethin' real bad. He shot at a woman, and he shot at an unarmed man. He deserved what he got."

The bearded man looked like he was foaming at the mouth. "You done this? You?"

When he started coming toward Miss Hattie, she leveled the gun at him, stopping him in his tracks.

"I can shoot two men as easy as one," she said.

"No, Jim, don't do it," Harvey begged. "Don't get yourself shot. Don't leave me alone."

Jim spat on the floor. "You're gonna hang for murder," he threatened Miss Hattie. "My daddy was a sheriff."

"Who was shot with *your* gun," she told him. "And I got a salon full o' happy regulars who'll swear it was in your hands at the time."

The men below voiced their agreement.

"So unless *you* want to hang for his murder," she told them, "you'd best get dressed and get out o' my town. You can take your daddy with you if you like or leave him here."

There was a bit of an argument over that. Harvey wanted to take him back to Shasta. But Jim said he'd be rotten by then. In the end, after charging Miss Hattie to give him a proper burial, they decided to leave him.

Long after they'd gone, Miss Hattie glared down at the

dead sheriff and muttered, "That's the only way that son o' the devil could possibly ever wind up in Paradise."

Then she sat down on the stair step with the pistol on her lap and rested her head in her hands.

Catalina sat down beside her. "You saved my life."

She shrugged it off. "He ain't the first man I shot. Prob'ly won't be the last."

Catalina only knew she was grateful Miss Hattie had fired the gun when she had. A split-second later and...

She shuddered at the thought.

"Truth is, Catalina," Miss Hattie said, "I've about had it with this business. I'm gettin' too old for this kind o' calamity."

"Oh, Miss Hattie, you are not old."

Miss Hattie patted her knee. "You're a fine young lady, Cat. You've got a good man and a bright future. Me? I got nothin' but this den of iniquity. When I die, I'm gonna be meetin' up with all the fellas I shot, 'cause I sure ain't gettin' into heaven."

Catalina frowned. That wasn't right. The madam was a good person.

Miss Hattie gazed around the room at the red wallpaper and the crystal chandeliers, the card tables and the mahogany bar, the big mirror on the wall and the overstuffed chairs in the salon.

"You know, if it weren't for my girls needin' to make a livin', I'd close down The Parlor tomorrow."

Catalina didn't know what to say to that. It was true that The Parlor was a *bordello,* a place that catered to the sinful appetites of men. But she had friends here. She couldn't imagine what Anne and Emily would do if Miss Hattie closed down The Parlor.

CHAPTER 32

Drew spit in his palms and got a good grip on the crate. "You ready?"

Across from him, Chase nodded and hefted up his end.

The ladies at The Parlor leaned over the balustrade, watching with interest as the twins hauled the heavy crate, step by step, up the stairs of The Parlor.

"Don't you ladies have gentlemen waitin' for you?" Miss Hattie asked.

Most of them reluctantly returned to their rooms.

"What's in here anyway, a railroad safe?" Chase asked with a grunt.

"You'll see," Drew replied.

It had taken two weeks, but the shipment had finally come in.

At Drew's suggestion and with Miss Hattie's permission, Catalina had taken the day off and gone to the Parker Ranch to visit Claire. When she returned, there would be a splendid surprise in her room.

Earning the money to buy it had been challenging, especially once Sheriff Campbell cornered Drew with an ultimatum.

It seemed that after the shooting death of Sheriff Jasper Brown by one of his sons—according to witnesses, though no one could prove it—Sheriff Campbell had done some investigating of his own. He'd made inquiries about a certain related incident at the Winsome Saloon in Shasta where the sheriff's youngest son Billy had been killed. The bartender admitted it had looked like an accident to him—an unlucky crack on the head—but Jasper, convinced the half-breed gambler had killed his boy, had come looking for Drew Hawk in Paradise.

It was a sticky business. A person could argue that Drew wasn't exactly innocent in all this. There was also some mention of Miss Hattie having confiscated the boys' guns. But Sheriff Campbell said he'd be willing to overlook some of the details and cover for Drew on one condition...

Drew had to play poker with him. The sheriff was still pining over his lost ladylove and convinced he was going to win back his money and his girl. No matter how Drew tried to persuade him that gambling was no way to impress Maggie Ellen, the sheriff insisted it was what he wanted to do.

Naturally, Drew had to agree...and he had to lose. He'd spent a week cheating—folding when he had a straight flush, betting a fortune on a pair of eights, *accidentally* letting the sheriff take a good gander at his cards—until he finally repaid every penny he'd profited.

Unfortunately, it had taken a toll on the savings he was trying to amass for his wedding. And he wasn't winning enough off of other players to make up for that. It seemed like it'd be months before they could afford to get married.

In the end, it was the brilliant Miss Hattie who'd come through for him.

He'd been standing on a step ladder one morning while Cat was out, bringing down the crystal chandelier for her to polish when the madam said, "You know, I never returned those two pistols to the Brown boys."

Drew hesitated, chandelier in hand.

"You aren't thinkin' o' clearin' your conscience, are you?" If she returned the murder weapon, she'd have no leverage over the sheriff's sons. "'Cause those boys might come lookin' to avenge their—"

"Hell, no." She reached her arms up to take the chandelier, setting it gently on the carpet. Then she dusted off her hands. "I got that revolver off o' their daddy too."

He smirked as he climbed down from the ladder. "Yeah, you got quite the gun collection, Miss Hattie."

"That's what the man from Chico said."

He folded up the ladder and set it against the wall. "What man?"

"The one who bought 'em off o' me."

"You sold 'em."

"I did. Got a nice bundle for 'em too. They weren't exactly pearl-handled revolvers. But they fetched a decent price."

"Well, good for you." Drew smiled. At least something good had come of the incident. "You need me for anything else?"

"Just this," she said.

Reaching over the bar, she brought out a small leather satchel and handed it to him. It was heavy.

"What's this?"

"It's yours. Go on, look inside."

When he opened the top of the satchel, silver coins winked up at him. "What the—?"

"Gun money. I figure with that and the money you've been makin' off cards, you should have enough to buy that pretty little bride o' yours what she's been wantin'."

"I can't take your—"

"You can and you will."

"But it ain't mine, not rightly."

"It ain't mine neither."

She had a point. For once, he was speechless...which greatly amused Miss Hattie.

"Go on then," she told him, chuckling. "Head down to Clark's and have him order the thing. It should be here in a couple weeks."

He'd bent down and given Miss Hattie a big, sloppy smack on the cheek, which made her giggle and blush and swat at him.

That had been two and a half weeks ago.

Cat had told him it would take her a month to make all the dresses for the wedding. So if all went well, in another four weeks, they'd officially be Mr. and Mrs. Hawk.

"Quit dawdling," Chase complained as he tugged on the crate.

"Dawdlin'?" Drew snickered. Chase was sounding more and more civilized all the time, now that he had a white sweetheart.

Chase shook his head. "What is this anyway? Did you buy a forge so you could work on your physique for your bride?"

"Ho ho." His blacksmith brother might have more muscles than he did, but Drew made up for it in charm.

Once they got the crate onto the landing, Anne and Emily rushed up to take a look.

"What is it?" Anne wanted to know. "No, don't tell me. Let me guess."

"Is it an icebox?" Emily asked.

Drew shook his head.

"It's a bridal chest," Anne said.

"No."

"A washtub?" Emily guessed.

"Nope."

Chase took a turn. "A piano," he groused.

The ladies laughed. The crate wasn't *that* big.

"Well, it's heavy enough to be a piano," Chase muttered.

"Is it a nightstand?" Anne asked.

"It's a commode!" Emily decided.

"A commode? Emily!" Anne jostled her friend. "Don't be silly. What man would get his bride..." Then she looked askance at Drew. "It ain't a commode, is it?"

"No," he assured her.

"Twelve anvils," Chase grumbled.

"Mr. Wolf," Emily chided, "honestly..."

"Oh, I know! I know what it is!" Anne announced. "It's a cradle!"

Mortified, Chase and Drew answered together, "A cradle?"

Chase pinned him with a glare. "Are you...?"

Drew blew out a steadying breath. "No. *No.* It ain't a cradle."

"Well, I'm stumped," Anne said.

They slid the crate into the bedroom and took a crowbar to it. Even after it was unpacked and the ladies were cooing over it, Chase had no idea what the strange wood and iron contraption was.

But that was fine. Cat would know exactly what it was.

CHAPTER 33

Getting ready for her wedding in Claire's upstairs bedroom at the Parker Ranch, Catalina could hardly contain her excitement.

But it was her soon-to-be sister-in-law who was squirming as Catalina arranged the long white veil over Claire's short blonde hair, pinning a violet spray of lupins across the top.

"Be still," she scolded with a laugh. "Ah, better. The pins, they are not biting you?"

"No, they're not biting me."

When she finished, she tugged Claire over to the full-length mirror. "So. Do you like?"

Originally, Catalina had wanted a fashionable white gown like the English Queen's. But Claire said that since the red Paradise dirt stained everything, she preferred darker colors. Catalina shuddered, remembering the ugly browns and grays of Claire's regular wardrobe.

They'd managed a compromise.

Sketching out the designs for their wedding dresses, Catalina had suggested the colors of the local wildflowers—

the vibrant hues of the lupins and poppies that draped the foothills in spring like brilliant swaths of cloth.

For green-eyed Claire, she'd designed a pale lavender gown with a high buttoned neckline and a darker violet insert in the skirt. Narrow cream-colored ruffles edged the flounces and belled sleeves. The vivid fresh lupins that anchored her veil drew attention to Claire's delicate face, and more lupins filled her bouquet.

For herself, she'd created a soft peach dress that seemed to float on her frame in layers of sheer silk, caught up with bows to reveal playful ruffles of orange beneath. Her dark hair made a good foil for the crown of bright orange poppies that secured her white veil.

"It's perfect," Claire murmured.

They exchanged smiles in their reflection.

Catalina loved having a sister. And she was suddenly very glad she'd insisted on a double wedding, considering the trouble they'd been given.

If people thought Catalina's bustle was scandalous, they were a hundred times more offended at the idea of a white woman marrying a half-breed. None of the churches would allow them to speak their vows at the altar.

To make things worse, despite Catalina's innocent association with The Parlor, most people judged her harshly for it.

As for Claire, many treated her as if she'd gotten herself kidnapped on purpose.

Many townsfolk would neither speak nor look at them.

In the end, they'd decided to face the fire—and the scorn of society—together. They would hold a double wedding in the new barn at the Parker Ranch. That way, they knew whoever attended would be true friends.

"I think we will be very beautiful flowers today," Catalina decided.

Claire turned sideways to the mirror and giggled. "Are you *sure* this looks right?"

Catalina wondered if Paradise would ever get accustomed to bustles. "Oh, *si, si,*" she assured Claire. "It is the latest fashion."

She turned to the side as well to make sure her own bustle was straight. Then, with a secret smile, she ran a hand over the front of her skirt. Fortunately, she wasn't showing too much yet.

A movement at the window caught her eye, and she rushed over to peer at the drive below. The guests were starting to arrive.

Catalina grinned and straightened with pride as she watched them. The ladies of The Parlor, mincing along the drive with their elegant parasols and their extravagant hats, could have passed for the aristocracy of Italy. She'd dressed them in so many beautiful colors, they looked like a lovely rainbow as they ambled past.

Then she spotted the twins.

"Come, come quickly," she said to Claire. "Come see our beautiful men."

Catalina had chosen their suits as well. She'd wisely dressed them in different colors. Though Claire and she could easily tell the brothers apart, most could not. Chase's suit was the deep rich brown of *espresso.* Drew's was the dark blue shade of the night sky.

Claire leaned against the window with a dreamy sigh.

She wasn't the only one appreciating the handsome twins. Catalina could see ladies whispering behind their gloves and young girls blushing as the brothers passed.

"I think the ladies cannot decide which man is the most beautiful," she told Claire.

Catalina knew exactly how they felt. Her own cheeks flushed as she let her gaze travel from the top of their curling black hair to the heels of their sturdy black boots, stopping to admire their broad shoulders and narrow hips.

But her heart thrilled to more than that. The idea that Drew belonged to *her,* that she was the lucky lady who was going to spend the rest of her life with him...that took her breath away.

"Wait," Claire said with a frown. "Didn't you say Drew was going to wear blue and Chase would be in brown?"

Drew knew he probably shouldn't have broken his new rule of never betting against a lawman. But easy money was so hard to resist. So when the jailer they'd fooled with the two-spirits game had popped into The Parlor the night before his wedding, claiming *nobody* could tell the difference between the twins, not even their brides, Drew couldn't help but take that bet.

Chase wasn't exactly happy about it.

"I mean to split the winnin's with you, you know," he told Drew as they walked along the drive of the Parker Ranch.

"What if there aren't any winnings? What if they *can't* tell us apart?"

Drew snorted. "O' course they can tell us apart. I'm as sure o' that as I am o' winnin' a hand o' poker with a full house."

What he didn't tell Chase was that a man couldn't necessarily always win a hand with a full house...if the other player had a royal flush...or a straight flush...or even four of a kind. In other words, there was a slim possibility that Claire and Cat might *not* be able to tell their grooms apart, especially since they'd swapped suits. But he was *reasonably* sure they could.

That was before Samuel Parker had come up, clapped Drew on the back, and called him "son."

While Chase glared at Drew in silent rage, Mr. Parker took the twins on a detour behind the ranch house.

They hiked across a field full of wildflowers and over a small hill to a spot where a solitary oak grew. At the bottom of the trunk was a hunk of stone sunk into the ground.

This was the spot, Mr. Parker said, where he'd gently laid Yoema, their beloved grandmother—Claire's spirit mother— to rest.

They took a few moments to pay their respects, and then headed back to the barn.

Drew murmured to Chase, "You know, I don't think it matters if Mr. Parker thinks I'm his son-in-law. We're the same blood, after all."

Chase gave him a sideways glare, biting out, "I don't much like being mistaken for a gambler living in a cathouse."

Drew arched a brow and muttered, "So you're Mr. Upstanding, are you?"

Chase sniffed. "I'm a local hero."

Drew narrowed his eyes, hissing, "Well, except for that part about kidnappin' a woman."

Chase elbowed him.

Drew shoved him back.

They were still grumbling at each other fifteen minutes later as they stood at the makeshift altar at the end of the barn, waiting for their brides to arrive.

The barn had come out nice. With lumber readily available from up on the ridge and all the townsfolk pitching in, the building went up fast. The new structure had six shuttered windows which were currently open to let the sunlight in. In fact, except for the sweet smell of hay and the lack of self-righteousness, Drew didn't see much difference between the barn and the church his mother used to take the twins to on occasion when they were young.

Drew wasn't even nervous until the preacher opened his

book, the fiddler started playing, and he heard the rustle of clothing behind him as people stood.

This was it, he thought, licking his lips. These were the cards he'd dealt himself. And he was all in.

He turned to look down the aisle. The moment he saw the beautiful blossoms floating toward him, his fears vanished.

Since Cat didn't have anyone, Samuel Parker was giving both brides away. Flanked by the lovely ladies, he definitely looked like a thorn between two roses.

Drew couldn't have described later what Cat was wearing, which he was sure would have upset her. All he knew was she looked like an angel, all pretty and glowing and full of light. Apparently, the townsfolk thought so too. He could hear their gasps of awe as Cat glided down the aisle, between the benches.

They were halfway down the path when Drew heard a strangling sound come out of Chase's throat. Drew cast a quick sidelong glance at his brother. Chase looked like smoke would come out of his ears any second.

Then Drew saw what he saw.

The ladies were gazing lovingly, longingly at the wrong twin.

His first thought was, Damn, he was going to lose the bet.

His second thought was, Shit! He was going to marry the wrong woman.

The brothers froze as the ladies stood beside them.

Then the preacher began to speak.

Hell! What was he going to do?

Chase cleared his throat.

Drew coughed.

As the preacher continued to drone on, Drew clenched his fists. From the corner of his eye, he could see Chase looking like he wanted to kill something.

"...to join together this man and this woman..." The

preacher nodded to Drew and Claire, then to Chase and Cat. "And *this* man and this woman..."

Suddenly, Claire burst out laughing.

Cat's eyes danced. "A moment, please."

Drew should have remembered that Cat gave as good as she got. The ladies traded places then, to the amusement of the townsfolk. Tucking their hands into the proper grooms' elbows, they smugly grinned at their bit of mischief.

He supposed he deserved it. It wasn't right playing the two-spirit game on their brides. And coming so close to marrying the wrong person made him realize how much he really wanted Cat...and no one else.

She was his one of a kind, his queen of hearts. She could be as playful as a kitten or as fierce as a wildcat, as delicate as a rose petal or as prickly as a thorn. One moment, he'd be struggling to understand her tangled words. And in the next, she was sending him an unmistakable message with her eyes alone. Cat was unpredictable, spirited, and exciting.

He guessed life would always be uncertain.

But though he might not know what was in the cards going forward, he was sure he wanted to share that life with Cat.

His chest swelled with joy as he smiled down at her, his beautiful bride, repeating the words that would seal their love and make them a pair of hearts forever.

EPILOGUE

On the second floor of the Parker house, in Claire's old bedroom, Catalina slowed the pedal on the treadle sewing machine, snipped the ends of the thread, and pulled out the tiny nightdress.

She held it up to the late summer light streaming in through the open window. Little yellow blossoms dotted the soft white cotton, and she planned to make a matching yellow nightcap.

She rubbed the slight curve of her abdomen. It was hard to believe that in another five months she was going to have a baby that would fit into this nightdress.

"It's a mite small for me, darlin'!" Drew called up from the yard below.

She grinned and waved from the windowsill. She never got tired of Drew's humor or his dashing good looks. Even as he was now—covered in dust, his jeans frayed, and his hair falling over his forehead—he could make her heart race with a wink of his dark, sparkling eyes.

"When will you be finished?" she called back.

"Soon," he promised.

Making sure none of the ranch hands were watching, Catalina blew him a sultry kiss.

"Very soon," he amended.

She smiled, waggled her fingers in farewell, and folded the little nightdress.

Things had certainly turned out differently than anyone expected. As Drew liked to say, it was a good thing he hadn't wagered on his future, because taking over the Parker Ranch had never been in his plans.

But the previous ranch manager Frank had been hanged. And Chase and Claire had decided to return to Hupa. So Samuel Parker was left without a man to run his ranch.

Drew was perfect for the job. He was clever, good with numbers, a fast learner, a hard worker, and handy with a gun.

He hadn't completely given up poker. He still played the occasional game with Sheriff Campbell. By some miracle, the sheriff *had* won back the heart of his Maggie Ellen. She'd forgiven him for his reckless gambling. She'd even promised to stay with him on the condition that he only played against Mr. Hawk, since, for some strange reason, he always seemed to win when he played against Mr. Hawk.

Catalina smiled as she tucked the nightdress into her sewing basket, atop the three other gowns she'd already made.

Of course, now, with so much to learn about the ranch and a baby on the way, Drew was up before dawn most mornings, working long into the night.

That was fine with Catalina. She was just as busy.

She'd had to limit her sewing to daytime, since Drew had complained her sewing machine sounded like a locomotive running through the bedroom.

So in the evenings, she designed. She scoured her weekly delivery of *La Mode Illustrée* from France for pictures of the latest fashions. But she also questioned Drew about the traditional clothing of his people. She began to create new ensembles inspired by a unique combination of the latest European trends—ruffles, bustles, pleats, and lace—and Hupa tradition—shells, feathers, doeskin, and fringe.

Ever since the women of Paradise had glimpsed the lovely creations at her wedding, she'd been swamped with dress orders. It was flattering. But she didn't know how she was going to keep up with them, especially once she had her child.

As she was daydreaming, she heard Drew outside again.

"Cat!"

When she moved to the window, she saw the mail wagon pulling out of the drive. Drew had a package in his arms.

"I think this is for you." He studied the box, frowning at the name. "It's from someplace called...Ferra-"

"Ferrara?" Her heart raced. Her father had answered her. "I'll be right down."

"No need. I'll bring it up. I'll just be a—"

"Hurry!"

He chuckled.

She whipped away from the window and began pacing back and forth across the room. What was it? What had her father sent?

She'd never spoken much about her father to Drew...or anyone, for that matter. At first, it was because she didn't want to be found. Her father's name was well-known enough that a decent detective could track her back to her estate in Italy.

Once she'd met Drew and he'd proposed, she knew her father couldn't command her any longer. He couldn't summon her home to marry the man of his choice, because she already had a husband.

But she didn't want any questions at the wedding. She didn't want her friends asking why her family hadn't come. So she'd let them believe she was an orphan.

Afterward, it had haunted her that she hadn't told her father about any of it. He might be a domineering, demanding man who thought his daughter was a prize to be used for political gain.

But he was generally good. He'd given her food and shelter, taught her right from wrong, and spoiled her with the comforts of nobility. He deserved to know the truth.

She chewed at her lip. When was Drew going to get here? She rushed to the window again. He was still down there with the package, chatting with Mr. Parker.

"Drew!" she yelled.

"On my way."

He gave a tip of his hat to Mr. Parker and then loped toward the house.

She turned her back to the window and began wringing her hands. What had her letter said? She closed here eyes, trying to remember.

She'd apologized for leaving in such haste, of course. But she hadn't apologized for leaving. She'd told him she couldn't marry the man of his choice and was following her dreams. That much was true.

But the crux of the letter, she was ashamed to admit, was intentionally misleading.

She'd told her father she was getting married to the grandson of a great lord in California.

It wasn't exactly *un*true. Drew's father had been the headman of his people, the Konkow.

What she'd omitted, however, was the fact that the Konkow were a small tribe of natives who lived in stick houses, wore doeskin skirts, and subsisted largely on acorns and deer.

271

She was sure her father would never approve.

She gulped. What if he was coming to visit? What if he showed up and had the marriage annulled, stripped off her wedding ring, and dragged her back to Ferrara?

The breath caught in her chest.

Then she heard steps on the stairs.

She rushed to the door, opening it before Drew had even reached for the doorknob, and snatched away the package.

"Greedy girl." He laughed and clucked his tongue. "I'd hate to see what you're like at Christmas."

She dropped the package on the bed and took the scissors out of her apron pocket to cut loose the strings.

"It is from my father," she explained to Drew.

"Your father?"

Her fingers were trembling. It was ridiculous, she knew. Even if the package contained something bad—a document disowning her or an official demand for her to return to Italy—it no longer had any legal effect on her. She was now the citizen of a new country.

Still, she held her breath as she unwrapped the paper and opened the box.

"What is it?" Drew whispered.

There was a note on top. She read the first sentence and lowered herself on shaky legs to the bed.

"Is everything all right?" Drew asked.

"I am not..." She read the rest quickly and then lowered the note to her lap.

"*Xongqot,* Cat, what does it say?"

She translated it for Drew. "To my daughter Catalina, to say I am displeased does not begin to describe my emotions. When I discovered you had run away, my heart was broken. Your dear mother, with her dying breath, demanded I find you a good husband. To my sorrow, you left before I could fulfill her wishes. I am sorry you found life here so unbearable. But now that you have found a husband, I hope you find pleasure in your new country. I am pleased that you have found your way and married a person of noble blood who will—"

"Wait. What? Noble blood? Where did he get that idea?"

She shrugged. "I may have told him your grandfather was a lord."

He winced at her lie and then reconsidered. "Well, that *is* true...sorta."

She scanned the letter, looking for where she left off. "...a person of noble blood who will provide for you and give you many children."

"Many?" Drew asked. "How many?"

She ignored him and kept translating. "But what I am most displeased about is that I was not invited to the wedding." Her voice caught on the touching words.

Drew put his arm around her, and she felt her eyes filling with tears. She didn't know why, but lately she got teary all the time.

She cleared her throat, sniffed, and continued. "I hope I am not too late to give you a wedding gift, a gift so you will never forget your home. One day I will come to California. I hope I will be welcome at your husband's estate. With loving regards..."

"Estate?"

That did make her laugh just a little through her tears.

Drew let out a low whistle. "I'm gonna have to work a lot harder if I'm gonna have that estate built by the time he comes to visit."

Catalina grinned up at him. He winked back. She didn't need an estate, and he knew it.

"What's in the package?" he asked.

She removed a crumpled wad of papers, noting with amusement that they were pages from her old fashion magazines. Then she looked at the bundle below, wrapped in parchment and tied with twine. She snipped the string and peeled back the parchment.

Beneath it was a bundle of gauze.

She gasped. She knew what it was.

Carefully, she loosened the parchment to uncover at least a dozen black lumps the size of a baby's fist.

"Coal?" Drew guessed.

"*Tartufi!*" she cried.

She burst into tears then—ridiculous, howling sobs of joy that startled Drew and made her wonder at her own sanity.

Of course, her weeping was about more than the *tartufi*. It was about making peace with her father, keeping her ties with the place of her birth while finding a new home in a new country.

Drew folded her in his arms, catching her sobs and letting her drench his shirt with her tears. She wept also for being blessed with an incredible husband who had given her a baby and bought her a beautiful sewing machine so she could do what she loved best.

When she ran out of tears, she pulled away to wipe her face with her hands. Sniffling, she told Drew, "You must try one."

"I don't know. The way you're carryin' on," he said with a wink, "I'm beginnin' to think they might be as dangerous as opium."

She smiled. "You have a knife?"

He pulled out his Bowie knife and handed it to her, handle first.

She picked up one of the black lumps and carried it on a piece of parchment to the marble-top dresser. Then she carefully cut two slices no thicker than a coin.

"You sure about this?" he asked as he took the slice, eyeing it as if it might contain poison.

"I will go first," she told him.

She took a small nibble, rolling her eyes as she savored the musky, garlicky flavor on her tongue. "Mmmm." It tasted like...home. "Now you."

She watched with amusement as he took a tiny bite. Seeing as it didn't poison him, he took another. His forehead creased as he considered the taste. Finally, he took a generous bite, chewing and frowning with the concentration of her father's wine-taster.

"Well?" she asked.

"Not bad. Better than I expected."

Her brows shot up. Not bad? She took another heavenly nibble. How could he not taste the forests of Ferrara in every bite?

But then she realized that was part of it. For her, it was more than a taste. It was an experience and a memory.

"*Tartufi* reminds me of home, of my childhood," she said. "What was your favorite food when you were a boy?"

"Mmm, *k'itust-dediwilliq'*."

"And this is...?"

"Acorn bread."

"Then I must try your acorn bread," she decided.

"That's a promise," he said. "O' course, my mother makes the best. She learned from the other women o' the—"

There was a knock on the door.

"Miss Catalina?" It was Mr. Parker.

She opened the door, *tartufo* in hand.

He nodded a greeting and extended an envelope. "It looks like a letter came for you today."

"Oh." Two letters in one day?

Mr. Parker gave the *tartufo* a skeptical glance.

"Would you like to try the *tartufo?*" she offered. "It is a delicacy from my country."

"No, thanks, ma'am. I'm more of a steak and potatoes man."

She shrugged. But as she took the letter with thanks, she couldn't help but wonder how steak and potatoes would be with little shavings of *tartufo* on top.

The letter was from Sacramento. She used Drew's knife to slice it open.

"It's from Jenny!" she cried when she saw the name.

"Jenny? Our little runaway Jenny?"

"*Si*. I will read it." It was good for Catalina to practice reading English. "My dearest Catalina, I cannot thank you enog..."

"Enough?"

"I cannot thank you enough for helping me to escape my woo-reh-ch...woo-reh-ch..."

"May I?" Drew asked.

She showed him the word.

"Wretched."

"For helping me to escape my wretched kirkum-, circumstances, and I want you to know your gen-, generosity has not been in vain. I am delig-..."

"Delighted?" he guessed.

She nodded. "Delighted to tell you that I have found myself a kind and upstanding gentleman, and I am now..." She gasped in wonder. "Married!"

She grinned up at Drew.

"Go on," he said.

"Because you were such a freen-...friend to me, I wish to repay your kindness. My new husband is in the retail bus-, bus-..."

He glanced at the page. "Business."

She blinked and shook her head. These Americans had very strange ways of spelling words.

"Retail business with a Mr. Wine-, Ween-, Weinstock?"

Drew shrugged. "No tellin'."

"They would be very interested to see your clothing

desi-..." She broke off, racing ahead to silently read the rest. "Designs?"

She nodded, barely able to contain her excitement. "They want to see my designs. It says they want to carry clothings made to order."

She stared up at him, stunned.

"Well, that's good news, right?" he asked.

"It is wonderful news!"

He gave her a big hug. But of course, her mind was already hundreds of miles away, planning.

"I'll send them what I have so far," she said. She had several designs drawn up.

She pulled out of Drew's embrace and went to rummage through her portfolio of designs.

Behind her, Drew unbuttoned his shirt.

"Sacramento is a very big city, yes?" she asked, as she pulled out a few of her papers and turned to him.

He shuffled out of his shirt, hanging it over the chair. "Yeah, pretty big."

Her forehead wrinkled with worry. "I wonder how many orders they will get."

"Hard to say." He sat on the bed and kicked off his boots.

She tapped on the papers in her hands. "What if I cannot fill all the orders?"

Drew began unbuttoning his trousers.

She sat on the edge of the bed, worrying her lip under her teeth.

"I wouldn't worry," Drew told her. "Things have a way o' workin' out."

That was easy for him to say. He wasn't responsible for filling the orders.

He pulled off his trousers, first one leg, then the other. "Look at the way things worked out for you at The Parlor. You wouldn't have dreamed o' workin' at a place like that. But if you hadn't, we would never have met. And if it weren't for Miss Hattie—"

She inhaled sharply, interrupting him. Of course, she thought.

"Miss Hattie," she said. "She said she wanted to get rid of The Parlor."

"Yeah?" Drew yanked off his socks and dropped them onto the floor.

Catalina's mind was working as fast as her treadle machine. "But she didn't want to put all the girls on the street."

Drew pulled off his undershirt. "What's that got to do with—"

"I can teach the ladies to sew," Catalina realized. "If I move my sewing machine back to The Parlor, I can have three shifts of ladies sewing, all day and all night."

Drew gazed at her, his eyes full of wonder and admiration. "Huh. That's pretty clever." He smiled. "You never cease to amaze me."

He made her blush, but her heart raced at the possibilities.

"If there are many, many orders, I can buy a second machine, and a third, and so on."

"You could transform The Parlor into a dressmaker's shop," Drew realized.

"Exactly!" She couldn't wait to break the happy news to Miss Hattie. She could already envision it. "The rooms upstairs can be for sewing, and the ladies can come for fittings in the salon below. I can display gowns all around the room. And behind the bar, I can stock gloves, hats, parasols, and reticules to match. Oh. And I can even serve tea and coffee to the ladies while they are waiting for alterations."

She beamed at Drew in triumph. It was only then she noticed that he was mostly undressed.

"What happened to your clothings, Drew?"

He gave her a sultry grin. "You may have been right about the *tartufo* makin' a person amorous."

She didn't believe the stories about *tartufi*. But even after all these weeks, Drew could make her heart flutter with just a glance.

She dipped her eyelids and then skewered him with a steamy stare. "You know I ate more than you did."

"That's true." He came close, letting his smoldering black gaze trace her lips and throat, settling on her cleavage. "So why are you still dressed?"

THE END

THANK YOU FOR READING MY BOOK!

Did you enjoy it? If so, I hope you'll post a review to let others know! There's no greater gift you can give an author than spreading your love of her books.

It's truly a pleasure and a privilege to be able to share my stories with you. Knowing that my words have made you laugh, sigh, or touched a secret place in your heart is what keeps the wind beneath my wings. I hope you enjoyed our brief journey together, and may ALL of your adventures have happy endings!

If you'd like to keep in touch, feel free to sign up for my monthly e-newsletter at www.glynnis.net, and you'll be the first to find out about my new releases, special discounts, prizes, promotions, and more!

If you want to keep up with my daily escapades:
Friend me at facebook.com/GlynnisCampbell
Like my Page at bit.ly/GlynnisCampbellFBPage
Follow me at twitter.com/GlynnisCampbell
And if you're a super fan, join facebook.com/GCReadersClan

Excerpt from

Native Wolf

California Legends Book 2

SPRING 1875
PARADISE, CALIFORNIA

Chase Wolf lifted his eyes to the grand mansion shining in the moonlight, and the corners of his mouth turned down.

Natives had built this princely manor for a white man who'd probably never soiled his hands on the Great Spirit's earth. While revered Konkow headmen and gifted shamans like his grandmother blistered their palms and bent their backs to serve the rancher, Parker and his family lived like spoiled children, untouched by harsh winds or scorching sun or the indignity of hard labor. He wondered how Parker would fare as a slave, sweating and toiling for the profit of another.

Then a dark inspiration took hold. His lips slowly curved into a grim smile.

The march to Nome Cult.

He would force Parker to endure the march, as his people had. He'd prod the rancher across a hundred miles of rugged land, without water, without food, without shelter, until there was nothing left of him. An eye for an eye, a tooth for a tooth, as his white mother's Bible preached. That was how his grandmother would be avenged. That was how her spirit would find peace.

Resolve—and liquor—made him bold. He silently climbed the steps and circled the porch until he found a window left open to capture the night breeze. He brushed aside the sheer curtain. Moonlight spilled over the sill and into the darkened house like pale acorn soup.

A sudden swell of vertigo tipped him off-balance as he climbed through the window. He made a grab for the curtain, tearing the frail fabric. Luckily, he had enough presence of mind to silence an angry curse, and his feet finally found purchase on the polished wood floor.

He swayed, then straightened, swallowing hard as he perused the sumptuous furnishings of the parlor in the moonlight, feeling as out of place as a trout in a tree.

A pair of sofas so plump they looked pregnant squatted on stubby legs carved with figures of leaves. Four rush-seat chairs stenciled with twining flowers sat against one wall. Delicate tables perched here and there on legs no thicker than a fawn's. A massive marble fireplace with an iron grate dominated the room, and an ornate clock ticked softly on the mantel. A huge chandelier hung from the ceiling like a giant crystal spider, and a dense, patterned carpet stretched in an oval pool over the floor. Sweeping down one side of the room was a mahogany staircase, and the walls were adorned with paper printed in pale vertical stripes.

His gaze settled on the enormous gilt-framed oil portrait hung above the mantel.

Letting the torn curtain fall closed, Chase ventured into the room to take a closer look. The title at the bottom read, SAMUEL AND CLAIRE PARKER. Hatred began to boil his blood as he let his eyes slide up to study the face of his enemy, the evil rancher who'd enslaved his grandmother.

Samuel Parker was a portly old man with a stern, wrinkled face, a balding head, dark eyes, and a trailing gray mustache that made him look even sterner. He was easy to hate. Chase's lip curled as he savored the thought of dragging the villain from his bed.

Then his gaze lit on Claire Parker. A wave of lightheadedness washed over him. It was only the whiskey, he told himself, yet he couldn't take his eyes off of the face in the painting. The woman was half her husband's age, as innocent and fair as Parker was darkly corrupt. She had long fair hair, partially swept up into a knot. Her features were delicate, and her eyes were serene and sweet. He'd never seen anyone so beautiful.

After a good minute of gawking, he finally squeezed his eyes shut against the image. The woman's looks didn't matter. Her heart was doubtless as evil as her husband's.

A flicker suddenly danced across the landing above, and Chase faded back into the wallpaper. The glow of a candle lit the top steps, making shadows flutter about the walls. And then, at the top of the stairs, the portrait of the woman appeared to come to life.

Claire Parker.

The flame illuminated her face, giving her creamy skin an ethereal glow. Her long hair had been cut since the painting. Short, blunt strands now caressed her chin. But the blonde locks shone in the candlelight like the halos of the angels in his mother's Bible. She wore a white lace-trimmed camisole, an ankle-length petticoat...and nothing else. Timidly she descended the steps in bare feet.

He stood frozen while the woman, unaware he lurked in the shadows, crept slowly closer. He didn't dare breathe as she brushed past him.

She hesitated, close enough for him to tell the portrait didn't do her justice. Claire Parker was breathtaking. Yet there were dark hollows beneath her eyes that painted her face in shades of unspeakable sorrow. His heart softened briefly, and he wondered what horrible tragedy haunted her.

Then, just as quickly, he remembered who she was, what she was, and the reason he'd come. He couldn't let a pretty face distract him from his vengeance.

But how was he going to steal past the lady to get to her husband? He couldn't afford to wait for her to go back to bed. The longer he remained in the house, the greater his chances were of getting caught.

Hell. He had to do something. And soon.

Instinct took over. It must have been instinct. Or the whiskey. Because if he'd thought about what he was doing for one minute, he never would have taken that first step.

Sliding his knife silently from its sheath, he slipped out of the shadows and came up behind her. Before she could wheel around in surprise, he clamped a hand over Claire Parker's mouth and set the sharp blade against her slim throat.

It happened in a heartbeat.

For one brief moment, Claire, hearing the soft sound from downstairs and sensing a shadowy presence in the room below, had foolishly believed it might be the spirit of her beloved Yoema. Hope filling her heart, she'd crept down the stairs.

But in an instant, those hopes were dashed. A huge hand closed over her mouth, choking off her gasp of shock. And a sharp edge of cold steel pressed against her neck.

She dropped the candle, extinguishing its light. Her heart jammed up against her ribs, fluttering like a singed moth. Air whistled through her flared nostrils. Her fingers splayed ineffectually as the blade threatened her with a menacing chill. Her throat clogged with panic, and she stared ahead with blind terror, sure the knife would end her gulping any moment.

She felt utterly helpless, not at all like the heroes of the dime novels she kept under her bed. She had no revolver. She had no Bowie knife. And she had no idea what her attacker intended.

For a long, drawn-out moment, the man did nothing, which was almost worse than killing her outright, for it gave her time to think, to dread.

Who was he? What did he want? Was he going to hurt her? Kidnap her? Murder her? The panicked whimper born in her throat was cut short by his tightening grip. Who *was* he?

The pungent smell of strong whiskey and wood smoke rose off of him, stinging her nose. The palm crushing her mouth tasted faintly of blood. His fingers, pressed into her cheek, were rough and callused. One thick-muscled arm, slung heavily across her bosom, trapped her. Where he secured her against his broad chest, he was as hard as a tree trunk.

She didn't dare resist, scarcely dared to breathe while the knife rested so close to her madly pulsing vein. If only she hadn't left her scissors in her bedroom...

The man moved his arm to struggle awkwardly with something behind her. She squeezed her eyes tight, praying he wasn't unfastening his trousers.

Then, for one moment, the cool blade disappeared from her throat. She stiffened like a clock spring, poised to bolt free. His hand fell away, and she sucked in a great gulp of air to scream.

But he was too quick for her. He jammed a wad of dusty cloth into her open mouth. She fought to keep from gagging, wincing as he knotted it tightly at the back of her head. Then he brandished the shiny silver blade in front of her eyes, flashing a silent threat in the moonlight.

This time, instead of cowering in fright, she let his gesture fuel her courage. Mustering her strength and calling to mind all the Buckskin Bill adventures she'd read, she swung her clasped hands across his forearm and brought her heel down hard on the top of his foot.

His forearm didn't budge, and she felt the bone-jarring impact of her bare heel upon his stiff boot all the way up her leg. She winced in pain. If only she'd had her Sunday church heels on, she despaired, she might have heard much more out of him than just an annoyed grunt.

Instead of thwarting him, her struggles seemed to increase his determination. He hugged her closer against him, so close she could feel his hot whiskey breath riffling her hair. He raised the knife in his huge fist till it glinted with menace before her. Then he began dragging her backward across the room.

In desperation, she tried to wrench out of his iron grasp, twisting enough to catch a glimpse of his shadowed face before he jerked her back against him.

What she'd seen surprised her. Even in the dim light, she could tell he was a native. His eyes, narrowed with intent, were as dark as the night, and his short, unkempt hair shone like ebony silk. His features were strongly sculpted and handsome, from the bold arch of his nose and his square jaw to the lean cords of his neck and his strong brow. And though she couldn't imagine why, he looked somehow familiar.

Why would an Indian attack her? The Indians who worked her father's ranch were as docile as sheep. Still, there had been tales of scalpings years ago, perpetrated by savages who'd learned such violence from vicious white settlers. Dear God, did he mean to take her scalp?

Suddenly she could draw no air into her lungs, and a hysterical thought kept circling her brain—she'd surely cheated the man of his prize if he meant to scalp her, for only moments ago, she'd cut her hair short in mourning.

Stunned and breathless, she hardly resisted as he

continued to lug her toward the open window. But when he climbed out and began to haul her over the sill, pushing her head down with one massive hand so she wouldn't bang it on the sashes, she awoke from her stupor.

Dear Lord, the man was abducting her!

They were halfway out of the house when panic made her fight in earnest. She grabbed hold of the window, refusing to let go. Kicking at the wall for all she was worth, she twisted and flailed against him until he hissed a guttural word at her, probably an epithet in his native tongue.

In a matter of seconds, of course, his strength won out. He unlatched her hands with a sweep of his arm and pulled her out onto the porch into the stark night.

Maybe she could still make noise, she thought in desperation. Her screams might not be heard through the gag, but if she stomped on the planks and made a huge fuss, surely her father or one of the ranch hands would come to investigate.

The man must have read her thoughts. Before she could make a single sound, he picked her up, tucked her between his arm and his hip like a sack of feed, and stole off the porch with the silent step that was a hallmark of the local Indians.

Suspended as she was, with her arms trapped against her sides, she couldn't do much more than squirm against him, which didn't hamper him in the least.

She peered between the blunt strands of her newly cropped hair. Though he weaved a bit, he seemed to be heading for the stables.

A slender slice of moonlight spilled in when he eased the door open, but the horses were unperturbed by the presence of an intruder. Hoping to startle them into a frenzy of neighing, Claire thrashed wildly in her captor's grip. He grunted and squeezed her tightly about the waist, cutting off her struggles and her air. Then he took a coil of rope from a nail in the wall and started forward.

He quickly found what he wanted—Thunder, her father's five-year-old prize stallion. He unlatched the gate and, stroking the horse's chest, nudged Thunder out of the stall. With one hand and his teeth, he managed to fashion a loop to slip over the horse's head.

She expected he'd make a break for it. He'd swing up bareback and throw her across his lap, slap Thunder's flank, let out a war whoop, and race into the night. As soon as he did, of course, a posse of her father's men would mount up and ride after him like the devil. They'd put a bullet in the villain before the moon rose even halfway across the sky.

But he did no such thing. He led Thunder out of the stable as stealthily as he'd come in. To her amazement, the normally headstrong stallion followed willingly, as if the two of them were partners in crime.

Still clamped firmly under the brute's huge arm and against his lean hip, Claire tried to calm her racing heart and make sense of things. Surely this couldn't be happening. Surely a stranger couldn't march up to the front door of the formidable Parker house in the middle of the night, snatch her from her own parlor, and make off with her by the light of the full moon.

Yet no one had heard him come. No one had roused when he left. It would be morning before anyone missed Claire. And, heaven help her, she'd left a note saying she was running away. Her father probably wouldn't come after her at all.

What were the man's intentions?

Obviously, he didn't mean to kill her. She'd be dead already if that were the case. Maybe he meant to hold her for ransom. Samuel Parker's prosperity was well known. This savage wouldn't be the first scoundrel to go after her father's wealth.

But he was by far the boldest.

They'd left the drive now, gone out the gate, onto the main

road. The land on the other side was wild, uncultivated and overgrown, and the Indian led Thunder straight into the weeds. Tall grasses brushed the horse's flanks and whipped at Claire's petticoat as she sagged in the man's grip.

Once they'd descended the rolling hill, out of sight of the Parker house, he stopped to remove the noose from Thunder's neck. Seizing the opportunity, Claire thrust out with her feet, kicking one of the beast's hocks, hoping to spook the horse into galloping back to the ranch.

But the Indian calmed the animal with a few murmurs and a pat to Thunder's flank, turning on Claire with a withering glare, as if she'd kicked the horse just for spite.

He righted her then, planting her atop the weed-choked ground. Before she could catch her balance, he dropped the noose about her, cinching it tightly around her waist.

When he casually swept up the hem of her petticoat, exposing her knees, Claire's eyes widened, and her heart skittered along her ribs. Perhaps she'd been mistaken about the man's intent after all.

But, drawing his knife, he slashed a long strip from the hem and let the garment fall. Then he put away the blade and seized one of her hands.

Instinctively she pulled away, but was caught fast in his great fist. He looped the cloth around her wrist, pulled it behind her, and crossed it over the other hand, knotting the cotton strips together.

Satisfied with his handiwork, he stepped back, his thumbs hooked insolently into the waistband of his trousers. She stared at him, wondering how intoxicated he must be to take pride in subduing a woman her size.

He must have read her mind. A scowl darkened his features, and for a moment, Claire thought she detected a hint of shame marring his drunken arrogance. Then he growled and turned his back on her, destroying all notions of civility.

In a movement surprisingly fluid for such a large man, he swung up atop Thunder. Coiling the loose end of the rope around his fist, he nudged the horse forward. The rope pulled taut, and Claire was forced to follow.

Caught off guard, she staggered and almost fell. What kind of abduction was this? Surely the man would want to flee as swiftly as possible to avoid capture. Why wasn't he sweeping her up and tearing off across the countryside?

He rode slowly, but keeping up was difficult. Claire was no longer accustomed to walking barefoot. Her father had cured her of that uncivilized habit years ago. The ground was rocky and uneven. Every few steps, she winced as star thistles bristled against her ankles and sharp pebbles poked her heels. Burrs caught in what was left of her lace hem, and her petticoat grew sodden with its harvest of dew.

She twisted her ankle on a stone and nearly went down again. The pain as she hobbled forward made her eyes water, but she didn't dare stop. She feared if she hesitated, he'd ride on anyway, dragging her through the thistles.

But despite her best efforts to be stoic, her eyes filled, and the stars and the moon and the ground blurred before her. A trickle wound its way down her cheek and was swallowed up by the cotton binding her mouth.

It wasn't the pain that triggered her crying. And it wasn't fear, not really. It was grief.

From the day that Yoema fell ill, Samuel Parker had insisted that Claire hide her sorrow. After all, no one knew the truth about Yoema's relationship to Claire. They assumed the native woman was a servant, no more. So for the sake of propriety and obedience to her father, Claire had kept a stiff upper lip and denied herself the catharsis of tears. When Yoema died, there had been no funeral, and Claire was expected to carry on as if nothing had happened.

But now she was removed from the eyes of society,

stripped of everything that had kept her sailing on a shaky but even keel. Her emotions felt as raw as the soles of her feet. And her father wasn't around to witness her weeping, to be disappointed in her. So all the pain she'd bottled up inside, all the bittersweet memories she'd repressed, all the tears she'd been unable to shed, gushed forth in a torrent so powerful that before long, her chest heaved with wrenching sobs and the gag grew wet with her weeping.

She no longer cared about the stones cutting her feet, no longer wondered about her captor. All she could think about was the woman who'd cared for her since she was a little motherless girl, who'd taught her the names of the animals, who'd held her when she was sad and lonely, who'd told her stories and sang her songs, and whose voice was now silent. Forever.

This time, when Claire tripped on the edge of a rock, she landed hard on her knees. She expected to be dragged through the weeds, and frankly she didn't care if he hauled her that way for ten miles. Now that the egg of her sorrow had been cracked, she realized that nothing could hurt her as much as the loss of the woman she'd called Mother.

The moment she struck the dirt, however, her captor halted, turning to see what delayed her.

Overcome with woe, she sank forward over her knees and buried her head. She didn't care if he watched her. He was nobody. She didn't have to keep a brave face for him like she did for her father. Her breath came in loud, wheezing gasps, filtered by the smothering cloth. Her throat ached with an agony of grief, and the sobs that racked her body felt as if they tore her soul asunder. Overwhelmed by heartache, she didn't notice that the Indian had dismounted and now loomed over her.

His fingers suddenly grazed the top of her head, startling her, and she almost choked on her tears as she glanced up at him. Though his face swam in her watery vision, he seemed shaken.

Of course he was shaken. Men never understood women's weeping. But she didn't care. She stared up at the frowning savage, openly defiant, tears streaming down her cheeks, silently daring him to ridicule her.

His scowl deepened, and he jutted out his chin. His mouth worked as if he were trying to decide whether to swallow or spit. Then, with a whispered expletive, he released her. Winding one arm around her waist, he hauled her to her feet and nodded sharply as if to tell her there would be no more falling down.

She wiped her wet cheek on her shoulder, staring coldly at him, but he refused to meet her eyes. He wrapped his end of the rope one more time around his hand, turned away, and remounted. His back expanded and released once with a deep breath before he clucked to the horse, urging it forward one step.

Claire stood her ground, refusing to move. Her grief was turning rapidly to anger. What kind of a brute abducted a woman by night, force her barefoot across rock-riddled hills, and ignored her tears of distress? In her novels, even the hero's worst nemesis possessed some shred of common decency. Damn his coal-black eyes! If he wanted her to move from this spot, he'd just have to drag her.

When he turned to peer at her, the corners of his mouth were drawn down. He tugged once more on the rope.

Raising her chin, she took a step backward.

His eyes widened. He tugged again, pulling her forward a step.

Incensed, she marshaled her strength and hauled back on the rope as hard as she could.

To her satisfaction, she managed to alter his look of annoyance to one of surprise, though for all her efforts, he didn't budge more than a few inches.

His amazement was short-lived. He simply let up on the

rope, and she sank with a plop onto her bottom. Before she could scramble upright, he slipped from Thunder, stalking toward her, muttering under his breath all the way.

Leaning forward, he upended her, slinging her over one ox-like shoulder. The air whooshed out of her, and she closed her eyes against the dizzying sensation of her precarious perch. Then he tossed her sidesaddle across the horse and swiftly mounted up behind her.

Flinging a possessive arm around her waist, he nudged Thunder forward, mumbling what sounded suspiciously like "damn fool Indian," and rode stonily into the deepening night.

At first she sat upright, stiff, unwilling to even think about letting her body come into contact with his. But as they rode on, mile after mile, her strength flagged. The sleep that had evaded her for days finally caught up with her, lulling her muscles into complacency and urging her eyes closed.

She stirred once along the gently rocking ride, fluttering her eyes open long enough to note that the sky had taken on the purple cast of the far side of midnight. Then she settled back in surrender against the stranger's chest. Her grief spent, she found curious comfort in dozing against the warm cotton shirt, safe from sorrow, safe from memories, safe from judgment.

Hours later, the sound of soft snoring woke her. Claire opened her eyes to a morning filled with apricot-colored light. Before her, the rolling hills lay silvered with dew and dotted with dark oaks, and the rising sun stretched fingers of gold across the emerald knolls. For one brief moment, she forgot where she was and simply enjoyed the glorious view.

Then the man—who was pressed far too intimately against her—snorted awake, and she remembered everything. Her captor had apparently slept for some time, for the horse had stopped to graze upon a patch of clover, and it looked like they were miles from anywhere.

"Shit!"

Claire flinched. So the savage did speak English…or at least knew one useful word. He shifted on Thunder's back, and she realized, much to her chagrin, that unless the man wore a Colt down his trousers, her hands, bound behind her, had just brushed the most private part of his anatomy. She curled her fingers in horror, relieved when he finally dismounted.

The stallion neighed, and then returned to chomping at the sweet grass. Her captor circled into her view, hitching up his trousers and scrubbing the sleep from his eyes. Then he lowered his hands from his face, and Claire saw him by the light of day for the first time.

He was truly massive, larger than any man she'd ever seen, broad of shoulder and chest. The muscles of his arms strained the blue flannel of his shirt, and his hands looked big enough to hide a whole poker deck.

But it wasn't his size that made her throat go suddenly dry.

The man was devilishly handsome. She could see now that he wasn't a full-blooded native. His short black hair had a slight curl to it, and his chin was dark with stubble. His skin was as golden as wild honey, and his teeth were snowy white where his lips parted. Deep, brooding eyes, shadowed by fatigue, shone like marbles of obsidian as he scrutinized her. And again, something about him looked curiously familiar.

"Ah, hell."

She blinked, impressed by his command of English, if not his vocabulary.

But the third word she pretended she didn't hear. He turned his back to her and kicked hard at the dirt, raking his hair back with both hands.

She wondered why he was upset. He had no reason to blacken the air with his cussing. *He* wasn't the one trussed up like a steer for branding. *He* wasn't the one stolen from a snug home and dragged across the hills half the night in his unmentionables. *His* throat wasn't as dry as gunpowder, and his legs weren't bloody with thistle scratches.

He spun back around, glaring at her as if she were somehow to blame. She tried to glare back at him. But Thunder chose that inopportune moment to amble forward, stretching his neck down for a choice bunch of clover. Claire's eyes widened as she began to slide inexorably, helplessly from her perch toward the hard-packed earth.

The instant Chase saw the panic in those big, beautiful green eyes, he instinctively lunged forward and caught the woman before she could slide off. Unfortunately, his efforts trapped her awkwardly between the horse's shoulder and his own chest. Her eyes widened even more, and he cursed, realizing that with her hands tied behind her, she could lend him no assistance whatsoever.

She slipped down his body, inch by delicious inch. Her soft breasts were crushed against his hard ribs, and her flimsy petticoat rode halfway up her legs before he could disentangle himself from her. At last he managed to get her feet on the ground.

Now if he could only regain his *own* balance.

What the hell had he been thinking last night, stealing a white woman? Whatever was in that whiskey, it must have robbed him of his last bit of sense, making him believe he had a hunger for vengeance and the stomach for violence.

Chase wasn't a killer. Or a kidnapper. Hell, he wouldn't go out of his way to step on a spider. Cruelty didn't come naturally to him.

Neither did embracing a beautiful woman. Women didn't come close to Chase much. His size usually scared them off. And if that didn't do it, his scowl would.

Not this one. The lady might be a tiny thing, as pale as a flower, as delicate as a fawn. But there was strength in her spirit, fire in her heart. Damn, even in his sleep, his body had gotten riled up over her.

A moment passed before Chase realized his arms were still wrapped around the woman. Outrage sparked in her eyes, and he released her like a white-hot poker.

She probably figured he meant to ravage her. He was sure white men did such things. But Chase would no sooner take a woman against her will than he'd brand an animal.

He stepped away, shaken, but managed to keep enough wits about him to gather the end of the rope in his fist so she wouldn't run off and get herself into worse trouble. Then he sank down onto the trunk of a fallen tree to consider his predicament.

Shit! Why hadn't he listened to Drew? Chase had had more whiskey than sense last night. And today, unlike the sweet flavor of revenge he'd imagined, the reality of holding a helpless woman captive left a bitter taste in his mouth.

He rubbed the back of his neck, glancing sideways at his hostage, who looked like some beautiful snow-white angel dropped out of heaven into the dirt. What the hell had he done?

A half-breed couldn't kidnap a white woman, particularly the wife of a rich rancher, and not expect half the population to come after him with guns blazing.

Worse, the horse he'd borrowed was a fine-looking animal, probably breeding stock. Hell, Parker might mourn the loss of his stallion more than his wife. Chase didn't know what they did to a man who took another man's woman, but they hanged you for horse thieving.

He scratched uneasily at his throat.

Vengeance had seemed like such a good idea last night. Now it felt like the biggest mistake of his life.

ABOUT THE AUTHOR

I'm a *USA Today* bestselling author of swashbuckling action-adventure historical romances, mostly set in Scotland, with over a dozen award-winning books published in six languages.

But before my role as a medieval matchmaker, I sang in *The Pinups,* an all-girl band on CBS Records, and provided voices for the MTV animated series *The Maxx,* Blizzard's *Diablo* and *Starcraft* video games, and *Star Wars* audiobooks.

I'm the wife of a rock star (if you want to know which one, contact me) and the mother of two young adults. I do my best writing on cruise ships, in Scottish castles, on my husband's tour bus, and at home in my sunny southern California garden.

I love transporting readers to a place where the bold heroes have endearing flaws, the women are stronger than they look, the land is lush and untamed, and chivalry is alive and well!

I'm always delighted to hear from my readers, so please feel free to email me at glynnis@glynnis.net. And if you're a super-fan who would like to join my inner circle, sign up to be part of Glynnis Campbell's Readers Clan on Facebook, where you'll get glimpses behind the scenes, sneak peeks of works-in-progress, and extra special surprises!

Made in the USA
Middletown, DE
25 October 2018